"IT IS NEVER TOO LATE TO MEND."

A MATTER OF FACT ROMANCE.

BY

CHARLES READE,
AUTHOR OF
"CHRISTIE JOHNSTONE," "PEG WOFFINGTON," ETC.

IN THREE VOLUMES.

VOL. III.

LONDON:
RICHARD BENTLEY, NEW BURLINGTON STREET.
1856.

[The Author reserves the right of Translation.]

'IT IS NEVER TOO LATE TO MEND

A MATTER OF FACT ROMANCE.

CHAPTER L

Mr. Meadows despatched his work in Shropshire twice as fast as he had calculated and returned home with two forces battling inside him—love and prudence. The battle was decided for him.

AVilliam Fielding's honest but awkward interference had raised in Susan Merton a desire to separate her sentiments from his by showing Mr. Meadows a marked respect. She heard of his arrival and instantly sent her father to welcome him home. Old Merton embraced the commission, for he happened to need Meadows's advice and assistance. The speculations into which he had been led by Mr. Clinton, after some fluctuations, wore a gloomy look, ' which could only be temporary' said that gentleman. Still a great loss would be incurred by selling out of them at a period ol

VOL. III. B

depression, and Mr. Clinton advised him to borrow a thousand pounds and hold on till things brightened.

Mr. Meadows smiled grimly as the fly came and buzzed all this in his web : ' Dear! dear! what a pity my money is locked up! Go to Lawyer Crawley. Use my name. He won't refuse my friend, for I could do him an ill turn if I chose.'

' I will. You are a true friend. You will look in and see us of course market-day ?'

'Why not?'

Meadows did not resume his visits at Grassmere without some twinges of conscience and a prudent resolve not to anchor his happiness upon Susan Merton. ' That man might come here any day with his thousand pounds and take her from me,' said he. ' He seems by his letters to be doing well, and they say any fool can make money in the colonies. Well, if he comes home respectable and well to do I'll go out. If I am not to have the only woman I ever loved or cared for, let thousands and thousands of miles of sea lie between me and that pair.' But still he wheeled about the flame.

Ere long matters took a very different turn. The tone of George's letters began to change. His repeated losses of bullocks and sheep were all recorded in his letters to Susan, and these letters were all read with eager anxiety by Meadows a day before they reached Grassmere.

The respectable man did not commit tliis action without some iron passing through his own soul—

Nemo repente turpissimus. The first letter he opened it was like picking a lock. He writhed and blushed and his uncertain fingers fumbled with another's property as if it had been red-hot. The next cost him some shame too, but the next less, and soon these little spasms of conscience began to be lost in the pleasure the letters gave him. ' It is clear he will never make a thousand pounds out there, and if he doesn't the old fanner won't give him Susan. Won't? He shan't! He shall be too deep in my debt to venture on it even if he was minded.' Meadows exulted over the letters and as he exulted they stabbed him, for by the side of the records of his ill-fortune the exile never failed to pour out his love and confidence in his Susan and to acknowledge the receipt of some dear letter from her which Meadows could see by George's must have assured him of undiminished or even increased affection.

Thus did sin lead to sin. By breaking a seal which was not his and reading letters which were not his Meadows filled himself with the warmest hopes of possessing Susan one day, and got to hate George for the stabs the young man innocently gave him. At last he actually looked on George as a sort of dog in the manger, who could not make Susan happy yet would come between her heart and one who could. All weapons seemed lawful against such a mere pest as this —a dog in the manger.

Meadows started with nothing better nor worse than a common-place conscience. A vicious habit is an iron that soon sears that sort of article. When he had opened and read about four letters his moral nature turned stone blind of one eye. And now he was happier (on the surface) than he had been ever since he fell in love with Susan.

Sure now that one day or another she must be his, he waited patiently, enjoyed her society twice a-week, got every body into his power, and bided his tijne. And one frightful thing in all this was that his love for Susan was not only a strong but in itself a good love. I mean it was a love founded on esteem; it was a passionate love and yet a profound and tender affection. It was the love which under different circumstances has often weaned men, aye and women too, from a frivolous, selfish, and sometimes from a vicious life. This love Meadows thought and hoped would hallow the unlawful means by which he must crown it. In fact he was mixing vice and virtue. The snow was to whiten the pitch, not the pitch blacken the snow. Thousands had tried this before him and wiU try it after him. Oh! that I could persuade them to mix fire and gunpowder instead! Men would bless me for this when all else I have written has been long long forgotten.

He felt good all over when he sat with Susan and thought how his means would enable that angel to satisfy her charitable nature and win the prayers of the poor as well as the admiration of the wealthy. * If ever a woman was cherished she shall be! If ever a woman was happy she shall be!' And as for him if he had done wrong to win her he would more than compensate it afterwards. In short he had been for more than twenty years selling, buying, swapping, driving every conceivable earthly bargain, so now he was proposing one to heaven.

At last came a letter in which George told Susan of the fatal murrain among his sheep, of his fever that had followed immediately, of the further losses while he lay ill, and concluded by saying that he had no right to tie her to his misfortunes and that he felt it would be more manly to set her free.

When he read this Meadows's exultation broke all bounds. * Ah ha!' cried he ' is it come to that at last ? Well he is a fine fellow after all and looks at it the sensible way, and if I can do him a good turn in business I always will.'

The next day he called at Grassmere. Susan met him all smiles and was more cheerful than usual. The watchful man was delighted. ' Come, she does not take it to heart.' He did not guess that Susan had cried for hours and hours over the letter and then had sat quietly down and written a letter and begged George to come home and not add separation to their other misfortunes, and that it was this decision and having acted upon it that had made her cheerful. Meadows argued in his own favour and now made sure to win.

The next week he called three times at Grassmere instead of twice and asked himself how much longer he must wait before he should speak out. Prudence said 'a little more patience;' and so he still hid in his

bosom the flame that burned him the deeper for this unnatural smothering. But he drank deep silent draughts of love and revelled in the bright future of his passion.

It was no longer hope, it was certainty. Susan liked him; her eye brightened at his coming; her father was in his power. There was nothing between them but the distant shadow of a rival; sooner or later she must be his. So passed three calm delicious weeks away.

(7)

CHAPTER 11.

Meadows sat one day in his study receiving Crawley's report.

' Old Mr. Merton came yesterday. I made difficulties as instructed. Is to come to-morrow.'

' He shall have the eight hundred.'

* That makes two thousand four hundred; why his whole stock won't cover it.'

'No!'

* Don't understand it, sir, it is too deep for me. What is the old gentleman doing ?'

' Hunting Will-o'-the-wisp. Throwing it away in speculations that are coloured bright for him by a man that wants to ruin him,'

* Aha!' cackled Crawley. ' And do him no harm.'

' Augh! How far is it to the bottom of the sea, sir, if you please ? I'm sure you know ?' Mr. Levi and you.'

' Crawley' said Meadows suddenly turning the conversation ' the world calls me close-fisted, have you found me so ?'

' Liberal as running water sir. I sometimes say how long will this last before such a great man breaks Peter

8 * IT IS NEVER TOO LATE TO MEND/

Crawley and flings him away and takes another ?' and Crawley sighed.

* Then your game is to make yourself necessary to me.'

' I wish I could' said Peter with mock candour. ' Sir' he crept on ' if the most ardent zeal, if punctuality, secresy, and unscrupulous fidelity—'

' Hold your gammon! Are we writing a book together? Answer me this in English. How far dare you go along with me ?'

' ^s far as your purse extends :—only—'

' Only what ? Only the thermometer is going down already, I suppose.'

' No sir, but what I mean is I shouldn't like to do any thing too bad.'

' What d'ye mean by too bad ?'

' Punishable by law.'

' It is not your own conscience you fear then ?' asked the other gloomily.

' Oh dear no sir, only the law.'

' I envy you. There is but one crime punishable by law, and that I shall never counsel you to.'

' Only one—too deep, sir, too deep. Which is that?'

' The crime of getting found out.

' What a great man! how far would I go with you, sir? To the end of the earth. I have but one regret, sir.'

' And what is that?'

' That I am not thought worthy of your confidence. That after so many years I am still only a too—I mean an honoured instrument, and not a humble friend.'

* Crawley' said Meadows solemnly ' let well alone Don't ask my confidence, for I am often tempted to give it you, and that would be all one as if I put the blade of a razor in your naked hand.'

' I don't care sir! You are up to some game as deep as a coal-pit; and I go on working and working all in the dark. I'd give any thing to be in your confidence.'

' Any thing is nothing; put it in figures' sneered Meadows incredulously.

' I'll give 20 per cent, off all you give me if you will let me see the bottom.'

'The bottom?'

* The reason sir,—the motive!—the why! — the wherefore. The what it is all to end in. The bottom!'

' Why not say you would like to read John Mea-dows's heart?'

' Don't be angry sir; it is presumption, but I can't help it. Deduct 20 per cent, for so great a honour.'

' Why the fool is in earnest.'

' He is; we have all got our little vanity, sir, and like to be thought worthy of confidence.'

' Humph!'

' And then I can't sleep for puzzling. Why should you stop every letter that comes here from Australia. Oh! bless me how neglectful I am; here is a letter from there, just come. To think of me bringing it and then forgetting.'

* Give it me directly.'

' There it is. And then sir, why on earth are we

mining old Mr. Merton without benefitting you, and you seem so friendly with him; and indeed you say he is not to be harmed—only ruined; it makes my head ache. Why what is the matter Mr. Meadows sir? What is wrong? No ill news I hope. I wish I'd never brought the letter.'

' That will do Crawley' said Meadows faintly, ' you may go.'

Crawley rose with a puzzled air.

* Come here to-morrow evening at nine o'clock, and you shall have your wish. All the worse for you' added he moodily. * All the worse for me. Now go without one word.'

Crawley retired dumb-founded. He saw the iron man had received some strange unexpected and terrible blow; but for a moment awe suppressed curiosity, and he went ofi' on tip-toe saying almost in a whisper * Tomorrow night at nine, sir.'

Meadows spread George's letter on the table and leaned on his two hands over it.

The letter was written some weeks after the last desponding one. It was full of modest but warm and buoyant exultation. Heaven had been very good to Susan and him. Eobinson had discovered gold: gold in such abundance and quality as beat even California. The thousand pounds so late despaired of was now a certainty.' Six montlis' work wi.th average good fortune would do it. Robinson said five thousand a-piece was the least they ought to bring home; but how could he (George) wait so long as that would take. ' And

Susan dear, if any thing could make this wonderlul luck sweeter it is to think that I owe it to you and to your goodness. It was you that gave Tom the letter, and bade me be kind to him, and keep him by me for his good; he has repaid me by making us two man and wife, please God. See what a web life is! Tom and I often talk of this. But Tom says it is Parson Eden I have to thank for it, and the lessons he learned in the prison; but I tell him if he goes so far back as that he should go further, and thank Farmer Meadows, for he 'twas that sent Tom to the prison, where he was converted and became as honest a fellow as any in the world, and a friend to your Greorge as true as steel.'

The letter concluded as it began with thanks to Heaven, and bidding Susan expect his happy return in six months after this letter. In short the letter was one " Hurrah!" tempered with simple piety and love.

Meadows turned cold as death in reading it, at the part where Farmer Meadows was referred to as the first link in the golden chain he dashed it to the ground and raised his foot to trample on it, but forbore lest he should dirty a thing that must go to Susan.

Then he walked the room in great agitation.

' Too late George Fielding' he cried aloud. ' Too late; I can't shift my heart like a weather-cock to suit the changes in your luck. You have been feeding me with hopes till I can't live without them. I never longed for a thing yet but what I got it, and I'll have this though I trample a hundred George Fieldings dead on my way to it. Now let me think.'

He pondered deeply his great brows knitted and lowered. For full half an hour invention and resource poured scheme after scheme through that teeming brain, and prudence and knowledge of the world sat in severe and cool judgment on each in turn, and dismissed the visionary ones. At last the deep brow began to relax, and the eye to kindle; and when he rose to ring the bell, his face was a sign-post with Eureka written on it in Nature's vivid hand-writing. In that hour he had hatched a plot worthy of Machiavel,—a plot complex yet clear. A servant girl answered the bell.

' Tell David to saddle Rachael directly.'

And in five minutes Mr. Meadows with a shirt a razor a comb and a map of Australia was gallopping by cross lanes to the nearest railway station. There he telegraphed Mr Clinton to meet him at Peel's Coffeehouse at two o'clock.

The message flashed up to town like lightning. The man followed it slowly like the wind.

(13)

CHAPTER III.

Meadows found Mr. Clinton at Peel's.

' Mr. Clinton, I want a man of intelligence to be at my service for twenty-four hours. I give you the first offer.'

Mr. Clinton replied that really he had so many irons in the fire that twenty-four hours—

Meadows put a fifty pound note on the table.

' Will all your irons iron you out fifty pounds as flat as that?'

* Why hem?'

' No nor five. Come sir, sharp is the word. Can you be my servant for twenty-four hours for fifty pounds, yes or no!'

' Why this is dramatic—yes!'

'It is half-past two. Between this and four o'clock I must buy a few hundred acres in Australia a fair bargain.'

'Humph ! Well that can be done. I know an old fellow that has land in every part of the globe.'

'Take me to him.'

In ten minutes they were in one of those dingy narrow alleys in the city of London that look the abode of decent poverty, and they could afford to buy Grosvenor Square for their stables; and Mr. Clinton introduced his friend to a blear-eyed merchant in a large room papered with maps; the windows were encrusted; mustard and cress might have been grown from them. Beauty in clean linen collar and wrist-bands would have shone here with intolerable lustre; but the blear-eyed men-chant did not come out bright by contrast; he had taken the local colour. You could see him and that was all. He was like a partridge in a furrow; a snuff-coloured man; coat rusty all but the collar which was greasy; poor as its c-olour was, his linen had thought it worth emulating; blackish nails, cotton wipe, little bald place on head but didn't shine for the same reason the windows didn't. Mr. Clinton approached this "dhirrrty money" this rusty coin in the spirit of flunkeyism.

'Sir' said he in a low reverential tone ' tliis party is disposed to purchase a few hundred acres in the colonies.'

Mr. Rich looked up from his desk and pointed with a sweep of his pen to the walls.

' There are the maps: the red crosses are my land. They are numbered. Refer to the margin of map and you will find the acres and the latitude and longitude calculated to a fraction. When you have settled in what part of the world you buy come to me again; time is gold.'

And the blear-eyed merchant wrote and sealed and filed and took no notice of his customers. They found red crosses in several of the United States, in Canada, in Borneo, in nearly all the colonies, and as luck would have it they found one small cross within thirty miles of Bathurst, and the margin described it as five hundred acres. Mr. Meadows stepped towards the desk. ' I have found a small property near Bathurst.'

'Bathurst? where is that?'

'In Australia.' ' Suit?'

'If the price suits. What is the price sir ?'

'The books must tell us that.'

Mr. Rich stretched out his arm and seized a ledger and gave it Meadows.

' I have but one price for land and that is five per cent, profit on my outlay. Book will tell you what it stands me in, you can add five per cent, to that and take the land away or leave it.'

With this curt explanation Mr. Rich resumed his work.

'It seems you gave five shillings an acre sir' said Mr. Clinton. ' Five times five hundred shillings, one hundred and twenty-five pounds. Interest at five per cent., six poimds five.'

' When did I buy it ?' asked Mr. Rich. ' Oh, when did you buy it sir?' Mr. Rich snatched the book a little pettishly and gave it to Meadows.

' You make the calculation,' said he; ' the figures are all there. Come to me when you have made it.'

The land had been bought twenty-seven years and some montlis ago. Mr. Meadows made the calculation in a turn of the hand and announced it. Rich rang a hand bell. Another snuffy figure with a stoop and a bald head and a pen came through a curtain.

' Jones, verify that calculation.'

' Penny half-penny two pence, penny half-penny two pence. Mum, mum ! Half-penny wrong, sir.'

' There is a half-penny wrong!' cried Mr. Rich to Meadows with a most injured air.

' There is sir' said Meadows, ' but it is on the right side for you. I thought I would make it even money against myself.'

' There are only two ways, wrong and right,' was the reply. ' Jones make it right. There that is the price for the next half hour; after business hours to-day add a day's interest; and, Jones if he does not buy write your calculation into the book with date—save time next customer comes for it.'

' You need not trouble Mr. Jones,' said Meadows. ' I take the land. Here is two hundred and fifty pounds—that is rather more than half the purchase-money.'

' Jones count.'

' When can I have the deeds ?' ' Ten to-morrow.'

' Receipt for two hundred and fifty pounds' said Meadows falling into the other's key. ' Jones write receipt—two five nought.' ' Write me an agreement to sell' proposed Meadows. ' No, you write it; I'll sign it Jones, enter transaction in the books. Have you anything to do young gentleman ?' addressing Clinton.

' No sir.'

' Then draw this pen through the two crosses on the map and margin. Good morning, gentlemen.'

And the money-making machine rose and dismissed them as he had received them with a'short sharp business conge.

Ye fair, who turn a shop head over heels, maul sixty yards of ribbon and buy six, which being sent home insatiable becomes your desire to change it for other six which you had fairly, closely, and with all the powers of your mind compared with it during the seventy minutes the purchase occupied, let me respectfully inform you that the above business took just eight minutes, and that 'when it was done 'twas done' \'7bShakespeare).

'You have given too much my friend,' said Mr. Clinton.

' Come to my inn,' was all the reply. ' This is the easy part, the game is behind.'

After dinner—' Now' said Meadows, ' business : do you know any respectable firm disposed towards speculation in mines?'

' Plenty.'

' Any that are looking towards gold ?'

' Why, no. Gold is a metal that ranks very low in speculation. Stop! yes, I know one tip-top house that has gone a little way in it, but they have burned their fingers, so they will go no farther.'

' You axe wrong; they will be eager to go on first to recover the loss on that article of account and next to show their enemies and in particular such of them as are their friends that they didn't blunder. You will go to them to-morrow and ask if they can allow you a commission for bringing them an Australian settler on whose land gold has been found.'

' Now my good sir' began Mr. Clinton a little superciliously, * that is not the way to gain the ear of such a firm as that. The better way will be for you to show me your whole design and leave me to devise the best means for carrying it into efiect.'

Up to this moment Meadows had treated Mr. Clinton with a marked deference as from yeoman to gentleman. The latter therefore was not a little surprised when the other turned sharp on him thus :—

' This won't do; we must understand one another. You think you are the man of talent and I am the clodhopper. Think so to-morrow night; but for the next twenty-four hours you must keep that notion out of your head or you will bitch my schemes and lose your fifty pounds. Look here, sir. You began life with ten thousand pounds; you have been all your life trying all you know to double it and where is it? The pounds are pence and the pence on the road to farthings. I started with a whip and a smock-frock and this,' touching his head, * and I have fifty thousand pounds in government securities. Which is the able man of these two—the bankrupt that talks like an angel and loses the game or the wise man that quietly wins it and pockets what all the earth are grappling with him for ? So much for that. And now which is master—the one who pays or the one who is paid ? I am not a liberal man, sir, I am a man that looks at every penny. I don't give fifty pounds. I sell it. That fifty pounds is the price of your vanity for twenty-four hours. I take a day's loan of it. You are paid fifty pounds per diem to see that there is more brains in my little finger than in all your carcass. See it for twenty-four hours or I won't fork out, or don't see it but obey me as if you did see it. You shan't utter a syllable or move an inch that I have not set down for you. Is this too hard ? then accept ten pounds for to-day's work and let us part before you bungle your master's game as you have done your own.'

Mr. Clinton was red with mortified vanity, but forty pounds ! He threw himself back in his chair.

* This is amusing,' said he. ' Well, sir, I will act as if you were Solomon and I nobody. Of course under these circumstances no responsibility rests with me.'

* You are wasting my time with your silly prattle' said Meadows very sternly. ' Man alive! you never made fifty pounds cash since you were calved. It comes to your hand to-day and even then you must chatter and jaw instead of saying yes and closing your fingers on it like a vice.'

' Yes!' shouted Clinton; * there.' ' Take that quire' said Meadows sharply. * Now I'll dictate the very words you are to say; learn them off by heart and don't add a syllable or subtract one or —no fifty pounds.'

Meadows being a general by nature (not Horse-Guards) gave Clinton instructions down to the minutest matters of detail, and he whose life had been spent in proving he would succeed—and failing, began to suspect the man who had always succeeded might perhaps have had something to do with his success.

Next morning well primed by Meadows, Mr. Clinton presented himself to Messrs. Bradthwaite and Stevens and requested a private audience. He inquired whether they were disposed to allow him a commission if he would introduce them to an Australian settler on whose land gold had been discovered.

The two members of the firm looked at one another. After a pause one of them said—

* Commission really must depend on bow such a thing turned out. They had little confidence in such statements, but would see the settler and put some questions to him.'

Clinton went out and introduced Meadows. This happened just as Meadows had told him it would. Outside the door Mr. Meadows suddenly put on a rustic carriage and so came in and imitated natural shyness with great skill; he had to be twice asked to sit down.

The firm cross-examined him. He told them gold had been discovered within a stone's throw of his land, thirty miles from Bathurst; that his firiends out there had said go home to England and they will give you a heavy price for your land now; that he did hope to get a heavy price, and so be able to live at home, didn't want to go out there again; that the land was worth money for there was no more to be sold in that part. Government land all round and they wouldn't sell, for he had tried them (his sharp eye had seen this fact marked on Mr. Eich's map).

'Well' said the senior partner * we have information that gold has been discovered in that district; the report came here two days ago by the " Anne Amelia." But the account is not distinct as yet. We do not hear on whose land it is found if at all. I presume you have not seen gold foimd.'

'Could I afford to leave my business out there and come home on a speculation?'

The eyes of the firm began to glitter.

'Have you got any gold to show us? *

'Nothing to speak of, sir; only what they chucked me for giving them a good dinner. But they are shovelling it about like grains of wheat I assure you.'

The firm became impatient.

'Show us what they gave you as the price of a dinner?'

Meadows dug into a deep pocket, and chased into a comer and caught and produced a little nugget of quartz and gold worth about four pounds, also another of somewhat less value.

'They don't look handsome gents,' said he, * but you may see the stuflp glitter here and there; and here is some of the dust. I had to buy this, gave them fifty shillings an ounce for it. I wish I had bought a hundredweight, for they tell me it is worth three pound ten here—'

* May we inspect these specimens.*

* Why not, sir? I'll trust it with you, I wouldn't with every body though.'

The partners retired with the gold, tested it with / mTU33aJaiS..jtcid, weighed it, and after a short excited interview one of them brought it back, and asked with great nonchalance the price of the land.

Meadows hung his head.

'Twenty thousand pounds,'

'Twenty thousand pounds' and the partner laughed in his face.

'I don't wonder you are surprised sir. I wonder at myself asking so much. Why before this if you had offered me five thousand I would have jumped into your arras as the saying is; but they all say I ought to have twenty thousand, and they have talked to me till they make me greedy.'

The partner retired and consulted, and the firm ended by offering ten thousand.

'I am right down ashamed to say no' was the answer, * but I suppose I must not take it.'

The firm undertook to prove that it was a magnificent offer. Meadows offered no resistance, he thought so too; but he must not take it, everybody told him it was worth more. At last when his hand was on the door they offered him twelve thousand five hundred.

He begged to consider of it.

No! they were peremptory. If he was off they were off.

He looked this way and that way with a frightened air.

* What shall I do sir' said he helplessly to Clinton, and nudged him secretly.

' Take it and think yourself very lucky,' said that gentleman, exchanging a glance with the firm.

' Well then if you say so I will. You shall have it gentleman, five hundred acres in two lots — 400 and 100.'

Clinton acting on his secret instructions now sought a private interview with the firm.

' I am to have a commission, gentlemen ?'

* Yes! fifty pounds; but really we can hardly afford it.'

' Well then as you give me an interest in it I say— pin him.'

'Why?'

' Don't you see he is one of those soft fellows who listen to everybody. If he goes away and they laugh at him for not getting more for it I really could hardly answer for his ever coming back here.'

The firm came in cheerfuUy.

' Well Mr.—Mr.'

* Not Mr., sir. Fielding, plain George Fielding.'

' We will terminate this affair with you. We will have a contract of sale drawn up and make you an advance. When can you give us the title deeds ?'

* In a couple of hours if the lawyer is at home.'

' By the by, you will not object to draw upon us at three months for one-half of the money.'

' Oh! dear no, sir. I should say by the look of you you were as good as the bank.'

* The other half by check in two hours.' The parties signed the contract respectively.

Then Meadows and Clinton went off to the Five per Center, completed with him, got the title deeds, brought them, received cheque and accepted draft. Clinton by Meadows's advice went in and dunned for his commission then and there and got it, and the confederates went oiF and took a hasty dinner together. After dinner they settled.

' As you showed me how to get this commission out of them it belongs to you' said Clinton sorrowfully.

' It does, sir. Give it to me. I return it you sir, do me the favour to accept it.'

' You are very generous, Mr. Meadows.'

' And here is the other fifty you have earned.'

' Thank you my good sir. Are you satisfied with the day's work ?'

' Amply sir. Your skill and ingenuity brought us through triumphant' said Meadows, resuming the deferential since he risked nothing by it now.

' Well I think I managed it pretty well. By the by that gold you showed them, was it really gold ?'

' Certainly.'

' Oh! because I thought—'

' No, sir, you did not. A man of your ability knows
I would not risk ten thousand pounds for want of a purchase I could not lose ten shillings by. Ore is not a fancy article.'

' Oh! ah! yes, very true; no, of course not. One question more. Where did the gold come from ?'

' California.'

' But I mean how did you get it ?'

' I bought it out of a shop-window those two knowing ones pass twice every day of their lives.'

'Ha! ha! ha!'

' You pass it oftener than that, sir. Excuse me, sir; I must catch the train. But one word before I go. My name must never be mentioned in this business.'

' Very well; it never shall transpire upon my honour.'

Meadows felt pretty safe. As he put on his greatcoat he thought to himself, ' When the story is blown and laughed over this man's vanity will keep my name out of it. He won't miss a chance of telling the world how clever he is. My game is to pass for honest, not for clever, no thank you.'

' Grood-bye sir' was his last word. ' It is you for hoodwinking them.'

' Ha! ha! ha! Good-bye farmer' (in a patronizing tone).

Soon after this Meadows was in a corner of a railway carriage, twelve thousand four hundred and fifty pounds in his pocket, and the second part of his great complex scheme boiling and bubbling in his massive head. There he sat silent as the grave, his hat drawn over his powerful brows that were knitted

VOL. III. C

all the journey by one who never knitted them in vain.

He reached home at eight and sat down to his desk and wrote for more than half an-hour. Then he sealed up the paper and when Crawley came he found him walking up and down the room. At a silent gesture Crawley took a chair and sat quivering with curiosity. Meadows walked in deep thought.

' You demanded my confidence. It is a dangerous secret, for once you know it you must serve me with red-hot zeal or be my enemy and be crushed out of life like a blind-worm or an adder Peter Crawley.*

' I know that dear sir' said Peter ruefully.

' First, how far have you guessed ?'

' I guess Mr. Levi is some how against us.'

' He is' replied Meadows carelessly.

' Then that is a bad job. He will beat us sir. He will beat us. He is as cunning as a fox.'

Meadows looked up contemptuously, but as he could not afford to let such a sneak as Crawley think him any thing short of invincible he said coolly, ' He is, and I have measured cunning with a fox.'

' You have, sir ? That must have been a tight match.'

* A fox used to take my chickens one hard winter; an old fox cautious and sly as the Jew you rate so high. The men sat up with guns for him—no; a keeper set traps in a triangle for him—no. He had the eye of a hawk, the ear of a hare, and his own nose. He would have the chickens and he would not get

himself into trouble. The woman complained to me of the fox. I turned a ferret loose into the rabbit-hutch and in half a-minute there was as nice a young rabbit dead as ever you saw.'

* Lookee there now' cried Crawley.

' I choked the ferret off but never touched the rabbit. I took the rabbit with a pair of tongs; the others had handled their baits and pug crept round 'em and nosed the trick. I poured twenty drops of croton oil into the little hole ferret had made in bunny's head and I dropped him in the grass near pug's track. Next morning rabbit had been drawn about twenty yards and the hole in his head was three times as big. Pug went the nearest way to blood; went in at ferret's hole. I knew he would.'

* Yes, sir! yes ! yes ! yes ! and there lay the fox.'

'No signs of him. Then I said "Go to the nearest water. Croton oil makes 'em dry. They went along the brook and on the very bank there lay an old dogfox blown up like a bladder as big as a wolf and as dead as a herring, now for the Jew. Look at that;' and he threw him a paper.

* Why this is the judgment on which I arrested Will Fielding, and here is the acceptance.'

* Levi bought them to take the man out of my power. He left them with old Cohen. I have got them again you see, and got young Fielding in my power spite of his foxy friend.'

* Capital sir capital!' cried the admiring Crawley. He then looked at the reconquered documents. ' Ah I'

c2

said he spitefully, * how I wish I could alter one of these names, only one!'

' What d ye mean ?'

' I mean that I'd give fifty pound (if I had it) if it was but that brute George Fielding that was in our power instead of this fool William.'

Meadows opened his eyes: * Why ?'

' Because he put an affront upon me,' was the somewhat sulky reply.

'What was that?'

* Oh no matter sir I'

' But it is matter. Tell me. I am that man's enemy.'

' Then I am in luck. You are just the enemy I wish him.'

' What was the afiront ?'

* He called me a pettifogger.' 'Oh! is that all?'

' No. He discharged me from visiting his premises.'

' That was not very polite.'

' And threatened to horsewhip me next time I came there.'

' Oh, is that where the shoe pinches ?'

' No, it is not!' cried Crawley almost in a shriek; ' but he altered his mind, and did horsewhip me then and there. Carse him !'

Meadows smiled grimly. He saw his advantage. ' Crawley' said he quickly * he shall rue the day he lifted his hand over you. You want to see to the bottom of me.'

* Oh Mr. Meadows that is too far for the naked eye to see,' was the despondent reply.

* Not when it suits my book. I am going to keep my promise and show you my heart.'

' Ah!'

' Listen and hear the secret of my life. Are you listening ?'

* What do you think, sir ?' was the tremulous answer.

' I—love—Miss—Merton,' and for once his eyes sunk before Crawley's.

' Sir! you—love—a—woman ?'

' Not as libertines love, nor as boys flirt and pass on. Heaven have mercy on me, I love her with all my heart and soul and brain I I love her with more force than such as you can hate!'

' The deuce you do !'

' I love the sweetheart—of the man—who lashed you —like a dog.'

Crawley winced and rubbed his hands.

' And your fortune is made if you help me win her.'

Crawley rubbed his hands.

' Old Merton has promised the woman I love to this Greorge Fielding if he comes back with a thousand pounds.'

' Don't you be frightened, sir; that he will never do.'

' Will he not ? Eead this letter.'

' Ah! the letter that put you out so. Let me see— Mum! mum! Found gold. Pheugh! Pheugh! Pheeeugh!!'

* Crawley, most men reading that letter would have given in then and there, and not fought against such luck as this. I only said to myself " Then it will cost me ten thousand pounds to win the day." Well between yesterday eleven forenoon and this hour I made the ten thousand pounds.*

He told him briefly how.

' Beautiful, sir! Beautiful! What did you make the ten thousand out of your own rival's letter ?'

' Yes, I taxed the enemy for the expenses of the war.'

' Oh Mr. Meadows what a fool what a villain I was to think Mr. Levi was as great a man as you. I must have been under a hallucination.'

' Crawley the day that John and Susan Meadows walk out of church man and wife I put a thousand pounds into your hand and set you up in any business you like; in any honest business, for from that day our underhand dealings must end. The husband of that angel must never grind the poor or wrong a living creature. If heaven consents to my being happy in this way, the least 1 can do is to walk straight and straight forward the rest of my days, and I will s'help me God.'

' That is fair. I knew you were a great man, but 1 had no idea you were such a good one.'

' Crawley,' said the other, with a sudden gloomy misgiving, ' I am trying to cheat the devil. I fear no man can do that,' and he himg his head.

' No ordinary man sir' replied the parasite, 'but your skill has no bounds. Your plan sir at once, that

I may co-operate and not thwart your great skill through ignorance/

' My plan has two hands: one must work here the other a great many miles from here. If I could but cut myself in two all would be well, but I can't; I must be one hand you the other. I work thus:—Post-office here is under my thumb. I stop all letters from him to her. Presently comes a letter from Australia telling among pork, grains, etc. how George Fielding has made his fortune and married a girl out there.'

* But who is to write the letter ?'

* Can't you guess ?'

' Havn't an idea. She won't believe it.' ' Not at first perhaps, but when she gets no more letters from him she will.'

* So she will. So then you will run him down to her.'

' Not such a fool, she would hate me. I shall never mention his name. I make one of my tools hang gaol over old Merton. Susan thinks George married. I strike upon her pique and her father's distress. I ask him for his daughter. Offer to pay my father-in-law's debts and start him afresh.'

' Beautiful! Beautiful!'

' Susan likes me already. I tell her all I suffered silent, while she was on with George. I press her to be mine. She will say no perhaps three or four times, but the fifth she will say yes!'

* She will! You are a great man.' ' And she will be happy.'

' Can't see it.'

' A man that marries a virtuous woman and loves her is no man at all if he can't make her love him; they can't resist our stronger wills except by flight or by leaning upon another man. I'll be back directly.'

Mr. Meadows returned with a bottle of wine and two glasses. Crawley was surprised. This was a beverage he had never seen his friend drink or offer him. Another thing puzzled him. When Mr. Meadows came back with the wine he had not so much colour as usual in his face—not near so much.

' Crawley' said Meadows in a low voice * suppose while I am working this George Fielding were to come home with money in both pockets ?'

' He would kick it all down in a moment.'

' I am glad you see that. Then you see one hand is not enough; another must be working far away.'

* Yes, but I don't see—'

' You will see. Drink a glass of wine with me my good friend—your health.'

' Same to you sir.'

' Is it to your mind ?'

' Elixir! This is the stuff that sharpens a chap's wit, and puts courage in his heart.'

' I brought it for that. You and I have no chicken's play on hand. Another glass.'

' Success to your scheme sir.'

* Crawley, George Fielding must not come back this year with one thousand pounds.'

* No he must not—thank you sir, your health.

Musn't, he shan't; but how on earth can you prevent him?'

* That paper will prevent him: it is a paper of instructions. My very brains lie in that paper—put it in your pocket.'

' In my pocket, sir ? Highly honoured—shall be executed to the letter. What wine !' ' And this is a cheque-book.'

* No! is it though ?'

* You will draw on me for one hundred pounds per month.'

' No! shall I though ? Sir, you are a king !'

* Of which you will account for fifty pounds only.'

' Liberal, sir; as I said before, liberal as running water.'

' You are going a journey.'

* Am I ? well! Don't you turn pale for that I'll come back to you,—^nothing but death shall part us. Have a drop of this sir, it will put blood into your cheek and fire into your heart. That is right. Where am I going, sir ?'

' What, don't you know ?'

' No! nor I don't care: so long as it is in your service I go.'

' Still it is a long journey.'

' Oh is it? Your health then, and my happy return.'

* You are not afraid of the sea or the wind ?'

' I am afraid of nothing but your wrath, and—and— the law. The sea be hanged and the wind be blowed ! When I see your talent and energy, and hold your

c3

cheque-book in my hand and your instructions in my pocket, I feel to play at foot-ball with the world. When shall I start?'

* To-morrow morning.'

' To-night if you like. Where am I to go to. ?'

* To Australia!'

That single word suspended the glass going to Crawley's lips, and the chuckle coming from them. A dead silence on both sides followed it. And now two colourless faces looked into one another's eyes across the table.

CHAPTER IV.

Three days the gold-finders worked alone upon the pre-Adamite river's bed. At evening on the third day they looked up and saw a figure perched watching them with a pipe in its mouth. It disappeared in silence. Next day there were men on their knees beside them digging, scraping, washing and worshipping gold. Soon they were the centre of a group,— soon after of a humming mob. As if the birds had really carried the secret North, South, East, and West men swarmed and buzzed and settled like locusts on the gold-bearing tract. They came in panting gleaming dusty and travel-stained, and flung ofl" their fatigue at sight, and running up dived into the gullies, and plied spade and pick-axe with clenched teeth and throbbing hearts. They seamed the face of Nature for miles; turned the streams to get at their beds; pounded and crushed the solid rock to squeeze out the subtle stain of gold it held in its veins;—hacked through the crops as through any other idle impediment; pecked and hewed and fought and wrestled with Nature for the treasure that lay so near yet in so tight a grip.

We take off our clothes to sleep and put them on to play at work, but these put on their clothes to sleep in and tore them off at peep of day, and labour was red-hot till night came and cooled it; and in this fight lives fell as quickly as in actual war, and by the same enemy — Disease : small wonder when hundreds and hundreds wrought the live-long day one-half in icy water, the other half dripping with sweat.

Men rotted like sheep, and died at the feet of that gold whom they stormed here in his fortress ; and some alas met a worse fate: for that befel which the world has seen in every age and land where gold has come to light upon a soil: men wrestling fiercely with Nature jostled each other, cupidity inflamed hate to madness, and human blood flowed like water over that yellow dirt. And now from this one burning spot gold-fever struck inwards to the heart of the land; burned its veins and maddened its brain: the workman sold his tools, bought a spade and a pick-axe, and fled to the gold: the lawyer flung down liis parchment and off to the gold: the penny-a-liner his brass pen and off to a greater wonder than he had ever fabricated: the schoolmaster, to whom little boys were puzzling out—

Quid non mortalia pectora cogis Auri sacra fames.

made the meaning perfectly clear; he dropped ferule and book and ran with the national hunt for srold. Shops were closed for want of buyers and sellers ; the grass crept up between the paving stones in great

thoroughfares; outward-bound ships lay deserted and helpless in the roads; the wilderness was peopled and the cities desolate. Commerce was paralyzed, industry contracted : the wise and good trembled for the destiny of the people, the Grovernment trembled for itself:— idle fear. That which shook this colony for a moment settled it firm as a granite mountain, and made it great with a i-apidity that would have astounded the puny ages cant appeals to as the days of wonders.

The sacra fames was not Australian but human; and so at the first whisper of gold the old nations poured the wealth they valued—their food and clothes and silk and coin—and the prime treasure they valued not, their men—into that favoured land.

Then did great labour, insulted and cheated so many years in narrow over-crowded corners of the huge unpeopled globe, lift his bare arm and cry, " Who bids for this ?" and a dozen gloved hands jumped and clutched at the prize: and in bargains where a man went on one side and money on the other, the money had to say, " thank you " over it instead of the man.

But still though the average value of labour was now full as high in the cities as in the mine, men flowed to the desert and the gold, tempted by the enormous prizes there, that lay close to all and came to fortune's favourites.

Hence a new wonder—a great moral phenomenon the world had never seen before on such a wide scale. At a period of unparalleled civilisation and refinement, society, with its artificial habits and its jealous class

distinctions on its back, took a sudden unprepared leap fix>m the heights it had been centuries constructing,— into a gold mine : it emerged, its delicate fabric crushed out of all recognizable shape, its petty prides annihilated and even its just distinctions turned topsy turvy. For mind is really more honourable than muscle, yet when these two met in a gold mine it fared ill with mind. Classical and mathematical scholars joined their forces with navvies to dig gold : and nearly always the scholars were found after a while cooking, shoe-cleaning, and doing generally menial offices for the navvies.

Those who had no learning, but had good birth genteel manners and kid gloves and feeble loins, sank lower and became the dregs of gold-digging society ere a week's digging had passed over their backs. Not that all wit yielded to muscle. Low cunning often held its own; hundreds of lazy leeches settled on labour's bare arm and bled it. Such as could minister to the digger's physical needs, appetites, vices, had no need to dig; they made the diggers work for them, and took toll of the precious dust as it fell into their hands.

One brute that could not spell chicoree to save himself from the gallows, cleared two thousand pounds a month by selling it and hot water at a pinch a cup. Thus ran his announcement—* Cofy alius rady.' Meantime Trigonometry was frying steaks and on Sunday blacking boots.

After a while lucky diggers returned to the towns clogged with gold and lusting and panting for plea-sm-e.

They hired carriages and sweet-hearts, and paraded the streets all day, crying ' We be the hairy-stocracy now!!'

The shopkeepers bowed down and did them homage.

Even here Nature had her say. The sexes came out —the 'men sat in the carriages in their dirty fustian and their chequered shirts and no jacket; their inamoratas beside them glittered in silk and satin, and some fiend told these poor women it was genteel to be short-sighted; so they all bought gold spy-glasses, and spied without intermission.

Then the old colonial aristocracy, who had been born in broad-cloth and silk and unlike the new had not been transported, but only their papas and mammas, were driven to despair: but at last they hit upon a remedy. They would be distinguished by hook or by crook, and the only way left now was always to go on foot. So they walked the pavement, wet or dry nothing could induce them to enter the door of a carriage. Item : they gave up being short-sighted; the few who for reasons distinct from fashion could not resign the habit concealed it as if it was a defect instead of a beauty.

This struggle of classes in the towns, with its hundred and one incidents, was an excellent theme for satire of the highest class. How has it escaped ? is it that even Satire, low and easy art, is not so low and easy as Detraction. But these are the outskirts of a great theme. The theme itself belonged not to little satire but to great epic.

In the sudden return of a society far more complex artificial and conventional than Pericles ever dreamed of, to elements more primitive than Homer had to deal with ; in this with its novelty, and nature, and strange contrasts,

In the old barbaric force and native colour of the passions as they burst out undisguised around the gold,

In the hundred and one personal combats and trials of cunning,

In a desert peopled, and cities thinned, by the magic of cupidity,

In a huge army collected in ten thousand tents, not as heretofore by one man's constraining will, but each human unit spurred into the crowd by his own heart,

In ' the siege of Gold,' defended stoutly by Rock and Disease,

In the world-wide effect of the discovery, the peopling of the earth at last according to lieaven's long-published and resisted design.

Fate offered poetry a theme broad and high, yet piquant, and various as the dolphin and the rainbow.

I cannot sing this song, because I am neither Lamar-tine nor Hugo nor Walter Scott. I cannot hum this song, because the severe conditions of my story forbid me even to make the adventurous attempt. I am here to tell not the great tale of gold but the little story of how Susan Merton was affected thereby. Yet it shall never be said that my pen passed close to a great man or a great thing without a word of homage and sympathy to set against the sneers of grovelling criticasters, the blindness of self-singing poetasters, and the national itch for detraction of all great things and men that live, and deification of dead dwarfs.

God has been bountiful to the human race in this age. Most bountiful to Poets; most bountiful to all of us who have a spark of nobleness in ourselves, and so can see and revere at sight the truly grand and noble (any snob can do this after it has been settled two hundred years by other minds that he is to do it). He has given us warlike heroes more than we can count—far less honour as they deserve; and valour as full of variety as courage in the Iliad is monotonous except when it takes to its heels.

He has given us one hero, a better man than Hector or Achilles. For Hector ran away from a single man: this hero was never known to run away at all. Achilles was a better egotist than soldier; wounded in his personal vanity he revenged himself, not on the man who had wronged him—-Prudence forbade—but on the army, and on his country. This antique hero sulked; my hero, deprived of the highest command, retained a higher still—the command that places the gi'eat of heart above all petty personal feeling. He was a soldier, and could not look from his tent on battle, and not plunge into it. What true soldier ever could ? He was not a Greek but a Frenchman, and could not love himself better than his country. Above all, he was not Achilles but Canrobert,

He has given us to see Nineveh disinterred by an English hero.

He has given us to see the north-west forced, and winter bearded on his everlasting throne by another. (Is it the hero's fault if self and snowdrop-singing poetasters cannot see this feat with the eyes of Camoens ?)

He has given us to see Titans enslaved by man; steam harnessed to our carriages and ships; and galvanism tamed into an alphabet a gamut, and its metal harp-strings stretched across the earth malgre mountains and the sea, and so men's minds defying the twin monsters Time and Space; and now, gold revealed in the east and west at once, and so mankind now first in earnest peopling the enormous globe. Yet old women and children of the pen say this is a bad, a small, a lifeless, an unpoetic age:—and they are not mistaken. For they lie.

As only tooth-stoppers, retailers of conventional phrases, links in the great cuckoo-chain, universal pill-venders, Satan, and ancient booksellers' ancient nameless hacks can lie, they lie.

It is they who are small-eyed. Now, as heretofore, weaklings cannot rise high enough to take a bird's-eye view of their own age, and calculate its dimensions.

The age, smaller than epochs to come, is a giant compared with the past, and full of mighty materials for any great pen in prose or verse.

My little friends aged nineteen and downwards— four-score and upwards, who have been lending your ears to the stale little cant of every age as chanted in this one by BufFo-Bombastes and other foaming at the pen old women of both sexes, take by way of a small

antidote to all that poisonous soul-withering drivel ten honest words.

I say before heaven and earth that the man who could grasp the facts of this day and do an immortal writer's duty by them, i. e., so paint them as a later age will be content to engrave them, would be the greatest writer ever lived : such is the force, weight, and number of the grand topics that lie this day on the world's face. I say that he who has eyes to see may now see greater and far more poetic things than human eyes have seen since our Lord and his apostles and his miracles left the earth.

It is very hard to write a good book or a good play, or to invent a good picture and having invented paint it. But it always was hard, except to those—to whom it was impossible. Bunglers will not mend matters by blackening the great canvasses they can't paint on, nor the impotent become any bodies by detraction.

' Justice !'

When we write a story or sing a poem of the great nineteenth century I give you my sacred word- of honour there is but one fear—not that our theme will be beneath us, but we miles below it; most of all, that we shall lack the comprehensive vision a man must liave from heaven to catch the historical the poetic the lasting features of the Titan events that stride so swiftly past IN THIS GIGANTIC AGE.

(44)

CHAPTEE V.

The life of George Fielding and Thomas Robinson for months could be composed in a few words; tremendous work from sunrise to sundown, and on Sunday welcome rest, a quiet pipe, and a book.

At night they slept in a good tent, with Carlo at their feet, and a little bag between them; this bag never left their sight; it went out to their work, and in to sleep.

It is dinner-time ; George and Tom are snatching a mouthful, and a few words over it.

' How much do you think we are, Tom ?'

* Hush! don't speak so loud, for heaven's sake;' he added in a whisper, ' not a penny under five hundred pounds worth.'

George sighed.

' It is slower work than I thought; but it is my fault, I am so unlucky.'

* Unlucky ! and we have not been five months at it.' ' But one party near us cleared four thousand pounds

at a haul; one thousand pounds a piece—ah !'

* And hundreds have only just been able to keep themselves. Come: you must not grumble, we are high above the average.'

George persisted.

' The reason we don't get on is, we try for nothing better than dust. You know what you told me, that the gold was never created in dust but in masses like all metals; the dust is only a trifle that has been washed off the bulk. Then you said we ought to track the gold dust coarser and coarser, till we traced the metal to its home in the great rocks.'

' Ay! Ay! I believe I used to talk so, but I am wiser now. Look here George, no doubt the gold was all in block when the world started, but how many million years ago was that. This is my notion George : at the beginning of the world the gold was all solid, at the end it is all to be dust; now which are we nearer the end or the beginning.'

' Not knowing can't say Tom.'

' Then I can, for his reverence told me. We are iitty times nearer the end than the beginning, follows there is fiity times as much gold dust in nature as solid gold.'

' What a head you ha' got Tom ? but I can't take it up so: seems to me this dust is like the grain that is shed from a ripe crop before it comes to the sickle, now if we could trace—'

* How can you trace syrup up to the lump when the lump is all turned to syrup ?'

George held, his peace—shut up but not convinced.

' Hallo! you two lucky ones ' cried a voice distant about thirty yards ' will you buy our hole, it is breaking our heart here.'

Robinson went up and found a large hole excavated to a great depth; it was yielding literally nothing, and this determined that paradoxical personage to buy it if it was cheap,' What there is must be somewhere all in a lump.'

He offered ten pounds for it, which was eagerly snapped at.

' Well done Gardiner' said one of the band. ' We would have taken ten shillings for it' explained he to Robinson.

Robinson paid the money, and let himself down into the hole with his spade. He drove his spade into the clay, and the bottom of it just reached the rock; he looked up. ' I would have gone just one foot deeper before I gave in' said he; he called George. ' Come George, we can know our fate in ten minutes.'

They shovelled the clay away down to about one inch above the rock, and there in the white clay they found a little bit of gold as big as a pin's head.

* We have done it this time' cried Robinson, ' shave a little more off not too deep, and save the clay. This time a score of little nuggets came to view sticking in the clay; no need for washing, they picked them out with their knives.'

The news soon spread, and a multitude buzzed round the hole and looked down on the men picking out peas and beans of pure gold with their knives.

Presently a voice cried ' Shame, give the men back their hole.'

' Gammon,' cried others, ' they paid for a chance, and it turned out well; a bargain is a bargain.' Gardiner and his mates looked sorrowfully down. Robinson saw their faces, and came out of the hole a moment. He took Gardiner aside and whispered ' Jump into our hole like lightning, it is worth four pound a-day.'

' God bless you !' said Gardiner. He ran and jumped into the hole just as another man was going to take possession. By digger's law no party is allowed to occupy two holes.

All that afternoon there was a mob looking down at George and Robinson picking out peas and beans of gold, and envy's satanic fire burned many a heart; these two were picking up at least a hundred pounds an hour.

Now it happened late in the afternoon that a man of shabby fiiure, evidently not a digger, observing that there was always more or less crowd in one pla<je, shambled up and looked down

with the rest; as he looked down George happened to look up; the new comer drew back hastily. After that his proceedings were singular, he remained in the crowd more than two hours not stationary but winding in and out. He listened to everything that was said, especially if it was muttered and not spoken out; and he peered into every face, and peering into every face it befell that at last his eye lighted on one that seemed to fascinate him; it belonged to a fellow with a great bull neck, and hair and

beard flowing all into one—a man more like the black-maned lion of North Africa than anything else. But it was not his appearance that fascinated the serpentine one, it was the look he cast down upon those two lucky diggers; a scowl of tremendous hatred—hatred unto death. Instinct told the serpent there must be more in this than extempore envy. He waited and watched, and when the black-maned one moved away, he followed him about everywhere till at last he got him alone. Then he sidled up, and in a cringing way said—

* What luck some men have, don't they ?' The man answered by a fierce grunt.

The serpent was half afraid of him, but he went on.

' There will be a good lump of gold in their tent tonight.'

The other seemed struck with these words.

' They have been lucky a long time' explained the other, * and now this added—'

' Well 1 what about it ?'

* Nothing ! only I wish somebody else had it instead.' 'Why?'

' That is a secret for the present. I only tell you, because I think somehow they are no friends of your's either.'

' Perhaps not! what then.'

'Then we might perhaps do business together; it will strike you singular, but I have a friend who would give money to any one that would take a little from those two.'

' Say that again.'

* Would give money to any one that would take it from those two.'

* And you won't ask for any share of the swag ?'

* Me ? I have nothing to do with it.'

* Ganmion ! well! your friend! will he ?' ' Not a farthing!'

' And what will he give, suppose I have a friend that will do the trick ?'

* According to the risk!'

The man gave a whistle. A fellow with forehead villainously low came from behind some tents.' ' What is it, Will ?' asked the new comer. ' A plant.' ' This one in it!'

* Yes! This is too public, come to Bevan's store.'

VOL. in.

(50)

CHAPTER VL

' George, I want to go to Bathurst/ 'AVliatfor?' ' To buy some things !' ' What things ?'

' First of all a revolver, there were fellows about our tent last night creeping and prowHng.' ' I never heard them.'

* No more you would an earthquake, but I heard them and got up, and pointed my revolver at them, so then they cut—all the better for them. We must mind our eye, George; a good many tents are robbed every week, and we are known to have a good swag.'

* Well I must start this moment if I am to be back.'

' And take a pound of dust and buy things that we can sell here to a profit'

George came back at night looking rather sheep-faced.

'Tom' said he ' I am afraid I have done wrong. You see there was a confounded auction, and what with the hammer and the folk bidding, and his palaver, I could not help it.'

* But what is it you have bought ?'

* A bit o' land Tom.'

Eobinson groaned; but recovering himself he said gaily,

' Well, have you brought it with you ?'

' No, it is not so small as all that; as nice a bit of grass as ever you saw Tom, and just outside the town of Bathurst; only I didn't ought to have spent your money as well as my own.'

' Stuff and nonsense—I accept the investment. Let me load your new revolver. Now look at my day's work. I wouldn't take a hundred pound for these little fellows.'

Greorge gloated over the little nuggets, for he saw Susan's eyes in them. To-night she seemed so near. The little bag was placed between them, the day's spoils added to it, and the tired friends were soon asleep.

d2

(52)

CHAPTER VII.

* Help ! help! murder! help! murder !'

Such were the cries that invaded the sleepers' ears in the middle of the night, to which horrible sounds was added the furious barking of Carlo.

The men seized their revolvers and rushed out of the tent. At about sixty yards distant they saw a man on the ground struggling under two fellows, and still crying though more faintly ' murder' and ' help.'

' They are killing him!' cried George; and Robinson and he cocked their revolvers and ran furiously towards the men. But these did not wait the attack. They started up and off like the wind, followed by two shots from Robinson that whistled unpleasantly near them.

* Have they hurt you my poor fellow ?' said Robinson.

The man only groaned for answer.

Robinson turned his face up in the moonlight, and recognised a man to whom he had never spoken, but whom his watchful eye had noticed more than once in the mine—it was in fact the pedlar Walker.

* Stop Greorge, I have seen this face in bad company. Oh! back to our tent for your life, and kill any man you see near it!'

They ran back. They saw two dark figures melting into the night on the other side the tent. They darted in—they felt for the bag. Gone! They felt convulsively all round the tent. Gone! With trembling hands Kobinson struck a light. Gone—the work of months gone in a moment—the hope of a life snatched out of a lover's very hand, and held out a mile off again !

The poor fellows rushed wildly out into the night. They saw nothing but the wretched decoy vanishing behind the nearest tents. They came into the tent again. They sat down and bowed to the blow in silence, and looked at one another, and their lips quivered, and they feared to speak lest they should break into unmanly rage or sorrow. So they sat like stone till day-break.

And when the first streak of twilight came in George said in a firm whisper,

' Take my hand Tom before we go to work.'

So the two friends sat hand in hand a minute or two; and that hard grip of two working men's hands, though it was not gently eloquent like beauty's soft expressive palm, did yet say many things good for the heart in this bitter hour.

It said, ' A great calamity has fallen: but we do not blame each other, as some turn to directly and do.

It is not your fault George. It is not your fault Tom.'

It said, ' We were lucky together; now we are unlucky together—all the more friends. We wrought together; now we have been wronged together—all the more friends.' With this the sun rose, and for the first time they crept to their work instead of springing to it.

They still found gold in it, but not quite so abundant or so large. They had raised the cream of it for the thieves. Moreover a rush had been made to the hole, claims measured off actually touching them; so they could not follow the gold-bearing strata horizontally— it belonged to their neighbours. They worked in silence—they eat their meal in silence. But as they rose to work again Eobinson said very gravely even solemnly,

G-eorge, now I know what an honest man feels when he is robbed of the fruits of his work and his self-denial and his sobriety. If I had known it fifteen years ago I should never have been a—what I have been.'

For two months the friends worked stoutly with leaden hearts, but did Httle more than pay their expenses. The bag lay between them light as a feather. One morning Tom said to George,

* George this won't do. I am going prospecting. Moore will lend me his horse for a day.'

That day George worked alone. Eobinson rode all over the country with a tin pan at his back, and tested

all the places that seemed likely to his experienced eye. At night he returned to their tent. George was just lying down.

*No sleep to-night George' said he instinctively lowering his voice to a whisper, ' I have found surface-gold ten miles to the southward.'

' Well we will go to it to-morrow.'

* What by daylight watched as we are ? We the two lucky ones' said Eobinson, bitterly. ' No. Watch till the coast is clear—then strike tent and away.'

At midnight they stole out of the camp. By peep of day they were in a little dell with a brook running at the bottom of it.

* Now George listen to me. Here is ten thousand pounds if we could keep this gully and the creek a fortnight to ourselves.'

' Oh Tom! and we will. Nobody will find us here, it is like a box.'

Robinson smiled sadly. The men drove their spades in close to the little hole which Robinson had made prospecting yesterday, and the very first cradle-full yielded an ounce of gold-dust extremely small and pure. They found it diffused with wonderful regularity within a few inches of the surface. Here for the first time George saw gold-dust so plentifiil as to be visible. When a spade-full of the clay was turned up it glittered all over. When they tore up the grass, which was green as an emerald, specks of bright gold came up clinging to the roots. They fell like spaded tigers on the prey.

' What are you doing George ?'

56 * IT IS NEVEK TOO LATE TO MEND/

' Going to light a fire for dinner. We must eat I suppose, though I do grudge the time.' ' We must eat, but not hot.'

* Why not?'

' Because if you light a fire the smoke will be seen miles ofi", and half the diggings will be down upon us. I have brought three days' cold meat—here it is.'

' Will this be enough ?' asked George simply, his mouth full.

' Yes, it will be enough' replied the other bitterly. ' Do you hear that bird George ? They call him a leather-head. What is he singing?'

George laughed. ' Seems to me he is saying " Off we go!" "Off we go!" "Off we go!"'

' That is it. And look now, off he is gone; and what is more, he has gone to tell all the world he saw two men pick up gold like beans.'

' Work!' cried George.

That night the little bag felt twice as heavy as last night, and Susan seemed nearer than for many a day. These two worked for their lives. They counted each minute, and George was a Goliath. The soil flew round him like the dust about a winnowing-machine. He was working for Susan. Eobinson wasted two seconds admiring him.

' Weir said he ' gold puts us all on our mettle, but you beat all ever I saw. You are a man.'

It was the morning of the third day, and the friends were filling the little bag fast; and at breakfast George quizzed Robinson's late fears.

' IT IS NEVER TOO LATE TO MEND.' 57

'The leather-head didn't tell anybody, for here we are all alone.'

Robinson laughed.

' But we should not have been if I had let you light a fire. However I really begin to hope now they will let us alone till we have cleared out the gully. Hallo !'

' What is the matter ?'

' Look there Greorge.'

* What is it ? Smoke rising—down the valley ?' ' We are done ! Didn't I tell you ?'

' Don't say so Tom. Why it is only smoke, and five miles oflf.

* What signifies what it is or where it is. It is on the road to us.'

* I hope better.'

' What is the use hoping nonsense ? Was it there yesterday ? Well then.'

' Don't you be faint-hearted ' said George. ' We are not caught yet. I wonder whether Susan would say it was a sin to try and mislead them ?'

* A sin ! I wish I knew how, I'd soon see. That was a good notion. This place is five hundred pound a day to us. We must keep it to-day by hook or by crook. Come with me quick. Bring your tools and the bag.'

George followed Robinson in utter ignorance of his design; that worthy made his way as fast as he could towards the smoke. When they got within a mile of it the valley widened and the smoke was seen rising from the side of the stream. Concealing themselves they saw two men beating the ground on each side

58 *TT IS NEVER TOO LATE TO MEND/

like pointers. Robinson drew back. ' They are hunting up the stream' said he, * it is there we must put the stopper on them.'

They made eastward for the stream which they had left.

* Come,' said Robinson, * here is a spot that looks likely to a novice, dig and cut it up all you can.'

George was mystified but obeyed, and soon the place looked as if men had been at work on it some time. Then Robinson took out a handful of gold-dust and coolly scattered it over a large heap of mould.

' What are you at? Are you mad Tom? Why there goes five pounds. What a sin!'

' Did you ever hear of the man that flung away a sprat to catch a whale ? Now turn back to our hole. Stop, leave your pickaxe, then they will think we are coming back to work.'

In little more than half an hour they were in their little gully working like mad. They ate their dinner working. At five o'clock Greorge pointed out to Robinson no less than seven distinct columns of smoke rising about a mile apart all down the valley.

' Ay !' said Robinson, ' those six smokes are hunting the smoke that is hunting us I but we have screwed another day out.'

Just as the sun was setting a man came into the gully with a pickaxe on his shoulder.

' Ah! how d'ye do ?' said Rx)binson in a mock friendly accent. ' We have been expecting you. Thank you for bringing us our pickaxe.'

The man gave a sort of rueful laugh, and came and delivered the pick and coolly watched the cradle.

' Why don't you ask what you want to know ?' said Robinson.

The man laughed. ' Is that the way to get the truth from a digger ?' said he.

' It is from me, and the only one.'

' Oh! then what are you doing mate ?'

' About ten ounces of gold per hour.' The man's mouth and eyes both opened.

' Come my lad' said Robinson good-naturedly, ' of course I am not glad you have found us, but since you are come, call your pals light fires and work all night. To-morrow it will be too late.'

The man whistled. He was soon joined by two more and afterwards by others. The whole party was eight. A hurried conference took place, and presently the captain, whose name was Ede, came up to Robinson with a small barrel of beer and begged him and his pal to drink as much as they liked. They were very glad of the draught and thanked the men warmly.

The new comers took Robinson's advice, lighted large fires, divided their company, and groped for gold. Every now and then came a shout of joy, and in the light of the fires the wild figures showed red as blood against the black wall of night, and their excited eyes glowed like carbuncles as they clawed the sparkling dust. George and Robinson fatigued already by a long day broke down about three in the morning. They reeled into their tent, dug a hole, piTt in their gold bag, stamped it down, tumbled dead asleep down over it, and never woke till morn.

Grn 1 r-r-r ! gn 1 r-r-r !

' What is the matter Carlo ?'

Grn 1 r-r-r.

Hum! hum! hum ! Crash ! crash I

At these sounds Eobinson lifted up the corner of his tent. The gully was a digging. He ran out to see where he was to work, and found the whole soil one enormous tan-yard, the pits ten feet square, and so close there was hardly room to walk to your hole without tumbling into your neighbour's. You had to balance yourself and move like boys going along a beam in a timber-yard. In one of these he found Ede and his gang working. Mr. Ede had acquired a black eye, ditto one of his mates.

' Good morning, Captain Eobinson' said this personage with a general gaiety of countenance that contrasted most drolly with the mourning an expressive organ had gone into.

' Well, was I right?' asked Eobinson, looking ruefully round the crowded digging.

' You were, Captain Eobinson, and thank you for last night.'

' Well, you have picked up my name somehow. Now just tell me how you picked up something else. How did you suspect us in this retired spot ?'

' We were working just clear of the great digging by the side of the creek and doing no good when your cork came down.'

' My cork ?'

' Cork out of your bottle.'

* I had no bottle. Oh yes ! my pal had a bottle of small beer.'

* Ay! he must have thrown it into the creek, for a cork came down to us. Then I looked at it and I said, " Here is a cork from Moore's store; there is a party working up stream by this cork." '

Eobinson gave a little groan. ' We are never to be at the bottom of gold digging' said he.

' So we came up the stream and tried several places as we came, but found nothing, at last we came to your pickaxe and signs of work, so my lads would stay and work there, and I let them an hour or two, and then I said, " Come now lads the party we are after is higher up.'

' Now how could you pretend to know that?' inquired Robinson with curiosity.

* Easy enough. The water came down to us thick and muddyish, so I knew you were washing up stream.'

' Confound my stupid head' cried Robinson, * I deserve to have it cut off after all my experience.' And he actually capered with vexation.

' The best may make a mistake' said the other soothingly. ' Well, captain, you did us a good turn last night, so here is your claim. We put your pal's pick in it—here close to us. Oh! there was a lot that made difficulties but we over-persuaded them.' * Indeed! How ?'

' Gave them a hiding, and promised to knock out any one's brains that went into it. Oh! kindness begets kindness, even in a gold-mine.'

' It does' cried Eobinson, ' and the proof is that I give you the claim. Here, come this way and seem to buy it of me. All their eyes are upon us. Now split your gang, and four take my claim.'

* Well, that is good of you. But what will you do captain ? Where shall you go ?' And his eyes betrayed his curiosity.

' Humph! Well I will tell you on condition that you don't bring two thousand after me again. You should look behind you as well as before, stupid.'

These terms agreed to, Robinson let Ede know that he was going this moment back to the old digging. The other was greatly surprised. Robinson then explained that in the old digging gold lay at various depths and was inexhaustible; that this afternoon there would be a rush made from it to Robinson's Gully (so the spot where they stood was already called); that thousands of good claims would thus by diggers' law be vacated; and that he should take the best before the rush came back, which would be immediately, since Robinson's Gully would be emptied of its gold in four hours.

* So clear out your two claims' said he. ' It won't take you two hours. All the gold lies in one streak four inches deep. Then back after me; I'll give you the office. I'll mark you down a good claim.'

Mr. Ede, who was not used to this sort of thing since he fought for gold, wore a ludicrous expression of

surprise and gratitude. Eobinson read it and grinned superior, but the look rendered words needless, so he turned the conversation.

' How did you get your black eye ?'

* Oh! didn't I tell you ? Fighting with the blackguards for your claim.'

It was now Robinson's turn to be touched.

' You are a good fellow. You and I must be friends. Ah ! if I could but get together about forty decent men like you, and that had got gold to lose.'

* Well,' said Ede, ' why not ? Here are eight that have got gold to lose, thanks to you, and your own lot that makes ten. We could easy make up forty for any good lay; there is my hand for one. What is it ?'

Robinson took Ede's hand with a haste and an energy that almost startled him, and his features darkened with an expression unusual now to his good-natured face. ' To put down thieving in the camp' said he sternly.

' Ah!' said the other half sadly (the desirableness of this had occurred to him before now) ; ' but how are we to do that?' said he incredulously. ' The camp is choke full of them.'

Robinson looked blacker, uglier, and more in earnest. So was his answer when it came.

' Make stealing death by the law.'

'The law! What law?'

* Lynch!'

CHAPTER VIII.

One evening about a fortnight after Robinson's return to the diggings two men were seated in a small room at Bevan's store. There was little risk of their being interrupted by any honest digger for it was the middle of the day.

* I know that well enough' growled the black-maned one, 'every body knows the lucky rip has got a heavier swag than ever, but we shan't get it so cheap if we do at all.'

'Why not?'

' He is on his guard now, night and day, and what is more he has got friends in the mine that would hang me or you either up to dry if they but caught us looking too near his tent.'

* The ruflBans. Well but if he has friends he has enemies.'

* Not so many; none that I know of but you and me: I wonder what he has done to you ?'

The other waived this question and replied, ' I have found two parties that hate him; two that came in last week.'

* IT IS NEVER TOO LATE TO MEND.' 65

' Have you ? then if* you are in earnest make me acquainted with them for I am weak-handed, I lost one of my pals yesterday.'

' Indeed ! how ?'

' They caught him at.work and gave him a rap over the head with a spade. The more fool he for being caught. Here is to his memory.'

' Ugh ! what is he is he—'

' Dead as a herring.'

' Where shall we all go to ? What lawless fellows these diggers are. I will bring you the men.'

For the last two months the serpentine man had wound in and out the camp, poking about for a villain of the darker sort, as minutely as Diogenes did for an honest man, and dispensing liquor and watching looks and words. He found rogues galore, and envious spirits that wished the friends ill, but none of them seemed game to risk their lives against two men, one of whom said openly he would kill any stranger he caught in his tent, and whom some fifty stout fellows called Captain Eobinson, and were ready to take up his quarrel like fire. But at last he fell in with two old lags who had a deadly grudge against the captain, and a sovereign contempt for him into the bargain. By the aid of liquor he wormed out their story. This was the marrow of it:—the captain had been their pal, and while they were all three cracking a crib had with unexampled treachery betrayed them, and got them laid by the heels for nearly a year; in fact if they had not broken prison they would not have been

here now. In short in less than half an hour he returned with our old acquaintances brutus and mephistophiles.

These two came half reluctant, suspicious, and reserved, but at sight of Black Will they were reassured, villain was so stamped on him. With instantaneous sympathy and an instinct of confidence the three compared notes, and showed how each had been aggrieved by the common enemy. Next they held a council of war, the grand object of which was to hit upon some plan of robbing the friends of their new swag.

It was a difficult and very dangerous job. Plans were proposed and rejected, and nothing agreed upon but this, that the men should be carefully watched for days to find out where they kept their gold at night and where by day, and an attempt timed and regulated accordingly. Moreover, the same afternoon a special gang of six was formed, including Walker, which pitiful fox was greatly patronised by the black-maned lion. At sight of him brutus, who knew him not indeed by name but by a literary transaction, was for ' laying on,' but his patron interposed, and having enquired and heard the offence bellowed with laughter, and condemned the ex-pedlar to a fine of half a crown in grog. This softened brutus, and a harmonious debauch succeeded. Like the old Egyptians they debated first sober and then drunk, and to stagger my general notion that the ancients were unwise candour compels me to own it was while stammering maudling stinking and in every sense drunk that mephistophiles drivelled

out a scheme so cunning and so new as threw everybody and everything into the shade. It was carried by hiccoughation.

To work this scheme mephistophiles required a beautiful large new tent; the serpentine man bought it. Money to feed the gang; serpent advanced it.

Robinson's tent was about thirty yards from his claim, which its one opening faced. So he and George worked with an eye ever upon their tent. At night two men of Robinson's party patrolled armed to the teeth; they relieved guard every two hours. Captain Robinson's orders to these men, if they saw anybody doing anything suspicious after dark, were these,—
First fire, Then enquire.

This general order was matter of publicity for a quarter of a mile round Robinson's tent, and added to his popularity and our rascals' perplexities.

These orders had surely the double merit of conciseness and melody; well for all that they were disgustingly offensive to one true friend of the captain's, viz., to Greorge Fielding.

'What is all the gold in the world compared with a man's life?' said he indignantly.

'An ounce of it is worth half a dozen such lives as some here' was the cool reply.

'I have heard you talk very different. I mind when you could make excuses even for thieves that were never taught any better, poor unfortunate souls.'

'Did I?' said the captain a little taken aback.

'Well perhaps I did; it was natural, hem, under the circumstances. No! not for such thieves as these, that haven't got any honour at all.'

'Honour, eh ?'

'Yes ! honour. Look here, suppose in my unconverted days I had broke into a jeweller's shop, that comes nearest to a mine, with four or five pals, do you think I should have held it lawful to rob my pals of any part of the swag just because we happened to be robbing a silversmith ? Certainly not; I assure you George the punishment of such a nasty sneaking dishonourable act would be death in every gang, and cheap too. Well we have broken into Nature's shop here, and we are to rifle her, and not turn to like unnatural monsters and rob our ten thousand pals.'

'Thieving is thieving in my view' was the prejudiced reply.

'And hanging is hanging as all thieves shall find if caught convenient'

'You make my flesh creep Tom: I liked you better when you were not so great a man, more humble like; have you forgotten when you had to make excuses for yourself; then you had Susan on your side and brought me round, for I was bitter against theft: but never so bad as you are now.'

'Oh! never mind what I said in those days; why you must be well aware I did not know what I was talking about. I had been a rogue and a fool and I talked like both, but now I am a man of property, and my eyes are open and my conscience revolts against

theft, and I am satisfied that the gallows is the finest institution going, and next to that comes a jolly good prison. I wish there was one in this mine as big as Pentonville, then property—'

Here the dialogue was closed by the demand the pick made upon the man of property's breath. But it rankled, and on laying down the pick he burst out: 'Well to think of an honest man like you having a word to say for thieving. Why it is a despicable trait in a gold-mine. I'll go farther, I'll prove it is the sin of sins all round the world. Stolen money never thrives, goes for drink and nonsense. Now you pick and I'll wash. Theft corrupts the man that is robbed as well as the thief; drives him to despair and drink and ruin temporal and eternal. No country could stand half an hour without law!! The very honest would turn thieves if not protected, and there would be a go. Besides this great crime is like a trunk railway, other little crimes run into it and out of it, lies buzz about it like these Australian flies, drat you! Drunkenness precedes and follows it, and perjury rushes to its defence.'

'Well, Tom, you are a beautiful speaker.'

'I haven't done yet: what wonder it degrades a man when a dog loses his dignity under it. Behold the dog who has stolen; look at Carlo yesterday when he demeaned himself to prig Jem's dinner; (the sly brute won't look at ours.) How mean he cut with his tail under his belly instead of turning out to meet folk all jolly and waggle-um-tail-um as on other occasions—

mmmmmimmmmm

70 'IT IS NEVER TOO LATE TO MEND.'

Hallo, you sir ! what are you doing so near our tent ?' and up jumped the man of property and ran cocking a revolver to a party who was kneeling close to the friends' tent.

The man looked up coolly; he was on his knees.

' We are newly arrived and just going to pitch, and a digger told us we must not come within thirty yards of the captain's tent, so we are measuring the distance.'

' Well measure it and keep it.'

Eobinson stayed by his tent till the man, whose face was strange to him, had measured and marked the ground. Soon after the tent in question was pitched, and it looked so large and new that the man of property's suspicions were lulled.

' It is all right' said he, ' tent is worth twenty pounds at the lowest farthing.'

While Black Will and his gang were scheming to get the friends' gold, Robinson, though conscious only of his general danger, grew more and more nervous as the bag grew heavier, and strengthened his defences every day.

This very day one was added to the cause of order in a very characteristic way. I must first observe that Mr. McLauchlan had become George's bailiff, that is on discovery of the gold he had agreed to incorporate George's flocks, to use his ground, and to account to him sharing the profits and George running the risks. George had however encumbered the property with Abner as herdsman: that worthy had come whining to him lame of one leg from a blow on the head, which he convinced George Jacky had given him with his battle-axe.

' I'm spoiled for life and by your savage. I have lost my place; do something for me.'

Good-hearted George did as related, and moreover promised to give Jacky a hiding if ever he caught him again. George's aversion to bloodshed is matter of history; it was also his creed that a good hiding did nobody any harm.

Now it was sheep-shearing time and McLauchlan was short of hands; he came into the mine to see whether out of so many thousands he could not find four or five who would shear instead of digging.

When he put the question to George, George shook his head doubtfully, ' however' said he, ' look out for some unlucky ones, that is your best chance, leastways your only one.'

So McLauchlan went cannily about listening here and there to the men who were now at their dinners, and he found Ede's gang grumbling and growling with their mouths full; in short enjoying at the same time a good dinner and an Englishman's grace.

' This will do ' thought the Scot, misled like continental nations by that little trait of ours; he opened the ball.

' I'm saying—my lads will ye gie ower this weary warrh a wee wJiilee and shear a wheen sheep to me.'

The men looked in his face, then at one another, and the proposal struck them as singularly droll. They burst out laughing in his face.

72 ' IT IS NEVER TOO LATE TO MEND.'

McLauchlan (keeping his temper thoroughly but not without a severe struggle). ' Oh fine I ken I'll ha'e to pay a maist deevelich price for your highnesses—aweel Ise pay—aw thing has its price; jaast name your wage for shearing five hunder sheep.'

The men whispered together. The Scot congratulated himself on his success; it would be a question of price after all.

' We will do it for—the wool.'

' Th' 'oo ? 00 ay! but hoo muckle o' th' 'oo ? for ye ken'—

' How muckle ? why all.'

' A the 'oo! ye blackguard, ye're no blate.'

' Keep your temper farmer, it is not worth our while to shear sheep for less than that.'

' De'il go wi ye then!' and he moved off in great dudgeon.

' Stop,' cried the captain,' you and I are acquainted —you lived out Wellington way—me and another wandered to your hut one day and you gave us our supper.'

' Ay lad, I mind o' ye the noo !' ' The jolliest supper ever I had—a haggis you called it.'

' Aye did I my fine lad. I cookit it till ye mysel. Ye meicht help me for ane.'

' I will' said Captain Ede, and a conference took place in a whisper between him and his men.

' It is a' reicht the noo!' thought McLauchlan.

' We have an offer to make to you,' said Eden respectfully.

' Let us hear't.'

' Our party is large, we want a cook for it, and we offer you the place in return for past kindness.'

' Me a cuik y' impudent vagabond I' cried the Caledonian red as a turkey-cock, and if a look could have crushed a party of eight their hole had been their grave.

McLauchlan took seven ireful steps—wide ones— then his hot anger assumed a cold sardonic form, he returned and with blighting satire speered this question by way of gratifying an ironical curiosity.

' An what would ye ha'e the cheek t'offer a McLauchlan to cuik till ye, you that kens sae fine the price o' wark?'

' Thirty shillings.*

' Thretty shilling the week for a M'Lauchlan!' ' The week,' cried Ede,' nonsense—thirty shillings a-day of course. We sell work for gold, sir, and we give gold for it; look here !' and he suddenly bared a sturdy brown arm and smacking it cried ' that is dirt where you come from but it is gold here.'

' Ye're a fine lad,' said the Scot smoothly, ' an ye've a boenny aerm,' added he looking down at it, ' I'se no deny that. I'm thinking I'll just come and cuik till ye a wee for auld lang syne—thretty schelln the day— an ye'U buy the flesh o' me. I'll seU it a hantle cheaper than thir warldly-minded fleshers.'

Bret, he came to be shorn and remained to fleece. He went and told George what he had done.

' Hech! hech!' whined he, ' thir's a maist awfu' VOL. III. E

come doon for the M'Lauclilans, but wha wadna' stuip toliftgowd?'

He left his head man a countryman of his own in charge of the flocks and tarried in the mine. He gave great satisfaction except that he used to make his masters wait for dinner while he pronounced a thim-dering long benediction; but his cookery compensated the delay.

Eobinson enrolled him in his police, and it was the fashion openly to quiz and secretly respect him.

Eobinson also made friends with the women, in particular with one Mary M'Dogherty wife of a very unsuccessful digger. Many a pound of potatoes Pat and she had from the captain, and this getting wind secured the goodwill of the Irish boys.

CHAPTER IX.

George was very home-sick. ' Haven't we got a thousand pounds a-piece yet ?' ' Hush! no ! not quite : but too much to bawl about.' ' And we never shall till you take my advice and trace the gold to its home in the high rocks. Here we are plodding for dust and one good nugget would make us.'

* Well! well!' said Robinson, ' the moment the dry weather goes you shall show me the home of the gold.' Poor George and his nuggets !

' That is a bargain,' said George, * and now I have something more to say. Why keep so much gold in our tent ? It makes me fret. I am for selling some of it to Mr. Levi.'

• What at three pounds the ounce ? not if I know it.' ' Then why not leave it with him to keep ?'

' Because it is safer in its little hole in our tent. What do the diggers care for Mr. Levi ? You and I respect him, but I am the man they swear by. No, George, Tom weasel isn't caught napping twice in the same year. Don't you see I have been working this four months past to make my tent safe and I've done

E 2

it. It is watched for me night and day and if our swag was in the Bank of England it wouldn't be safer than it is. Put that in your pipe. Well Carlo, what is the news in your part ?'

Carlo came running up to George and licked his face, which just rose above the hole.

' What is it Carlo ?' asked Greorge in some astonishment.

* Ha! ha!' laughed the other, ' here is the very dog come out to encourage his faint-hearted master.'

' No !' said George, ' it can't be that—he means something,—be quiet Carlo licking me all to pieces,—but what it is heaven only knows; don't you encourage him; he has no business out of the tent—go back Carlo—go into kennel sir,' and off slunk Carlo back into the tent, of which he was the day sentinel.

' Tom,' remarked George thoughtfully, ' I believe Carlo wanted to show me something; he is a wonderful wise dog.'

* Nonsense' cried Eobinson sharply, * he heard you at the old lay grumbling, and came to say Cheer up old fellow.'

While Robinson was thus quizzing George, a tremendous noise was suddenly heard in their tent. A scuffle—a fierce muffled snarl—and a human yell; with a cry almost as loud the men bounded out of their hole and the blood running like melting ice down their backs with apprehension burst into the tent; then they came upon a sight that almost drew the eyes out of their heads.

In the centre of the tent, not six inches from their buried treasure, was the head of a man emerging from the bowels of the earth and cursing and yelling, for Carlo had seized his head by the nape of the neck and bitten it so deep that the blood literally squirted, and was stamping and going back snarling and pulling and hauling in fierce jerks to extract it from the earth, while the burly-bearded ruffian it belonged to, cramped by his situation and pounced on unawares by the fiery teeth, was striving and battling to get down into the earth again. Spite of his disadvantage, such was his strength and despair that he now swung the dog backwards and forwards. But the men burst in. Greorge seized him by the hair of his head, Tom by the shoulder, and with Carlo's help wrenched him on to the floor of the tent, where he was flung on his back with Tom's revolver at his temple, and Carlo flew round and round barking furiously and now and then coming flying at him; on which occasions he was always warded off by George's strong arm and passed devious, his teeth clicking together like machinery, the snap and the rush being all one design that must succeed or fail together.

Captain Eobinson put his lips to his whistle and the tent was full of his friends in a moment.

'Get me a bullock rope,'

'Aye!'

'And drive a stout pole into the ground.'

'Aye!'

In less than five minutes brutus was tied up to a

78 ' IT IS NEVER TOO LATE TO MEND.

post in the sun with a placard on his breast on which was written in enormous letters—THIEF (and underneath in smaller letters—)

Caught trying to shake Captain Eobinson's tent. First offence. N.B.—To be hanged next time.

Then a crier was sent through the mine to invite inspection of brutus's features, and ere sunset thousands looked into his face, and when he tried to lower it pulled it savagely up.

* I shall know you again my lad * was the common remark, ' and if I catch you too near my tent, rope or revolver one of the two.'

Captain Eobinson's men did not waste five minutes with brutus. They tied him to the stake and dashed into their holes to make up lost time, but Robinson and George remained quiet in their tent.

* George ' said Tom in a low contrite humble voice, ' let us return thanks to heaven, for vain is man's skill'

And they did.

* George' said Tom rising from his knees, ' the conceit is taken out of me for about the twentieth time; I felt so strong and I was nobody. The danger came in a way I never dreamed and when it had come we were saved by a friend I never valued. Give a paw. Carlo.'

Carlo gave a paw.

* He has been a good friend to us this day,' said

George. ' I see it all now; he must have heard the earth move and did not imderstand it, so he came for me, and when you would not let me go he went back, and says he—" I dare to say it is a rabbit burrowing up." So he waited still as death watching and nailed six feet of vermin instead of bunny.'

Here they both iell to caressing Carlo who jumped and barked and finished with a pretended onslaught on the captain as he was kneeling looking at their so late em-perilled gold, and knocked him over and slobbered his face when he was down. Opinions varied, but the impression was he knew he had been a clever dog. This same evening Jem made a collar for him on which was written, ' Policeman C

The fine new tent was entered and found deserted, nothing there but an enormous mound of earth that came out of the subterranean, which Eobinson got a light and inspected all the way to its debouchure in his own tent. As he returned holding up his light and peering about he noticed something glitter at the top of the arch; he held the light close to it and saw a speck or two of gold sparkling here and there. He took out his knife and scraped the roof in places and brought to light in detached pieces a layer of gold-dust about the substance of a sheet of blotting paper and full three yards wide; it crossed the subterranean at right angles, dipping apparently about an inch in two yards. The conduct of brutus and co. had been typical. They had been so bent on theft that they were blind to the pocketsful of honest safe easy gold they rubbed their very eyes and their tliick skulls against on their subterranean path to danger and crime.

Two courses occurred to Eobinson; one was to try and monopolize this vein of gold, the other to take his share of it and make the rest add to his popularity and influence in the mine. He chose the latter, for the bumptiousness was chilled in him. This second attack on his tent made him tremble.

'I am a marked man' said he. 'Well if I have enemies the more need to get friends all round me.'

I must here observe that many men failed altogether at the gold diggings and returned in rags and tatters to the towns; many others found a little, enough to live like a gentleman anywhere else but too little for bare existence in a place where an egg cost a shilling, a cabbage a shilling, and baking two pounds of beef one shilling and six pence, and a pair of mining boots eight pounds, and a frying-pan thirty shillings, and so on.

Besides the hundreds that fell by diarrhoea, their hands clutching in vain the gold that could not follow them, many a poor fellow died of a broken heart and hardships suffered in vain, and some, long unlucky but persevering, suddenly surprised by a rich find of gold fell by the shock of good fortune, went raving mad on the spot, dazzled by the gold, and perished miserably. For here all was on a great heroic scale: starvation wealth industry crime retribution madness and disease.

Now the good-natured captain had his eye upon four unlucky men at this identical moment.

No. 1, Mr. Miles his old master, who having run through his means had come to the diggings. He had joined a gang of five; they made only about three pounds a-week each and had expelled him, alleging that his work was not quite up to their mark. He was left without a mate and earned a precarious livelihood without complaining, for he was game, but Eobinson's quick eye and ear saw his clothes were shabby and that he had given up his ha! ha! ha!

No. 2, Jem, whose mate had run away and robbed him and he was left solus with his tools.

No. 3, Mr. Stevens, an accomplished scholar and above all linguist, broad in the forehead but narrow in the chest, who had been successively rejected by five gangs and was now at a discount. He picked up a few shillings by interpreting, but it was a suspicious circumstance that he often came two miles from his end of the camp to see Robinson just at dinner-time, Then a look used to pass between these two good-hearted creatures, and Mr. Stevens was served first and Carlo docked till evening. Titles prevailed but little in the mine. They generally addressed the males of our species thus—

'Hi! man!'

The females thus—

'Hi! woman!'

The Spartans! but these two made an exception in favour of this reduced scholar. They called him '* Sir," and felt abashed his black coat should so rusty; and they gave him the gristly bits for he was not working but always served him first.

mffmtrrmrm

wffmmmm

82 'IT IS NEVER TOO LATE TO MEND.'

No. 4. Unlucky Jack, a digger. This man really seemed to be unlucky. Grangs would find the stuiF on four sides of him, and he none; his last party had dissolved, owing they said to his ill-luck, and he was forlorn. These four Eobinson convened, with the help of Mary M'Dogherty, who went for Stevens ; and made them a little speech, telling them he had seen all their four ill-lucks, and was going to end that with one blow. He then, taking the direction of brutus's gold-vein, marked them out a claim full forty yards off, and himself one close to them; organized them, and set them working in high spirits tremulous expectation and a fervour of gratitude to him, and kindly feeling towards their unlucky comrades.

' You won't find anything for six feet' said the captain. ' Meantime, all of you turn to and tell the rest how you were the unluckiest man in the whole mine—till you fell in with me—he ! he !'

And the captain chuckled. His elastic vanity was fast recovering from brutus, and his spirits rising.

Towards evening he collected his ^whole faction, got on the top of two cradles, made a speech, thanked them for their good-will, and told them he had now an opportunity of making them a return. He had discovered a vein of gold which he could have kept all to himself, but it was more just and more generous to share it with his partisans.

' Now, pass through this little mine one at a time,' said he, ' and look at the roof, where I have stuck the

two lighted candles, and then pass on quick to make room for others.'

The men dived one after another, examined the roof, and rushing wildly out at the other end in great excitement ran and marked out claims on both sides of the subterranean.

But with all their greediness and eagerness, they left ten feet square untouched on each side the subterranean.

'What is this left for?'

* That is left for the clever fellow that found the gold after a thief had missed it' cried one.

* And for the generous fellow that parted his find ' roared another from a distance.

Eobinson seemed to reflect.

* No! I won't spoil the meat by cutting myself the fat—no ! I am a digger, but not only a digger, 1 aspire to the honour of being a captain of diggers; my claim lies out there.'

' Hurrah ! three cheers for Captain Robinson !'

* Will you do me a favour in return ?' ' Hurrah! won't we ?'

' I am going to petition the governor to send us out police to guard our tents.'

' Hurrah!'

' And even beaks, if necessary—(doubtful murmurs) And above all, soldiers to take our gold safe down to Sydney.'

' Hurrah!'

* Where we can sell it at three fifteen the ounce.'

' Hurrah! hurrah! hurrah!'

* Instead of giving it away here for three pounds, and then being robbed. If you will all sign, Mr. Stevens and I will draw up the petition; no country can stand without law!'

* Hurrah for Captain Eobinson the digger's friend.' And the wild fellows jumped out of the holes, and

four seized the digger's friend, and they chaired him in their rough way, and they put Carlo into a cradle, and raised him high, and chaired him; and both man and dog were right glad to get safe out of the precarious honour.

The proceedings ended by brutus being loosed and set between two long lines of men with lumps of clay, and pelted and knocked down, and knocked up again, and driven bruised battered and bleeding out of that part of the camp. He found his way to a little dirty tent not much bigger than a badger's hole, crawled in, and sunk down in a fainting state, and lay on his back stiff and fevered and smarting soul and body many days.

And while Robinson was exulting in his skill, his good fortune, his popularity, his swelling bag, and the constabulary force he was collecting and heading, this tortured ruffian, driven to utter desperation by the exposure of his features to all the camp with ' Thief blazing on him, lay groaning stiff and sore but lived for revenge.

' Let him keep his gold—I don't care for his gold now. I'll have his blood !'

(85)

CHAPTEK X.

' I WONDER at you giving away the claim that lay close to the gold ; it is all very well to be generous, but you forget—Susan.'

' Don't you be silly George: the vein dips, and those that cut down on it where it is horizontallish will get a little; we, that nick it nearly verticallish, will get three times as much out of a ten foot square claim.'

' Well! you are a sharp fellow, to be sure; but if it is so, why on earth did you make a favour to them of giving them the milk and taking the cream ?'

' Policy George ! policy !'

(86)

CHAPTER XI.

Sunday.

* Tom, I invite you to a walk.'

* Ay! ay! I'd give twenty pounds for one; but the ?'

* Leave it this one day with Mr. Levi; he has got two young men always armed in his tent, and a little peevish dog, and gutta percha pipes running into all the Jews' tents that are at his back like chicks aftcr the old hen.'

* Oh ! he is a deep one.'

* And he has got mouth-pieces to them, and so he could bring thirty men upon a thief in less than half a minute.'

' Well then, Greorge! a walk is a great temptation this beautiful day.'

In short, by eight o'clock the gold was deposited, and the three friends, for Policeman C must count for one, stepped lustily out in the morning air.

It was the month of January ; a blazing-hot day was beginning to glow through the freshness of morning f

the sky was one cope of pure blue, and the southern air crept slowly up its wings clogged with fragrance, and just tuned the trembling leaves—no more.

' Is not this pleasant, Tom—isn't it sweet ?'

' I believe you, Greorge! and what a shame to run down such a country as this. There they come home, and tell you the flowers have no smell, but they keep dark about the trees and bushes being haystacks of flowers. SnufF the air as we go, it is a thousand English gardens in one. Look at all those tea-scrubs, each with a thousand blossoms on it as sweet as honey, and the golden wattles on the other side, and all smelling like seven o'clock; after which flowers be hanged 1'

' Ay, lad! it is very refreshing—and it is Sunday, and we have got away from the wicked for an hour or two; but in England, there would be a little white church out yonder, and a spire like an angel's forefinger pointing from the grass to heaven, and the lads in their clean smockfrocks like snow, and the wenches in their white stockings and new shawls, and the old women in their scarlet cloaks and black bonnets, all going one road, and a tinkle tinkle from the bellfry, that would turn all these other sounds and colours and sweet smells holy as well as fair on the Sabbath morn. Ah! England. Ah!'

' You will see her again—no need to sigh.'

' Oh, I was not thinking of her in particular just then.'

' Of who?'

' Of Susan!'

* Prejudice be hanged, this is a lovely land/

' So 'tis, Tom, so 'tis. But I'll tell you what puts me out a little bit; nothing is what it sets up for here. If you see a ripe pear and go to eat it, it is a lump of hard wood. Next comes a thing the very sight of which turns your stomach, and that is delicious, a loquot for instance. There now look at that magpie! well it is Australia—so that magpie is a crow and not a magpie at all. Everything pretends to be some old friend or other of mine, and turns out a stranger. Here is nothing but surprises and deceptions. The flowers make a point of not smelling, and the bushes that nobody expects to smell or wants to smell they smell lovely.'

' What does it matter where the smell comes from, so that you get it ?'

* Why, Tom,' replied Greorge opening his eyes, ' it makes all the difference. I like to smell a flower— flower is not complete without smell—but I don't care if I never smell a bush till I die. Then the birds they laugh and talk like Christians; they make me split my sides, God bless their little hearts: but they won't chirrup. Oh dear no, bless you they leave the Christians to chirrup, they hold conversations and giggle, and laugh and play a thing like a fiddle—it is Australia! where everything is inside out and topsy turvy. The animals have four legs so they jmnp on two. Ten foot square of rock lets for a pound a month; ten acres of grass for a shilling a year. Eoasted at Christmas, shiver o' cold on Midsummer-day. The lakes are grass, and the rivers turn their backs on the sea and run into the heart of the land; and the men would stand on their heads, but I have taken a thought, and I've found out why they don't.'

^Why?'

' Because if they did their heads would point the same way a man's head points in England.'

Eobinson laughed, and told Greorge he admired the country for these very traits. ' Novelty for me against the world. Who'd come twelve thousand miles to see nothing we couldn't see at home ? Hang the same old story always; where are we going George ?'

' Oh, not much farther, only about twelve miles from the camp ?'

' Where to ?'

' To a farmer I know. I am going to show you a lark, .Tom,' said George, and his eyes beamed benevolence on his comrade.

Eobinson stopped dead short. ' George,' said he,' no! don't let us. I would rather stay at home and read my book. You can go into temptation and come out pure : I can't. I am one of those that if I go into a puddle up to my shoe, I must splash up to my middle.'

' What has that to do with it ?'

' Your proposing to me to go in for a lark on the Sabbath-day.'

' Why Tom, am I the man to tempt you to do evil ?' asked George hurt.

' Why no ! but you proposed a lark.'

' Aye but an innocent one, one more likely to lift your heart on high than to give you ill thoughts.'

' Well, this is a riddle;' and Eobinson was intensely puzzled.

' Carlo,' cried Greorge suddenly, ' come here, I will not have you hunting and tormenting those Kangaroo rats to-day. Let us all be at peace if you please. Come to heel.'

The friends strode briskly on, and a little after eleven o'clock they came upon a small squatter's house and premises. ' Here we are ' said George, and his eyes glittered with innocent delight.

The house was thatched and white-washed, and English was written on it and on every foot of ground round it. A furze bush had been planted by the door. Vertical oak palings were the fence, with a five-barred gate in the middle of them. From the little plantation all the magnificent trees and shrubs of Australia had been excluded with amazing resolution and consistency, and oak and ash reigned safe from over-towering rivals. They passed to the back of the house, and there George's countenance fell a little, for on the oval grass-plot and gravel walk he found from thirty to forty rough fellows, most of them diggers.

* Ah well' said he on reflection, ' we could not expect to have it all to ourselves, and indeed it would be a sin to wish it you know. Now, Tom, come this way ; here it is, here it is—there.' Tom looked up, and in a gigantic cage was a light brown bird.

He was utterly confounded. ' What is it this we came twelve miles to see ?'

' Aye! and twice twelve wouldn't have been much to me.'

* Well, but where is the lark you talked of?'

' This is it.'

'This? This is a bird.'

' Well, and isn't a lark a bird ?'

' Oh, ay! I see! ha! ha! ha! ha!'

Robinson's merriment was iuterrupted by a harsh remonstrance from several of the diggers, who were all from the other end of the camp.

' Hold your cackle,' cried one, ' he is going to

sing;' and the whole party had their eyes turned with expectation towards the bird.

Like most singers he kept them waiting a bit. But at last, just at noon when the mistress of the house had warranted him to sing, the little feathered exile began as it were to tune his pipes. The savage men gathered round the cage that moment, and amidst a dead stillness the bird uttered some very uncertain chirps, but after a while he seemed to revive his memories, and call his ancient cadences back to him one by one, and string them sotto voce.

And then the same sim that had warmed his little heart at home came glowing down on him here, and he gave music back for it more and more, till at last amidst breathless silence and glistening eyes of the rough diggers hanging on his voice, outburst in that distant land his English song.

It swelled his little tkroat and gushed from him with thrilling force and plenty, and every time he checked his song to think of its theme, the green meadows, the quiet stealing streams the clover he first soared from and the spring he sang so well, a loud sigh from many a rough bosom many a wild and wicked heart told how tight the listeners had held their breath to heai him: and when he swelled with song again, and poured with all his soul the green meadows the quiet brooks the honey clover and the English spring, the rugged mouths opened and so stayed, and the shaggy lips trembled, and more than one drop trickled from fierce unbridled hearts down bronzed and rugged cheeks.

Dulce domimi!

And these shaggy men full of oaths and strife and cupidity had once been curly-headed boys, and some had strolled about the English fields with little sisters and little brothers, and seen the lark rise and heard him sing this very song. The little playmates lay in the church-yard, and they were full of oaths and drink and lusts and remorses, but no note was changed in this immortal song. And so for a moment or two years of vice rolled away like a dark cloud from the memory, and the past shone out in the song-shine: they came back bright as the immortal notes that lighted them those faded pictures and those fleeted days; the cottage, the old mother's tears when he left her without one grain of sorrow; the village-church and its simple chimes— ding dong bell ding dong bell ding dong bell; the

clover field hard by in whicli he lay and gambolled, while the lark praised God overhead; the chubby playmates that never grew to be wicked, the sweet sweet hours of youth and innocence and home.

CHAPTEE XIL

'What will you take for him mistress ? I will give you five pounds for him.'

'No ! no ! I won't take five pounds for my lark !'

'Of course she won't,' cried another, ' she wouldn't be such a flat. Here missus,' cried he, ' I'll give you that for him,' and he extended a brown hand with at least thirty new sovereigns glittering in it.'

The woman trembled ; she and her husband were just emerging from poverty after a hard fight; she threw her white apron over her head. ' Oh !' she cried * it is a shame to tempt a poor woman with so much gold. We had six brought over, and all died on the way but this one.'

' you put the blunt' up and don't tempt the

woman,' was the cry. Another added, ' Why you fool it wouldn't live a week if you had it,' and they all abused the merchant: but the woman turned to him kindly and said,

' You come to me every Sunday and he shall sing to you. You will get more pleasure from him so' said she sweetly * than if he was always by you.'

'So I will old girl' replied the rough in a friendly tone.

George stayed till the lark gave up singing altogether and then he said ' Now I am off. I don't want to hear bad language after that, let us take the lark's chirp home to bed with us;' and they made off, and true it was the pure strains dwelt upon their spirits, and refreshed and purified these sojourners in a godless place. Meeting these two figures on Sunday afternoon armed each with a double barrelled gun and a revolver, you would never have guessed what gentle thoughts possessed them wholly. They talked less than they did coming, but they felt so quiet and happy.

' The pretty bird,' purred George (seeing him by the ear,) ' I feel after him—there—as if I had just come out o' church.'

' So do I George, and I think his song must be a psalm, if we knew all.'

' That it is, for heaven taught it him. We must try and keep all this in our hearts when we get among the broken bottles and foul language, and gold,' says George. * How sweet it all smells, sweeter than before.

' That is because it is afternoon.'

' Yes ! or along of the music; that tune was a breath from home that makes everything please me ; now this is the first Sunday that has looked and smelled and sounded Sunday.'

' George, it is hard to believe the world is wicked: everything seems good and gentle, and at peace with heaven and earth.'

A jet of smoke issued from the bush, followed by the report of a gun, and Carlo, who had taken advantage of George's reverie to slip on a-head, gave a sharp howl, and spun round upon all fours.

'The scoundrels!' shrieked Robinson. And in a moment his gun was at his shoulder, and he fired both barrels slap into the spot whence the smoke had issued.'

Both the men dashed up and sprang into the bush revolver in hand, but ere they could reach it the dastard had run for it; and the scrub was so thick pursuit was hopeless. The men returned full of anxiety for Carlo.

The dog met them, his tail between his legs, but at sight of Greorge he wagged his tail, and came to him and licked Greorge's hand, and walked on with them licking George's hand every now and then.

'Look Tom, he is as sensible as a Christian. He knows the shot was meant for him, though they didn't hit him.'

By this time the men had got out of the wood and pursued their road, but not with tranquil hearts. Sunday ended with the noise of that coward's gun. They walked on hastily, guns ready, fingers on trigger: at war. Suddenly Robinson looked back, and stopped and drew George's attention to Carlo. He was standing with all his four legs wide apart like a statue. George called him; he came directly, and was for licking George's hand, but George pulled him about and examined him all over.

'I wish they may not have hurt him after all the butchers; they have too. See here Tom, here is one

streak of blood on his belly ; nothing to hurt though I do hope. Never mind Carlo' cried Greorge, ' it is only a single shot by what I can see, 'tisn't like when Will put the whole charge into you rabbit shooting, is it Carlo? No, says he; we don't care for this, do we Carlo ?' cried George, rather boisterously.

'Make him go into that pool there' said Robinson, * then he won't have fever.'

* I will; here—cess! cess !' He threw a stone into the pool of water that lay a little off the road, and Carlo went in after it without hesitation, though not with his usual alacrity : afler an unsuccessful attempt to recover the stone he swam out lower down, and came back to the men and wagged his tail slowly, and walked behind George.

They went on.

* Tom ' said George, after a pause, ' I don't like it.' ' Don't like what ?'

' He never so much as shook himself.'

' What of that ? He did shake himself I should say.'

* Not as should be. Who ever saw a dog come out of the water and not shake himself Carlo, hie Carlo!' and George threw a stone along the ground, after which Carlo trotted; but his limbs seemed to work stiffly : the stone spun round a sharp comer in the road, the dog followed it.

* He will do now ' said Eobinson.

They walked briskly on. On turning the corner they found Carlo sitting up and shivering with the stone between his paws.

VOL. III. F

' We must not let him sit' said Tom, * keep his blood warm. I don't think we ought to have sent him into the water.'

* I don't know' muttered George gloomily. 'Carlo,' cried he cheerfully ' don't you be downhearted; there is nothing so bad as faint-heartedness for man or beast. Come, up and away ye go, and shake it off like a man.'

Carlo got up and wagged his tail in answer, but he evidently was in no mood for running, he followed languidly behind.

'Let us get home' said Robinson; * there is an old pal of mine that is clever about dogs, he will cut the shot out if there is one in him, and give him some physic'

The men strode on, and each to hide his own uneasiness chatted about other matters, but all of a sudden Robinson cried out, 'Why where is the dog?' They looked back, and there was Carlo some sixty yards in the rear, but he was not sitting this time, he was lying on his belly.

* Oh! this is a bad job' cried George. The men x-an up in real alarm: Carlo wagged his tail as soon as they came near him but he did not get up.

'Carlo' cried George despairingly, * you woul^'t do it, you couldn't think to do it. Oh! my dear Carlo, it is only making up your mind to live; keep up your heart old fellow; don't go to leave us alone among these villains. My poor dear darling dog. Oh no! he won't live, he can't live ; see how dull his poor dear eye is getting. Oh! Carlo! Carlo!'

At the sound of his master's voice in such distress Carlo whimpered, and then he began to stretch his limbs out. At the sight of this Eobinson cried hastily—

* Bub him George, we did Avrong to send him into the water.'

George rubbed him all over. After rubbing him awhile he said—

'Tom, I seem to feel him turning to dead under my hand.'

George's hand in rubbing Carlo came round to the dog's shoulder, then Carlo turned his head and for the third time began to lick George's hand. George let him lick his hand and gave up rubbing him, for where was the use ? Carlo never left off licking his hand, but feebly, very feebly, more and more feebly.

Presently, even while he was licking his hand, the poor thing's teeth closed slowly on his loving tongue, and then he could lick the beloved hand no more. Breath fluttered about his body a little while longer-; but in truth he had ceased to live when he could no longer kiss his master's hand.

And so the poor single-hearted soul was gone.

George took it up tenderly in his arms. Eobinson made an effort to console him.

'Don't speak to me if you please,' said George -gently, but quickly. He carried it home silently, and laid it silently down in a corner of the tent.

Robinson made a fire and put some stakes on, and made George slice some potatoes to keep him from

f2

looking always at what so little while since was Carlo. Then they sat down silently and gloomily to dinner, it was long past their usual hour and they were work' ing men. Until we die we dine come what may. The first part of the meal passed in deep silence. Then Robinson said sadly—

'We will go home Greorge. I fall into your wishes now. Gold can't pay for what we go through in this hellish place.'

'Not it' replied George quietly.

* We are surrounded by enemies.'

'Seems so,' was the reply in a very languid tone.

* Labour by day and danger by night.' ' Ay !' but in a most indifferent tone.

* And no Sabbath for us two.' ' No I'

'I'll do my best for you, and when we have five hundred poimds more you shall go home to Susan.' • ' Thank you. He was a good friend to us that lies there under my coat; he used to lie over it and then who dare touch it.'

'No! but don't give way to that George, do eat a bit, it will do you good.'

'I will Tom, I will. Thank you kindly. Ah! now I see why he came to me and kept licking my hand so the moment he got the hurt He had more sense than we had; he knew he and I were to part that hour : and I tormented his last minutes sending him into the water and after stones, when the poor thing wanted to be bidding me good-bye all the while. Oh dear! oh dear!'

and George pushed his scarce tasted dinner from him, and left the tent hurriedly his eyes thick with tears.

Thus ended this human day so happily begim; and thus the poor dog paid the price of fidelity this Sunday afternoon.

Siste viator iter and part with poor Carlo, for whom there are now no more little passing troubles no more little simple joys. His duty is performed, his race is run: peace be to him, and to all simple and devoted hearts. Ah me! how rare they are among men.

'What are you doing, Tom, if you please ?'

'Laying down a gut line to trip them up when they get into our tent.'

'When—who?'

'Those that shot Carlo.'

'They won't venture near me.'

'Won't they. What was the dog shot for ? I'hey will come and come to their death; tonight I hope. Let them come ! you will hear me cry " Carlo " in their ears as I put my revolver to their sculls and pull the trigger.'

George said nothing, but he clenched his teeth. After a pause he muttered—

'We should pray against such thoughts.'

Robinson was disappointed, no attack was made; in fact even if such a thing was meditated the captain's friends watched his tent night and day, and made such a feat a fool-hardy enterprise full of danger from without and within.

In the course of the next week a good deal of rain

fell and filled many of the claims, and caused much inaction and distress among the diggers, and Robinson guarded the tent and wrote letters and studied Australian politics, with a view to being shortly a member of congress in these parts. George had his wish at last and cruised about looking for the home of the gold. George recollected to have seen what he described as a river of quartz sixty feet broad, and running between two black rocks. It ran in his head that gold in masses was there locked up, for argued he all the nuggets of any size I have seen were more than half quartz. Robinson had given up arguing the point.

George was imeasy and out of spirits at not hearing from Susan for several months, and Robinson was for indulging him in everything.

Poor George! he could not even find his river of quartz. And when he used to come home day after day empty-handed and with this confession, the other's lips used to twitch with the hard struggle not to laugh at him; and he used to see the struggle and be secretiy more annoyed than if he had been laughed out at.

One afternoon Tom Robinson, internally despising the whole thing, and perfectly sure in his own mind, that there was no river of quartz, but paternal and indulgent to his friend's one weakness, said to him—

'I'll tell you how to find this river of quartz if it is anywhere except in your own head.'

'I shall be much obliged to you. How ?'

'Jem has come back to camp, and he tells me that Jacky is encamped with a lot more close to the gully he is working, it was on the other side the bush there, and Jacky inquired very kind after you.'

' The little viper.'

' He grinned from ear to ear Jem tells me; and says he, " Me come and see Greorge a good deal soon," says he.'

' If he does George will tan his black hide for him.'

' What makes you hold spite so long against poor Jacky ?'

* He is a little sneaking varmint.'

* He knows every part of this country, and he would show you " the home of the gold,"' said Robinson, restraining his merriment with great difficulty.

This cock would not fight, as vulgar wretches say. Jacky had rather mortified George by deserting him upon the first discovery of gold. ' Dis a good deal stupid,' was that worthy's remark on the second day. * When I hunt tings run, and I rim behind and catch dem. You hunt it not run yet you not catch it always. Dat a good deal stupid. Before we hunt gold you do many tings, now do one: dat a good deal stupid. Before, you go so (erecting a fore-finger); now you always so (crooking it). Dat too stupid.' And with this—whirr ! my lord was off to the woods.

On the head of this came Abner limping in, and told how a savage had been seen creeping after him with a battle-axe, and how he had lain insensible for days, and now was lame for life. George managed to forgive Jacky's unkind desertion, but for creeping after Abner and " spoiling him for life," to use Abner's phrase, he vowed vengeance on that black hide and heart.

Now if the truth must be told, Jacky had come back to the camp with Jem, and would have marched before this into George's tent. But Robinson knowing how angry George was with him, and not wishing either Jacky to be licked or George to be tomahawked, insisted on his staying with Jem till he had smoothed down his friend's indignation. Soon after this dialogue Robinson slipped out, and told Jacky to stay with Jem and keep out of George's way for a day or two.

And now the sun began to set red as blood, and the place to sparkle far and wide with the fiery rays emitted from a hundred thousand bottles that lay sown broad-cast over the land; and the thunder of the cradles ceased, and the accordions came out all over five miles of gold-mine. Their gentler strains lasted till the sun left the sky; then just at dusk came a tremendous discharge of musketry roaring rattling and re-echoing among the rocks. This was tens of thousands of diggers discharging their muskets and revolvers previous to reloading them for the night; for calm as the sun had set to the music of accordions, many a deadly weapon they knew would be wanted to defend life and gold ere that same tranquil sun should rise again.

Thus the tired army slept; not at their ease like other armies guarded by sentinels and pickets but every man in danger every night and every hour of it. Each man lay in his clothes with a weapon of death in

his hand; Robinson with two, a revolver, and a cutlass ground like a razor. Outside it was all calm and peaceful. No boisterous revelry—all seemed to sleep innocent and calm in the moonlight after the day of Herculean toil.

Perhaps if any one eye could have visited the whole enormous camp the children of theft and of the night might have been seen prowling and crawling from one bit of shade to another. But in the part where our friends lay the moon revealed no human figures but Robinson's patrol, three men who with a dark lantern and armed to the teeth went their rounds and guarded forty tents above all the captain's. It was at his tent that guard was relieved every two hours. So all was watched the livelong night.

Two pointed rocks connected at the base faced the captain's tent. The silver rays struck upon their foreheads wet with the vapours of night, and made them like frost seen through phosphorus. It was startling. The soul of silver seemed to be sentinel and eye the secret gold below.

And now a sad a miserable sound grated on the ear of night. A lugubrious quail doled forth a grating dismal note at long but measured intervals, offending the ear and depressing the heart. This was the only sound Nature afforded for hours. The neighbouring bush, though crammed with the merriest souls that ever made feathers vibrate and dance with song, was like a tomb of black marble; not a sound—only this little raven of a quail tolled her harsh lugubrious crake.

Those whose musical creed is Time before Sentiment might have put up with this night-bird ; for to do her justice she was a perfect timeist—one crake in a bar the livelong night; but her tune—ugh ! She was the mother of all files that play on iron throughout the globe—Crake I—crake !—crake ! untuning the night.

An eye of red light suddenly opened in the silver stream shows three men standing by a snowy tent. It is the patrol waiting to be relieved. Three more figures emerge from the distant shade and join them. The first three melt into the shade.

Crake!

The other three remain and mutter. Now they start on their rounds.

' What is that?' mutters one.

' I'll go and see.' Click.

' Well r

' Oh, it is only that brown donkey that cruise§ about here. She will break her neck in one of the pits some day.'

' Not she. She is not such an ass.'

These three melted into the night, going their rounds; and now nothing is left in sight but a thousand cones of snow, and the donkey paddling carefully among the pits.

Craake!

Now the donkey stands a moment still in the moonlight—now he paddles slowly away and disappears on the dark side the captain's tent. What is he doing ? He stoops—he lies down—he takes off* bis head and

skin, and lays them down. It is a man ! He draws his knife and puts it between his teeth. A pistol is in his hand—he crawls on his belly—the tent is between, him and the patrol. His hand is inside the tent—he finds the opening and winds like a serpent into the tent. Craake!

(108)

CHAPTER XIII.

Black Will no sooner found himself inside the tent than he took out a dark lantern and opened the slide cautiously. There lay in one comer the two men last asleep side by side. Casting the glare around he saw at his feet a dog with a chain round him. It startled him for a moment—but only for a moment. He knew that dog was dead, mephistophiles had told him within an hour after the feat was performed. Close to his very hand was a pair of miner's boots. He detached them from the canvas and passed them out of the tent; and now looking closely at the ground he observed a place where the soil seemed loose. His eye flashed with triumph at this. He turned up the openings of the tent behind him to make his retreat clear if necessary. He made at once for the loose soil, and the moment he moved forward Robinson's gut-lines twisted his feet from under him. He fell headlong in the middle, and half-a-dozen little bells rang furiously at the sleepers' heads.

Up jumped Tom and George weapons in hand, but not before Black Will had wrenched himself clear and bounded back to the door. At the door in his rage at
being baulked he turned like lightning and levelled his pistol at Kobinson, who was coming at hira cutlass in hand. The ex-thief dropped on his knees and made a furious upward cut at his arm. At one and the same moment the pistol exploded and the cutlass struck it and knocked it against the other side of the tent: the bullet passed over Robinson's head. Black Will gave a yell so frightful that for a moment it paralysed the men, and even with this yell he burst backward through the opening, and with a violent wrench of his left hand brought the whole tent down and fled, leaving George and Robinson struggling in the canvas like cats in an empty flour-sack.

The baffled burglar had fled but a few yards when casting his eye back he saw their helplessness. Losing danger in hatred he came back, not now to rob but murder his left hand lifted high and gleaming like his cruel eye—to plunge it through the canvas.

Flash bang! flash bang I bang! came three pistol shots in his face from the patrol, who were running right slap at him not thirty yards ofi", and now it was life or death. He turned and ran for his life, the patrol blazing and banging at him. Eighteen shots they fired at him, one after another; more than one cut his clothes, and one went clean through his hat, but he was too fleet, he distanced them; but at the reports diggers peeped out of distant tents and at sight of him running flash bang went a pistol at him from every tent he passed, and George and Robinson, who had struggled out into the night, saw the red flashes
issue, and then heard the loud reports bellow and reecho as he dodged about down the line, and then all was still and calm as death under the cold pure stars.

Craake I

They put up their tent again. The patrol came panting back. ' He has got off but he carries some of our lead in him. Go to bed, captain, we won't leave your tent all night.'

Eobinson and George lay down again thus guarded. The patrol sat by the tent: two slept one loaded the arms again and watched. In a few minutes the friends were actually fast asleep again, lying silent as the vast camp lay beneath the silver stars.

Craake 1

And now it was cold, much colder than before, darker too, no moon now, only the silver stars; it makes one shiver. Nature seemed to lie stark and stiff and dead, and that accursed craake is her dirge. All tends to shivering and gloom. Yet a great event approached.

Craake!

A single event a thousand times weightier to the world each time it comes than if with one fell stroke all the kingdoms of the globe became republics and all the republics empires so to remain a thousand years. An event a hundred times more beautiful than any other thing the eye can hope to see while in the flesh, yet it regaled the other senses too and blessed the universal heart.

Before this prodigious event came its little heralds
sweeping across the face of night. First came a little motion of cold air, it was dead still before; then an undefinable freshness; then a very slight but rather grateful smell from the soil of the conscious earth. Next twittered from the bush one little hesitating chirp.

Craake! went the lugubrious quail, pooh-poohing the suggestion. Then somehow rocks and forest and tents seemed less indistinct in shape; outlines peeped where masses had been.

Jug! jug! went a bird with a sweet jurgle in his deep throat. Craake! went the ill-omened one directly, disputing the last inch of nature. But a gray thrush took up the brighter view; otock otock tock! o tuee o o ! 0 tuee 0 o! o chio chee ! o chio chee ! sang the thrush with a decision as well as a melody that seemed to say * Ah! but I am sure of it; I am sure, I am sure, wake
P' joy J joy!'
From that moment there was no more craake: the lugubrious quail shut up in despair, perhaps in disdain,* and out gurgled another jug! jug! jug! as sweet a chuckle as Nature's sweet voice ever uttered in any land; and with that a mist like a white sheet came to light, but only for a moment for it dared not stay to be inspected, ' I know who is coming, I'm off,' and away it crept off close to the ground, and little drops of dew peeped sparkling in the frost powdered grass.
Yock! yock ! 0 chio faliera po ! Otock otock tock ! 0 chio chee! o chio chee!
Jug! jug! jug! jug!
* Like anonymous detraction before vox popuh.
Off we go! off we go!
And now a thin red streak came into the sky, and perfume burst from the bushes, and the woods rang, not only with songs some shrill some as sweet as honey, but with a grotesque yet beautiful electric merriment of birds that can only be heard in this land of wonders. The pen can give but a faint shadow of the drollery and devilry of the sweet merry rogues that hailed the smiling morn. Ten thousand of them, each with half a dozen songs, besides chattering and talking and imitating the fiddle, the fife, and the trombone. Niel gow! niel gow I niel gow! whined a leather-head. Take care o' my hat! cries a thrush in a soft melancholy voice; then with frightful harshness and severity, where is your bacca-box! your box! your box! then before any one could answer, in a tone that said devil may care where the box is or anything else, gyroc de doc! gyroc de doc! roc de doc! cheboc cheboc! Then came a tremendous cackle ending with an obstreperous hoo! hoo! ha I from the laughing jackass who had caught sight of the red streak in the sky—harbinger, like himself, of mom; and the piping crows or whistling magpies modulating and humming and chanting, not like birds but like practised musicians with rich barytone voices, and the next moment creaking just for all the world like Punch or barking like a pug dog. And the delicious thrush with its sweet and mellow tune. Nothing in an English wood so honey sweet as his otock otock tock! o tuee o o! 0 tuee 0 01 0 chio chee! o chio chee !
But the leatherheads beat all. Niel gow ! niel gow ! niel gow ! oiF we go ! off we go ! off we go ! followed by rapid conversations, the words unintelligible but perfectly articulate, and interspersed with the oddest chuckles, plans of pleasure for the day perhaps. Then ri tiddle tiddle tiddle tiddle tiddle tiddle tiddle ! playing a thing like a fiddle with wires ; then ' off we go' again, and bow! wow! wow! jug! jug! jug! jug! jug! and the whole lot in exuberant spirits, such extravagancies of drollery, such rollicking jollity, evidently splitting their sides with fun, and not able to contain themselves for it.
Oh! it was twelve thousand miles above the monotonous and scanty strains of an European wood, and when the roving and laughing and harshly demanding bacca boxes and then as good as telling you they didn't care a feather for bacca-boxes or anything else; gyroc de doc! cheboc cheboc cheboc! and loudly announcing their immediate departure, and perching in the same place all the more ; and sweet low modulations ending in putting on the steam and creaking like Punch, and then almost tumbling off the branches with laughing at the general accumulation of nonsense. When all this drollery and devilry, and joy and absurdity were at their maddest, and these thousand feathered fountains bubbling song were at their highest, then came the cause of all the merry hubbub, the pinnacles of rock glowed burnished gold ; Nature that had crept from

gloom to pallor, burst from pallor to light and life and burning colour, the great sun's forehead came with one gallant stride into the sky, and it was day !

Outshone ten thousand tents of every size and hue and shape, from Isaac Levi's rood of white canvas down to sugar loaves, and even to miserable roofs built on the bare ground with slips of bark, under which imlucky diggers crept at night like badgers—roofed beds—no more, the stars twinkling through chinks in the tester. The myriad tents were clustered for full five miles on each side of the river, and it wound and sparkled in and out at various distances, and shone like a mirror in the distant back-ground.

At the first ray the tents disgorged their inmates and the human hive began to hum; then came the fight, the manoeuvring, the desperate wrestle with Nature, and the keen fencing with their fellows, in short the battle, to which that nothing might be wanting, out burst the tremendous artillery of ten thousand cradles louder than thunder, and roaring and crashing without a pause.

The base of" the two-peaked rock that looked so silvery in the moon is now seen to be covered with manuscript advertisements posted on it; we can only read two or three as we run to our work :—

^Immense eeduction in eggs only one shilling EACH!!! Bevan's store.'

' Go-ahead library and registration office for NEW CHUMS. Tom Long in the dead-horse gully.'

' If this meets the i of Tom Bowles he will ear OF is pal in the iron-bark gully.'

'it is never too late to mend.' 115

' This is to give notice that whereas my wife
Elizabeth Sutton has taken to drink and gone
off with my mate bob, i will not be answerable
for your debts nor hold any communication with
you in future.'

' James Sutton.'

A young Jew, Nathan, issued from Levi's tent with a rough table and two or three pair of scales and other paraphernalia of a gold assayer and merchant. This was not the first mine by many the old Jew had traded in.

His first customers this morning were George and Robinson.

' Our tent was attacked last night Mr. Levi.'

' Again ? humph!'

' Tom thinks he has got enemies in the camp."*

' Humph! the young man puts himself too forward not to have enemies.'

' Well ' said George quickly, ' if he makes bitter enemies he makes warm friends.'

George then explained that his nerve and Eobinson's were giving way under the repeated attacks.

' We have had a talk and we will sell the best part of our dust to you, sir. Give him the best price you can afibrd for Susan's sake.'

And away went George to look for his quartz river, leaving the ex-thief to make the bargain and receive the money.

In the transaction that followed Mr. Levi did not appear to great advantage. He made a little advance on the three pounds per ounce on account of the quantity, but he would not give a penny above three guineas. No! business was business, he could and would have given George a couple of hundred pounds in day of need, but in buying and selling the habits of a life could not be shaken off. Wherefore Robinson kept back eight pounds of gold dust and sold him the rest for notes of the Sydney Bank.

' Well sir' said Tom cheerfully ' now my heart is light; what we have got we can carry round our waists now by night or day. Well friend, what do you want poking your nose into the tent ?'

Coming out suddenly he had run against a man who was in a suspicious attitude at the entrance.

' No offence' muttered the man, ' I wanted to sell a little gold-dust.'

Levi heard what Robinson said, and came quickly out.

He seated himself behind the scales.

* Where is your gold ?'

The man fumbled and brought out about an ounce. All the time he weighed it the Jew's keen eye kept glancing into his face; he lowered his eyes and could not conceal a certain uneasiness. When lie was gone Levi asked Robinson whether he knew that face.

' No ' said Robinson ' I don't.'

Levi called Nathan out.

' Nathan look at that man, follow him cautiously, and tell me where we have seen him; above all know him again. Surely that is the face of an enemy.'

Then the old man asked himself where he had seen

such an eye and brow and shambling walk as that; and he fell into a brown study and groped among many years for the clue.

' What! is Erin-go-bragh up with the sun for once ' cried Eobinson to Mary M'Dogherty, who passed him spade on shoulder.

' Sure if she warn't she'd never keep up with New-gut,' was the instant rejoinder.

■ Hem! how is your husband, Mary ?'

' Och captain it is a true friend ye are for inquiring. Then it's tied in a knot he is.'

' Mercy on us, tied in a knot ?'

* Tied in a knot intirely—wid the rheumatism, and it's tin days I'm working for him and the childhre, and my heart's broke against gravel' and stone intirely. I wish it was pratees we are digging, I'd may be dig up a dinner any way.'

' There is no difficulty, the secret is to look in the right place.'

*Ay! ay! take your divairsion ye sly rogue, I wish ye had my five childhre.'

' Oh! you spiteful cat!'

' Well Ede, come to sell ?'

* A little.'

' What is to do out there ? seems a bit of a crowd.'

* What haven't you heard ? it is your friend Jem! he has got a slice of luck, bought a hole of a stranger, saw the stuff glitter, so offered him thirty pounds; he was green and snapped at it; and if Jem didn't wash four ounces out the first cradleful I'm a Dutchman.'

118 ' IT IS NEVER TOO LATE TO MEND.'

' Well, I am right glad of that.' A young digger now approached respectfully. ' Police report, captain.'

* Hand it here. May I sit at your table a minute Mr. Levi?' Mr. Levi bowed assent.

* No clue to the parties that attacked our tent last night?'

* None at present captain, but we are all on the look out. Some of us will be sure to hear

of something course of the day, and then I'll come and tell you. Will you read the report? There is the week's summary as well.'

* Of course I will. Mum ! mum ! " Less violence on the whole this week; more petty larceny." That is bad. I'll put it down Mr. Levi. I am determined to put it down. What an infernal row the cradles make. What is this? '* A great flow of strangers into the camp, most thought to be honest, but some great roughs; also a good many Yankees and Germans come in at the south side." What is this ? " A thief lynched yesterday. Flung head foremost into a hole and stuck in the clay. Not expected to live after it." Gro it my boys! Didn't I say law is the best for all parties thieves included? Leave it Andrew, I will examine it with the utmost minuteness.'

The dog used fine words on these occasions, that he might pass for a pundit with his clique, and being now alone he pored over his police-sheet as solemn and stern as if the nation depended on his investigations.

A short explosion of laughter from Andrew inter-

rupted this grave occupation. The beak looked up with offended dignity, and in spite of a mighty effort fell a sniggering: for following Andrew's eyes he saw two gig-umbrellas gliding erect and peaceful side by side among the pits.

' What on earth are they ?'

' Chinamen, captain. They are too lazy to dig. They go about all day looking at the heaps and poking all over the camp. They have got eyes like hawks. It is wonderful I am told what they contrive to pick up first and last. What hats! Why one of 'em would roof a tent.'

' Hurroo!'

' What is up now ?'

* Hurroo!' And up came Mary M'Dogherty dancing and jumping as only Irish ever jumped. She had a lump of dim metal in one hand and a glittering mass in the other. She came up to the table with a fantastic spring and spanged down the sparkling mass on it, bounding back one step like India-rubber even as she struck the table.

' There ould gintleman, what will ye be after giving me for that. Sure the luck is come to the right colleen at last.'

* I deal but in the precious metals and stones,' replied Isaac quietly.

* Sure and isn't gould a precious metal ?'

' Do you offer me this for gold ? This is not even a metal. It is mica—yellow mica.'

* Mikee ?' cried Mary ruefully, with an inquiring look.

At this juncture in ran George hot as fire. ' There!' cried he triumphantly to Robinson, * was I right or wrong ? What becomes of your gold-dust ?' And he laid a nugget as big as his fist on the table.

' Ochone I' cried the Irishwoman, ' they all have the luck barrin' poor Molly M'Dogherty.' , The mica was handled, and George said to her compassionately, ' You see my poor girl the first thing you should do is to heft it in your hand. Now see, your lump is not heavy like—'

' Pyrites!' said Isaac drily, handing George back his lump. ' No! pyrites is heavier than mica, and gold than pyrites.'

' Mr. Levi, don't go to tell me this is not a metal' remonstrated George rather sulkily, * for I won't have it.'

* Nay, it is a metal,' replied Levi calmly, ' and a very useful metal, but not of the precious metals. It is iron.'

* How can it be iron when it is yellow ? And how is one to know iron from gold at that rate ?'

' Be patient ray son' said the old Jew calmly, ' and learn. Take this needle. Here is a scale of gold; take it up on the needle-point. You have done it. Why? Because gold is a soft metal. Now take up this scale from your pyrites ?'

' I can't.'

' No, because iron is a hard metal. Here is another childish test—a blood-stone, called by some the touchstone. Rub the pyrites on it. It colours it not—a hard metal. Now rub this little nugget of pure gold I have just bought.'

* Ay! this stains the stone yellow.'

A soft metal. Here in this little phial is muriatic acid. Pour a drop on my nugget? The metal defies it. Now pour on your pyrites ? See how it smokes and perishes. It cannot resist the acid. There are many other tests, but little needed. No metal, no earthly substance resembles gold in the least.'

* Not to a Jew's eye' whispered Eobinson.

* And much I marvel that arry man or even any woman who has been in a gold-mine and seen and handled virgin gold should take mica (here he knocked the mica clean off the table), or pyrites (here he spanged that in another direction) for a royal metal.'

' I'll tell you what to do Mary,' began Robinson cheerfully. ' Hallo! she is crying. Here is a faint heart.'

' Och! captain dear, Pat an' me we are kilt right out for want of luck Oh! oh ! We niver found but one gould and that was mikee. We can't fall upon luck of any sort—good, bad, or indifferent that is where I'm broke aud spiled and kilt hintirely. Oh! oh! oh!'

' Don't cry. You have chosen a bad spot.'

' Captain avick, they do be turning it up like carrots on both sides of huz. And I dig right down as if I'd go through the orld back to dear old Ireland again. He! he! he! oh! oh! An I do be praying to the Virgin at every stroke of the spade I do, and

VOL. III. G

she sends us no gould at all at all barrin mikee bad cess to't. Oh!'

' That is it. You are on two wrong tacks. You dig perpendicular and pray horizontal. Now you should dig horizontal and pray perpendicular.'

' Och! captain, them's hard words for poor Molly M'Dogherty to quarry through.'

' What is that in your hand ?'

' Sure it is an iligant lump of lead I found,' replied poor Mary; the base metal rising in estimation since her gold turned out dross. ' Ye are great with the revolver captain' said she coaxingly, ' ye'U be afther giving me the laste pinch in life of the rale stuff for it?'

Eobinson took the lump. ' Good heavens! what a weight!' cried he. He eyed it keenly. ' Come Mr. Levi' cried he, ' here is a find; be generous. She is unlucky.'

* I shall be just' said the old man gravely. He weighed the lump and made a calculation on paper, then handed her forty sovereigns.

She looked at them. ' Oh now, it is mocking me ye are old man;' and she would not take the money. On this he put it coolly down on the table.

* What is it at all ?' asked she faintly.

* Platinum' replied Isaac coldly.

* And a magnificent lump of it!' cried Robinson warmly.

' Och captain! och captain dear! and what is platinum at all—if ye plaze ?'

* It is not like your mica,' said Isaac. * See it is heavier than gold, and far more precious than silver. It has noble qualities. It resists even the simple acid that dissolves gold. Fear not to

take the money. I give you but your metal's value, minus the merchant's just profit. Platinum is the queen of the metals.'

* Och captain avick! och! och! come here till I eat you!' And she flung her arm round Eobinson's neck, and bestowed a little furious kiss on him. Then she pranced away; then she pranced back. ' Platinum, you are the boy; y'are the queen of the mitals. May the Lord bless you ould gentleman, and the Saints BLESS YOU! and the VIRGIN MARY BLESS Y OU !'* And she made at Isaac with the tears in her eyes, to kiss him; but he waived her off with calm repulsive dignity. ' Hurroo!' And the child of Nature bounded into the air like an antelope, and frisked three times; then she made another set at them. * May you live till the skirts of your coat knock your brains out the pair of ye ! hurroo !' Then with sudden demureness An here's wishing you all sorts of luck, good bad an indifferent my darlins. Plateenum for iver, and gould to the divil,' cried she suddenly with a sort of musical war-shout, the last words being uttered three feet high in air, and accompanied with a vague kick, utterly impossible in that position except to

* These imprecations are printed on the ascending scale by way of endeavour to show how the speaker delivered them.

g2

Irish, and intended, it is supposed, to send the obnoxious metal off the surface of the globe for ever. And away she danced.

Breakfast now! and all the cradles stopped at once.

' What a delightful calm' said Eobinson, * now I can study my police-sheet at my ease.'

This morning, as he happened to be making no noise, the noise of others worried him.

' Mr. Levi, how still and peaceful they are when their time comes to grub. " The still sow sups the kail," as we used, to say in the north; the English turn the proverb differently, they say, " The silent hog-"'

' Jabber ! jabber! jabber!—aie ! aie!'

* Hallo! there's a scrimmage! and there go all the fools rushing to see it. I'll go too !'

Alas! poor human nature; the row was this.

The peaceful children of the moon, whom last we saw gliding side by side vertical and seemingly imperturbable, had yielded to the genius loci, and were engaged in bitter combat, after the manner of their nation. The gig umbrellas were resolved into their constituent parts; the umbrellas proper, or hats, lay on the ground, the sticks or men rolled over one another scratching and biting. Europe wrenched them asunder with much pain, and held them back by their tails grinning horribly at eacli other and their long claws working unamiably.

The diggers were remonstrating; their morality was shocked.

' Is that the way to fight ? What are fists given us for, ye varmint ?'

Robinson put himself at the head of the general sentiment. ' I must do a bit of beak here!' cried he, ' bring those two tom-cats up before me !'

The proposal was received with acclamation. A high seat was made for the self-constituted beak, and Mr. Stevens was directed to make the orientals believe that he was the lawful magistrate of the mine.

Mr. Stevens, entering into the fun, persuaded the orientals, who were now gig umbrellas again, that Robinson was the mandarin who settled property, and possessed, among other trifles, the power of life and death. On this they took off their slippers before him, and were awe-struck, and secretly wished they had not kicked up a row, still more that they had stayed quiet by the banks of the Hoang-ho.

Robinson settled himself, demanded a pipe, and smoked calm and terrible, while his myrmidons kept their countenances as well as they could. After smoking in silence awhile, he demanded of the Chinese ' What was the row ?'

1st Chinaman. ' Jabber ! jabber! jabber !'

2nd Chinaman. ' Jabber ! jabber ! jabber !'

Both. ' Jabber ! jabber ! jabber !' ■ ' What is that ? can't they speak any English at all ?'

* No!'

126 'it is never too late to mend.'

' No wonder they can't conduct themselves, then!' remarked a digger.

The judge looked him into the earth for the interruption.

' You get the story from them, and tell it.'

After a conference Mr. Stevens came forward.

* It is about a nugget of gold, which is claimed by both parties.'

Robinson. * Stop! bring that nugget into court; that is the regular course.'

Great interest began to be excited, and all their necks were craned forward, when Mr. Stevens took from one of the Chinese the cause of so sanguinary a disturbance, and placed it on the judge's table. A roar of laughter followed, for it was between a pea and a pin's head in magnitude.

Robinson. ' You know this is shocking. Asia, I am ashamed of you. Silence in the court! Proceed with the evidence.'

Mr. Stevens. ' This one saw the gold shining, and he said to the other—" Ah!— "

Robins&n. (Writing his notes.) ' Said—to—the— other—" Ah !"—Stop! what was the Chinese for *'ah?"'

Stevens. ' " Ah!" '

Robinson. * Oh!'

Andrew. ' Come! the beggars have got hold of some of our words!'

Bobinson. * Silence in the court!'

Andrew. * I ask pardon captain.'

Stevens. ' But the other pounced on it first, so they both claim it.'

Robinson. * Well! I call it a plain case.'

Stevens. * So I told them.'

Robinson. ' Exactly ! Which do you think ought to have it ?'

Stevens. * Why, I told them we have a proverb— " Losers seekers finders keepers."'

Robinson. ' Of course ; and which was the finder ?'

Stevens. ' Oh! of course this one that — hum ! Well to be sure he only said " ah !" he did not point. Then perhaps—but on the other hand—himi!'

Robinson. ' Why, don't you see ? but no !—^yes ! why it must be the one that—ugh ! Drat you both ! why couldn't one of you find it, and the other another ?'

Eobinson was puzzled. At last, he determined that this his first judgment should satisfy both parties.

' Remove the prisoners,' said he; ' are they the prisoners or the witnesses? remove them any way, and keep them apart.'

Robinson then searched his pockets, and produced a little gold swan-shot scarce distinguishable from the Chinese. He put this on the table, and took up the other.

' Fetch in number one !'

The Chinaman came in with obeisances and misgivings ; but when the judge signed to him to take up the gold, which he mistook for the cause of quarrel, his face lightened with a sacred joy, he receded, and with a polite gesture cleared a space; then advancing one foot with large and lofty grace, he addressed the judge, whose mouth began to open with astonishment, in slow balanced and musical sentences. This done, he retired with three flowing salaams, to which the judge replied with three little nods.

'What on earth did the beggar say? What makes you grin, Mr. Stevens?'

Stevens. 'He said—click!'

MoMnson. 'Come! tell me first, laugh after.'

Stevens. 'He said—*' May your highness flourish like a tree by the side of a stream that never overflows, yet is never dry, but glides—(click!)—even and tranquil as the tide of your prosperity—"'

Robinson. 'Well, I consent!'

Stevens. '" May dogs defile the graves of your ene-mies!—

Robinson. 'With all my heart! provided I'm not dancing over them at the time.'

Stevens. '" When satiated with earthly felicity may you be received in paradise by seventy dark-eyed houris—"'

Robinson. 'Oh! my eye!'

Stevens. 'Click! " Each bearing in her hand the wine of the faithful, and may the applause of the good at your departure resemble the waves of the ocean beating musically upon rocky caverns. Thy servant, inexperienced in oratory, retires abashed at the great-ness of his subject, and the insignificance of his expressions." So then he cut his stick!'

Rohinson. 'A very sensible speech! Well, boys, I'm not greedy j I take the half of that offer, and give you the rest—bring in the other gentleman!'

No. 2 advanced with reverences and misgivings. Robinson placed the gold on the table and assigned it to him. A sacred joy illumined him, and he was about to retire with deep obeisances.

'Where is his speech?' cried the judge ruefully.

Stevens explained to him that the other had returned thanks. On this No. 2 smiled asscntingly, and advancing delivered the ibllowing sentences—

'Your slave lay writhing in adversity, despoiled by the unprincipled. He was a gourd withered by the noonday sun until your virtues descended like the dew, and refreshed him with your justice and benignity.

'Wherefore hear now the benediction of him wliom your clemency has raised from despair,

'May your shadow increase and cover many lands. May your offspring be a nation dwelling in palaces with golden roofs and walls of ivory, and on the terraces may peacocks be as plentiful as sparrows are to the undeserving. May you live many centuries shining as you now shine; and at your setting may rivulets of ink dug by the pens of poets flow through meadows of paper in praise of the virtues that embellished you here on earth. Sing-tu-Che, a person of small note but devoted to your service, wishes these frivolous advantages to the Pearl of the West, on whom be honour.'

Chorus of diggers —'My eye!'

Robinson rose with much gravity and delivered himself thus—

'Sing-tu-Che, you are a trump, an orator, and a humbug. All the better for you. May felicity attend you. Heichster guchster—honi soit qui mal y pense— donner und blitzen—

tempora mutantur—0 mia cara and pax vobiscum. The court is dissolved.'

It was, and I regret to add that Judge Robinson's concluding sentences raised him greatly in the opinion of the miners.

' Captain knows a thing or two.'

' If ever we send one to parliament that is the man.'

* Hallo! you fellows come here! come here!'

A rush was made towards Jem, who was roaring and gesticulating at Mr. Levi's table. When they came up they found Jem black and white with rage, and Mr. Levi seated in calm indifference.

' What is it ?' asked Robinson.

* The merchant refuses my gold.'

' I refuse no man's gold' objected Levi coolly, ' but this stuff is not gold.'

' Not gold dust,' cried a miner; and they aU looked with wonder at the rejected merchandise.

Mr. Levi took the dust and poured it out from one hand to the other; he separated the particles and named them by some mighty instinct.

* Brass—or-molu—gilt platinum to give it weight; this is from Birmingham not from Australia, nor nature*'

' Such as it is it cost me thirty pounds/ cried Jem. ' Keep it. I shall find him. My spade shall never go into the earth again till I'm quits with this one.'

' That is right/ roared the men, ' bring him to us, and the captain shall sit in judgment again;' and the men's countenances were gloomy, for this was a new roguery and struck at the very root of gold digging.

' I'll put it down Mr. Levi' said Robinson, after the others had gone to their work; ' here is a new dodge, Brummagen planted on us so far from home. I will pull it down with a tenpenny cord but I'll end it.'

Crash! went ten thousand cradles: the mine had breakfasted. I wish I could give the European reader an idea of the magnitude of this sound whose cause was so humble. I must draw on Nature for a comparison.

Did you ever stand upon a rocky shore at evening when a great storm has suddenly gone down, leaving the waves about as high as they were while it raged ? Then there is no roaring wind to dull the clamour of the tremendous sea as it lashes the long re-bellowing shore. Such was the sound of ten thousand cradles; yet the sound of each one was insignificant. Hence an observation and a reflection—the latter I dedicate to the lovers of antiquity—that multiplying sound magnifies it in a way science has not yet accounted for; and that though men are all dwarfs, Napoleon included, man is a giant.

The works of man are so prodigious they contradict all we see of any individual's powers; and even

m

132 * IT IS NEVER TOO LATE TO MEND.'

SO when you had seen and heard one man rock one cradle, it was all the harder to believe that a few thousand of them could rival thunder, avalanches, and the angry sea lashing the long re-echoing shore at night. These miserable wooden cradles lost their real character when combined in one mighty human effort; it seemed as if giant labour had stretched forth an arm huge as an arm of the sea and rocked one enormous engine, whose sides were these great primeval rocks and its mouth a thundering sea.

Crash! from meal to meal!

The more was Robinson surprised when full an horn-before dinner-time this mighty noise all of a sudden became feebler and feebler, and presently himian cries of a strange character made their way to his ear through the wooden thunder.

' What on earth is up now' thought he, ' an earthquake ? '

Presently he saw at about half a mile off a vast crowd of miners making towards him in tremendous excitement. They came on swelled every moment by fresh faces, and cries of vengeance and excitement were now heard, which the wild and savage aspect of the men rendered truly terrible. At last he saw and comprehended all at a glance.

There were Jem and two others dragging a man along whose white face and knocking knees betrayed his guilt and his terror. Eobinson knew him directly, it was Walker, who had been the decoy-duck the night his tent was robbed.

' Here is the captain! Hurrah! I've got him, captain. This is the beggar that peppered the hole for me, and now we will pepper him.'

A fierce burst of exultation from the crowd. They thirsted for revenge. Jem had caught the man at the other end of the camp and his ofience was known by this time to half the mine.

' Proceed regularly Jem,' said Eobinson. ' Don't condemn the man unheard.'

' Oh, no! He shall be tried and you shall be the judge.'

' I consent' said Robinson somewhat pompously.

Then arose a cry that made him reflect: ' Lynch ! Lynch! a seat for Judge Lynch!' and in a moment a judgment-seat was built with cradles and he was set on high, with six strange faces scowling round him for one of his own clique. He determined to back out of the whole thing.

' No! no !' cried he; ' that is impossible. I cannot be a judge in such a serious matter.'

' Why not ?' roared several voices.

' Why not ? Because I am not a regular beak; because I have not got authority from the Crown.'

There was a howl of derision.

' We give you authority !'

' We order you to be judge !'

' We are King, Lords, and Commons!'

' Do what we bid you, or,' added a stranger, ' we will hang you and the prisoner with one rope!'

Grim assent of the surrounding faces.—Robinson
sat down on the judgment-seat not a little discomposed.

' Now then,' remonstrated one; ' what are you waiting for ? Name the jury.'

' Me!' ' Me!' ' Me!' ' I!' 'I!' and there was a rush for the office.

' Keep cool,' replied another. ' Lynch law goes quick, but it goes by rule. Judge, name the jury.'

Eobinson, a man whose wits seldom deserted him, at once determined to lead since he could not resist. He said with dignity, ' I shall choose one juryman from each of the different countries that are working in this mine that no nation may seem to be slighted, for this gold belongs to all the world.'

' Hurrah! Well done, judge. Three cheers for Judge Lynch!'

' When I call a country give me a name, which I will inscribe on my report of the proceedings. I want a currency lad first.'

' Here is one. William Parker.'

'Pass over. France.'
'Present. Pierre Chanot.'
'Germany.'
'Here. Hans Muller.'
'Holland.'
'Here. Jan Van der Stegen.'

Spain and Italy were called, but no reply.

'United States.'
'Here. Nathan Tucker.'

Here Robinson, casting his eyes round, spied McLauchlan, and being minded to dilute the severity of his jury he cried out 'Scotland. McLauchlan, you shall represent her.'

No answer.

'McLauchlan,' cried several voices, 'where are ye ? Don't you hear Judge Lynch speak to you ?'

'Come McLauchlan, come over; you are a respectable man.'

Mr. McLauchlan intimated briefly in his native dialect that he was, and intended to remain so; by way of comment on which he made a bolt from the judgment-hall, but was rudely seized and dragged before the judge.

'For heaven's sake don't be a fool, McLauchlan. No man must refuse to be juryman in a trial by lynch. I saw a Quaker stoned to death for it in California.'

'I guess I was there^ said a voice behind the judge, who shifted uneasily.

McLauchlan went into the jury-box with a meaning look at Eobinson but without another audible word.

'Mercy ! mercy !' cried Walker.

'You must not interrupt the proceedings,' said Judge Lynch.

'Haud your whisht ye gowk. Ye are no land guilty yet' remonstrated a juror.

The jury being formed, the judge called the plaintiff.

'The man sold me a claim for thirty pound. I gave him the blunt because I saw the stuff was glittery. Well, I worked it, and I found it work rather easy, that is a fact.'

'Haw! haw! haw !' roared the crowd, but with a horrible laughter, no placability in it.

'Well, I found lots of dust and I took it to the merchant, and he says it is none of it gold. That is my tale.'

'Have you any witnesses ?'

'I don't know. Yes, the nigger; he saw it. Here Jacky, come and tell them.'

Jacky was thrust forward, but was interrupted by McLauchlan as soon as he opened his mouth. The Scottish juror declined to receive evidence but upon ©ath. The judge allowed the objection.

'Swear him in then' cried a hundred voices.

'Swear ?' inquired Jacky innocently.

Another brutal roar of laughter followed.

Jacky was offended.

'What for you laugh you stupid fellows ? I not a common black fellow. I been to Sydney and learn all the white man knows. Jacky will swear,' added he.

'Left your hand,' cried McLauchlan. 'It is no swearing if you dinna left your hond.'

'Dat so stupid' said Jacky, lifting his hand peevishly. This done, he delivered his evidence thus. ' Damme I saw dis fellow sell dirt to dis fellow, and damme I saw dis fellow find a good deal gold, and damme I heard him say dis is a dam good job, and den damme he put down his spade and go to sell, and directly he come back and say damme I am done.'

' Aweel,' said McLauchlan; ' we jaast refuse yon lad's evidence, the deevelish heathen.'

A threatening murmur.

' Silence! Hear the defendant.'

Walker, trembling like an aspen, owned to having sold the claim, but denied that the dust was false. ' This is what I dug out of it,' said he, and he produced a small pinch of dust.

' Hand it to me,' said the judge. ' It seems genuine.'

' Put it to the test. Call the merchant for a witness,' cried another.

A party ran instantly for Levi. He refused to come. They dragged him with fearful menaces.

' A test old man ! a test of gold 1'

The old Jew cast his eyes around, took in the whole scene, and with a courage few of the younger ones would have shown, defied that wild mob.

* I will give you no test. I wash my hands of your mad passions and your mockeries of justice, men of Belial!'

A moment's silence and wonder, a yell of rage, and a dozen knives in the air.

The judge rose hastily, and in a terrible voice that governed the tumult for an instant said, ' Down knives! I hang the first man that uses one in my court.' And during the momentary pause that followed this he cried out, ' He has given me a test. Kun and fetch me the bottle of acid on his table.'

* Hurrah! Jvidge Lynch for ever!' was now the cry, and in a minute the bottle was thrust into the judge's hand.

' Young man,' said Isaac solemnly, ' do not pour, lest heaven bring your soul to as keen a test one day. Who are you that judge your brother ?'

Judge Lynch trembled visibly as the reverend man rebuked him thus, but fearing Isaac would go further and pay the forfeit of his boldness, he said calmly ' Friends, remove the old man from the court, but use respect. He is an aged man.'

Isaac was removed. The judge took the bottle and poured a drop on that small pinch of dust the man had last given him.

No effect followed.

* I pronounce this to be gold.*

' There,' put in M'Lauchlan, ' ye see the lad was no deceiving you; is it his faut if a' the gowd is no the same ?'

'No!' whimpered Walker, eagerly, and the crowd began to whisper and allow he might be innocent.

The man standing behind the judge said with a cold sneer, ' That is the stuff he did not sell, now pour on the stuff he sold.'

These words brought back the prejudice against the prisoner, and a hundred voices shouted ' Pour !' while their eyes gleamed with a terrible curiosity.

Judge Lynch, awe-struck by this terrible roar, now felt what it is to be a judge; he trembled and hesitated.

' Pour!' roared the crowd still louder and more fiercely.

M'Lauchlan read the judge's feeling, and whimpered out, * let it fa' lad—^let it fa'!'

' If he does our knives fall on him and you. Pour!'

Eobinson poured : all their fierce eyes were fixed on the experiment. He meant to pour a drop or two, but the man behind him jogged his arm and half the acid in the bottle fell upon Walker's dust.

A quantity of smoke rose from it, and the particles fizzed and bubbled under the terrible test.

' Trash ! a rope—no! dig a hole and bury him—no! fling him off" the rock into the water.'

* Silence!' roared Eobinson, * I am the judge, and it is for me to pronounce the verdict.'

* Silence! hear Judge Lynch !' Silence was not obtained though for full five minutes.

* I condemn him to be exposed all day with his dust tied round his neck, and then drummed out of the camp.'

This verdict was received first with a yell of derisive laughter, then with a roar of rage.

* Down with the judge !' ' We are the judges !'

' To the rock with him!'

' Ay, to the rock with him.'

With this an all-over-powering rush was made, and Walker was carried off up the rock in the middle of five himdred infuriated men.

The poor wretch cried ' Mercy ! mercy !'

' Justice! dog,' was the roar in reply. The raging crowd went bellowing up the rock like a wave; and gained a natural platform forty feet above the great deep pool that lay dark and calm below. At the sight

of it the poor wretch screamed to wake the dead, but the roars and yells of vengeance drowned his voice.

' Put his dust in his pocket,' cried one crueller than the rest.

Their thirst of vengeance was too hot to wait for this diabolical proposal, in a moment four of them had him by the shoulders and heels; another moment and the man was flung from the rock, uttering a terrible death-cry in the very air; then down his body fell like lead, and struck with a tremendous plunge the deep water that splashed up a moment then closed and bubbled over it.

From that moment the crowd roared no longer, but buzzed and murmured, and looked down upon their work half-stupidly.

' Hush!'

'What is that?'

' It is his head !'

' He is up again!'

* Can he swim !'

* Fling stones on him.'

' No! Let him alone, or we'll fling you a top of him.'

' He is up, but he can't swim. He is only struggling ! he is down again!'

He was down, but only for a moment; then he appeared again choking and gurgling.

' Mercy ! mercy!'

* Justice thieving dog!' was the appalling answer as before.

' Save me ! save me! oh save me! save me!'

' Save yourself! if you are worth it!' was the savage reply.

The drowning despairing man's head was sinking again, his strength exhausted by his idle struggles, when suddenly on his left hand he saw a round piece of rock scarce a yard from him, he made a desperate effort and got his hand on it. Alas ! it was so slimy, he could not hold by it; he fell off it into the water; he struggled up again, tried to dig his feet into the rock, but after a convulsive cling of a few seconds, fell back, the slimy rock mocked his grasp. He came up again and clung, and cried piteously for help and mercy. There was none !—but a grim silence and looks of horrible curiosity at his idle struggles. His crime had struck at the very root of their hearts and lives. Then this poor cowardly wretch made up his mind that he must die. He gave up praying to the pitiless, who could look down and laugh at his death agony, and he cried upon the absent only. ' My children! my wife! my poor Jenny !' and with this he shut his eyes, and struggling no more, sank quietly down ! down ! down. First his shoulders disappeared, then his chin, then his eyes, and then his hair. Who can fathom human nature? that sad despairing cry which was not addressed to them, knocked at the bosoms that all his prayers to them for pity had never touched. A hasty low and uneasy murmur followed it almost as a report follows a flash.

' His wife and children!' cried several voices with surprise; but there were two men this cry not only touched, but pierced—the plaintiff and the judge.

142 'it is never too late to mend.'

* The man has got a wife and children' cried Jem, in dismay as he tried to descend the rock by means of some diminutive steps. ' They never offended me, he is gone down.—me if I see the man drowned like a rat Hallo!—Splash!'

Jem's foot had slipped, and as he felt he must go, he jumped right out, and fell twenty feet into the water.

At this the crowd roared with laughter, and now was the first shade of good-nature mixed with the guffaw. Jem fell so near Walker, that on coming up he clutched the drowning man's head and dragged him up once more from death. At the sight of Walker's face above water again, what did the crowd think you !

They burst into a loud hurrah! and cheered Jem till the echoes rang again.

* Hurrah! Bravo! Hurrah!' pealed the fickle crowd. Now Walker no sooner felt himself clutched than he

clutched in return with the deadly grasp of a drowning man. Jem struggled to get free in vain. Walker could not hear or see, he was past all that; but he could cling, and he got Jem round the arms and pinned them. After a few convulsive efforts Jem gave a loud groan. He then said quietly to the spectators, ' He will drown me in another half-minute.' But at this critical moment, out came from the other extremity of the pool Judge Lynch swimming with a long rope in his hand: one end of this rope he had made into a bight ere he took the water. He swam behind Walker and Jem, whipped the noose over their heads and tightened it

under their shoulders. * Haul 1' cried he to Ede, who held the other end of the rope. Ede hauled and down went the two heads.

A groan of terror and pity from the mob—their feelings were reversed.

' Haul quick Ede' shouted Robinson ' or 'you will drown them.'

Ede hauled hand over hand, and a train of bubbles was seen making all across the pool towards him; and the next moment two dripping heads came up to hand close together like cherries on a stalk; and now a dozen hands were at the rope, and the plaintiff and defendant were lifted bodily up on to the flat rock, which came nearly to the water's edge on this side the pool.

' Augh! augh! augh ! augh 1' gasped Jem.

Walker said nothing: he lay white and motionless, water trickling from his mouth nose and ears.

Robinson swam quietly ashore. The rocks thundered with cheers over his head.

The next moment ' the many-headed beast' remembered that all this was a waste of time, and bolted under ground like a rabbit, and dug and pecked for the bare life with but one thought left, and that was Gold.

' How are you, Jem?'

* Oh, captain, oh !' gasped poor Jem, ' I am choked, I am dead, I am poisoned, why I'm full of water; Bring this other beggar to my tent, and we will take a nanny-goat together.'

So Jem was taken off hanging his head, and deadly sick supported by two friends, and Walker was carried

to the same tent, and stripped and rubbed and rolled up in a blanket; and lots of brandy poured down Mm and Jem, to counteract the poison they had swallowed.

Eobinson went to Mr. Levi to see if he would lend him a suit, while he got his own dried. The old Jew received my lord judge with a low ironical bow, and sent Nathan to borrow the suit from another Israelite. He then lectured my lord Lynch.

' Learn from this young man, how easy it is to set a stone rolling down hill, how hard to stop it half way down. Law must always be above the mob, or it cannot be law. If it fall into their hands it goes down to their own level, and becomes revenge, passion, cruelty, any thing but law. The madmen! they have lost two thousand ounces of gold—to themselves and to the world, while they have been wasting their time and risking their souls over a pound of brass, and aspiring to play the judge and the executioner, and playing nothing but the brute and the fool as in the days of old.'

Mr. Levi concluded by intimating that there was YGiy little common sense left upon earth, and that little it would be lost time to search for among the Gentiles. Finally his discourse galled Judge Lynch, who thereupon resolved to turn the laugh against him.

' Mr. Levi' said he ' I see you know a thing or two, will you be so good as to answer me a question ?'

* If it come within my knowledge,' replied the senior with grave politeness.

* Which weighs the heaviest sir, a pound of gold or

a pound of feathers ?' and he winked at Nathan, but looked in Isaac's face as demure as a Quakeress.

' A pound of feathers' replied Isaac.

Eobinson looked half-puzzled—half-satirical.

* A childish question' said Isaac sternly. *What boy knows not that feathers are weighed by avoirdu-poids, and gold by Troy weight, and consequently that a pound of feathers weighs sixteen ounces, and a pound of gold but twelve ?'

' Well that is a new answer' cried Eobinson. * Goodbye sir, you are too hard for me;' and he made off to his own tent. It was a day of defeats.

The moment he was out of hearing Isaac laughed! The only time he had done it during six years. And what a laugh! How sublimely devoid of merriment! a sudden loud cackle of three distinct laughs not declining into a chuckle, as we do, but ending sharp in abrupt and severe gravity.

' I discomfited the young man, Nathan,—I mightily discomfited him. Ha! ha! ho! Nathan, did you as I bade you ?'

' Yes, master, I found the man and I sent Samuel, who went hastily to him, and cried out Mr. Meadows is in the camp and wishes to speak to you. Master, he started up in wonder, and his whole face changed; without doubt he is the man you suspected.'

' Yes' said Isaac reflecting deeply. ' The man is Peter Crawley ; and what does he here ?

Some deep villainy lies at the bottom of this, but I will fathom it, aye and thwart it, I swear by the God of Abraham.

Let me think awhile in my tent. Sit you at the receipt of gold.'

The old man sat upon a divan in his tent, and pondered on all that had happened in the mine; above all on the repeated attacks that had been made on that one tent.

He remembered too that George had said sorrowfully to him more than once,—' No letters for me Mr. Levi, no letter again this month.' The shrewd old man tied these two threads together directly.

' All these things are one ' said Isaac Levi.

Thus pondering, and patiently following out his threads the old man paced a mile down the camp to the post-office, for he had heard the postman's horn, and he expected important letters from England, from his friend and agent at Famborough, old Cohen.

There were letters from England, but none in old Cohen's hand. He put them in his bosom with a disappointed look, and paced slowly and deeply pondering back towards his tent. He was about half way, when much to his surprise a stone fell close to him. He took however no notice—did not even accelerate his pace or look round; but the next moment a limip of clay struck him on the arm. He turned round quivering with rage at the insult, and then he saw a whole band of diggers behind him, who the moment he turned his face began to hoot and pelt him.

* Who got poor Walker drowned ? Ah! ah! ah!' ' Who refused to give evidence before Judge Lynch' cried another * Ah! ah ! ah!'

There were clearly two parties in the mob.

' Down with the Jew—the blood-sucker. We do all the work, and he gets all the profit. Ah! ah! ah!'

And a lump of clay struck that reverend head, and almost stunned the poor old man. He sunk upon his knees, and in a moment his coat was torn to shreds, but with unexpected activity he wriggled himself free, and drew a dagger long bright and sharp as a needle. His assailants recoiled a moment. The next a voice was heard from behind—" Get on both sides of him at once!'

Isaac looked and saw Peter Crawley. Then the old man trembled for his life, and cried ' Help! help!' and they hemmed him in and knocked his dagger out of his hand, and hustled and pommeled him, and would have torn him in pieces, but he slipped down, and two of them got in front and dragged him along the ground.

' To Walker's pool,' cried brutus, putting himself at the head of those who followed.

All of a sudden Isaac, though half insensible, heard a roar of rage that seemed to come from a lion—a whizz, a blow like a thunder-clap—saw one of his assassins driven into the air, and falling like a dead clod three yards ofi", found himself dropped and a man striding over him. It was George Fielding, who stood a single moment snorting and blowing out his cheeks with rage, then went slap at the mob as a lion goes at sheep; seized one of the small ruffians by the knees, and by a tremendous effort of strength and rage, actually used him as a flail, and struck brutus with the man's head, and

knocked that ruffian down stunned and Ms nose levelled with his cheeks. The mob recoiled a moment from this one hero. George knew it could be but for a moment, so he had no sooner felled brutus, and hurled the other's carcass in all their faces, than he pounced on Isaac whipped him on his back and ran off with him.

He had got thirty yards with him ere the staggered mob could realize it all.

The mob recovered their surprise, and with a yell like a pack of hounds bursting covert dashed after the pair. The young Hercules made a wonderful effort, but no mortal man could run very fast so weighted. In spite of his start they caught him in about a hundred yards. He heard them close upon him—put the Jew down and whispered hastily, ' Kun to your tent,' and instantly wheeled round and flung himself at thirty men. He struck two blows and disabled a couple; the rest came upon him like one battering-ram and bore liim to the ground; but even as he went down he caught the nearest assailant by the throat and they rolled over one another, the rest kicking savagely at George's head and loins. The poor fellow defended his head with one arm and his assailant's body for a little while, but he received some terrible kicks on the back and legs.

' Give it him on the head!'

' Kick his life out!'

' Settle his hash !'

They were so fiercely intent on finishing George
that they did not observe a danger that menaced themselves.

As a round shot cuts a lane through a column of infantry so clean came two files of special constables with their short staves severing the mob in two—crick, crack, crick, crick, crick, crick, crack, crack. In three seconds ten heads were broken with a sound just like glass bottles under the short deadly truncheon, and there lay half-a-dozen ruffians writhing on the ground and beating the devil's tattoo with their heels.

* Charge back!' cried the head-policeman as soon as he had cut clean through.

But at the very word the cowardly crew fled on all sides yelling. The police followed in different directions a little way, and through this error three of the felled got up and ran staggering off. When the head-policeman saw that he cried out,

' Back, and secure prisoners.'

They caught three who were too stupified to run, and rescued brutus from George, who had got him by the throat and was hammering the ground with his head.

' Let go George,' cried policeman Eobinson in some anxiety ' you are killing the man.'

' Oh, I don't want to kill him neither,' said George.

And he slowly withdrew his grasp and left off hammering with the rascal's head, but looked at him as if he would have preferred to have gone on a little longer. They captured the three others.

' Now secure them' cried Ede. ' Out with your wipes.'

' There is no need of wipes,' said Robinson.

He then with a slight blush, and rather avoiding George's eye, put his hand in his pockets and produced four beautiful sets of handcuffs bran new—polished to the nine. With a magical turn of the hand he handcuffed the three men, still avoiding George's eye. Unnecessarily. George's sense of humour was very faint, and so was his sweetheart's—a sad defect.

Perhaps I may as well explain here how Robinson came so opportunely to the rescue. The fact is, that a week ago he had ordered a lot of constables' staves and four sets of handcuffs. The staves were nicely painted and lettered " Captain Robinson's Police, A, B, C," &c. They had just come home, and Robinson was showing them to Ede and his gang, when a hullahbaloo was heard and Levi was seen full half-a-mile off being hunted. Such an opportunity of trying the new staves was not to be neglected. Ede and his men jumped out of their claim and ran with Robinson to the rescue. But they would have been too late if George, who had just come into the camp at that very part, had not made his noble and desperate assault and retreat, which baffled the assailants for two precious minutes.

Robinson, ' What shall we do with them now we have got them ?'

G-eorge. * Give them a kick a-piece on their behinds, and let them go—the rubbish.'

Robinson. * Not if I know it/

Ude. * I say blackguard 'em.'

Robinson. ' No, that would be letting ourselves down to their level. No—we will expose them as we did my old pal here before.'

Ede. * Why, that is what I mean. Ticket them—put a black card on them with their offence wrote out large.'

No sooner said than done. All four were tied to posts in the sun and black-carded, or as some spell it placarded, thus: —

COWARD. Attacked and abused an old man.

N.B.—Not hanged this time because they got a licking then and there.

* Let us go and see after Mr. Levi, George.' ' Well Tom, I had rather not.'

' Why not ? He ought to be very much obliged to you.'

' That is it, Tom. The old man is of rather a grateful turn of mind, and it is ten to one if he doesn't go and begin praising me to my face, and then that makes me I don't know which way to look. Wait till he has cooled upon it a bit.'

' You are a rum one. Well, Greorge, I have got one proposal you won't say no to. First I must tell you there really is a river of quartz in the country.'

'Didn't I tell you?'

• Yes, and I didn't believe it. But I have spoken to Jacky about it, and he has seen it; it is on the other side of the bush. I am ready to start for it to-morrow, ibr there is little good to be done here now the weather has broken.'

George assented with joy; but when Eobinson suggested that Jacky would be very useful to pilot them through the bush his countenance fell.

' Don't think of it,' said he. ' I know he is here Tom, and I shan't go after him. But don't let him come near me, the nasty little creeping murdering varmint. Poor Abner will never get over his tomahawk—not if he lives fifty years.'

In short it was agreed they should go alone at peep of day.

' I have talked it over with Jem already, and he will take charge of our tent till we come back.'

' So be it.'

' We must take some provisions with us, George.'

' 111 go and get some cold meat and bread, Tom.'

' Do. I'm going to the tent.'

Robinson, it is to be observed, had not been in his tent since George and he left it and took their gold out of it just before sunrise. As he now carried their joint wealth about his person his anxiety was transferred.

Now at the door of the tent he was intercepted by Jem, very red in the face, partly with brandy, partly with rage. Walker, whose life he had saved, whom he had taken to his own tent, and whom Robinson had seen lying asleep in the best blanket, this Walker had absconded with his boots and half a pound of tobacco.

* Well, but you knew he was a rogue. Why did you leave him alone in your tent ?'

' I only left him for a minute to go a few steps with you if you remember, and you said yourself he was

asleep. Well the moment our backs were turned he must have got up and done the trick.' ' I don't like it,' said Eobinson.

* No more don't I,' said Jem.

* If he was not asleep he must have heard me say I was going to cross the bush with my mate to-morrow at day-break..'

'Well! and what if he did?'

' He is like enough to have gone and told the whole gang.'

* And what if he has ?'

Robinson was about to explain to Jem that he now carried all the joint gold in his pockets, but he forbore, ' It is too great a stake for me to trust anybody unless 1 am forced,' thought he. So he only said ' Well it is best to be prudent. I shall change the hour for starting.'

' You are a cunning one captain, but I really think you are over careful sometimes.'

' Jem ' said the other gravely * there is a mystery in this mine. There is a black gang in it and that Walker is one of them. I thin^ they have sworn to have my gold or my life, and they shan't have either if I can help it. I shall start two hours before the sun.'

He was quite right; Walker had been shamming sleep, and full four hours ago he had told his con^ federates as a matter of course all that he had heard in the enemy's camp.

Walker, a timid villain, was unprepared for the burst of savage exultation from brutus and Black Will that

h3

followed this intelligence. These two, by an instinct quick as lightning, saw the means of gratifying at one blow their cupidity and hate. Crawley had already told them he had seen. Robinson come out of Levi's tent after a long stay, and their other spies had told them his own tent had been left unguarded for hours. They put these things together and conjectured at once that the men had now their swag about them in one form or other.

' When do they go ?'

' To-morrow at break of day' he said.

' The bush is very thick !'

' And dark too!'

' It is just the place for a job.'

' Will two of you be enough ?'

' Plenty, the way we shall work.'

' The men are strong and armed.'

' Their strength will be no use to them, and they shan't get time to use their arms.'

' For heaven's sake shed no blood imnecessarily,' said Crawley, beginning to tremble at the pool of crime to who^e. brink he had led these meji.

' Do you think they will give up their swag while they are alive ?' asked brutus scornfully.

' Then I wash my hands of it all' cried the little self-deceiving caitiff; and he affected to have nothing to do with it.

Walker was then thanked for his information, and he thought this was a good opportunity for complaining of his wrongs and demanding redress. This fellow

was a thorough egotist, saw everything from his own point of view only.

Jem had dragged him before Judge Robinson; Robinson had played the beak and found him guilty; Levi had furnished the test on which he had been convicted. All these had therefore cruelly injured and nearly killed him.

Himself was not the cause. He had not set all these stones rolling by forging upon Nature and robbing Jem of thirty pounds. No! he could not see that, nor did he thank Jem one bit for jumping in and saving his life at risk of his own. ' Why did he ever get him thrown in, the brute ? if he was not quite drowned he was nearly, and Jem the cause.'

His confederates soothed him with promises of vengeance on all these three his enemies, and soon after catching sight of one of them, Levi, thy kept their word; they roused up some of the other diggers against Isaac on the plea that he had refused to give evidence against Walker, and so they launched a mob and trusted to mob nature for the rest. The recoil of this superfluous villainy was, as often happens, a blow to the head scheme.

brutus, who was wanted at peep of day for the dark scheme already hinted at, got terribly battered by George Fielding, and placarded, and what was worse chained to a post by Robinson and Ede. It became necessary to sound his body and spirit. One of the gang was sent by Crawley to enquire whether he felt strong enough to go with Black Will on that difficult

and dangerous work to-morrow. The question put in a passing whisper was answered in a whisper.

' I am as strong as a lion for revenge. Tell them I would not miss to-morrow's work for all the gold in Australia.' The lowering face spoke loud enough if the mouth whispered.

The message was brought back to Black Will and Crawley.

* What energy !' said Crawley admiringly.

' Aye !' said Black Will» * that is your sort; give me a pal with his skin smarting and his bones aching for the sort of job that wood shall see to-morrow. Have they marked him ?' he enquired with a strange curiosity.

' I am afraid they have ; his nose is smashed frightful.'

' I am glad of it; now wc are brothers and will have blood for blood.'

' Your expressions are dreadfully terse,' said Crawley, trying to smile but looking scared instead; ' but I don't understand your remark; you were not in the late unsuccessful attack on Mr. Levi, and you escaped most providentially in the night business, the men have not marked you my good friend.'

' Haven't they ?' yelled the man with a tremendous oath. ' Haven't they ? Look here !' A glance was enough. Crawley turned wan and shuddered from head to foot.

CHAPTEE XIV.

We left Robinson and Jem talking at the entrance to the tent.

* Come in,' said* Robinson, ' you will take care of this tent while we are gone.'

Jem promised faithfully.

He then asked Robinson to explain to him the dodge of the gut lines. Robinson showed him, and how the bells were rung at his head by the thiefs foot.

Jem complimented him highly.

Robinson smiled, but the next moment sighed. ' They will be too clever for us some of these dark nights—see how nearly they have nicked us again and again!!'

' Don't be down on your luck, captain!'

' Jem, what frightens me is the villains getting off so ; there they are to try again, and next time the luck will be theirs—it can't be always ours—why should it? Jem, there was a man in my tent last night.'

'There is no denying that, captain.'

'Well, Jem, I can't get it off my heart that I was to kill that man, or he me. Everything was on my side. I had my gut lines, and I had a revolver and a cutlass, and I took up the cutlass like a fool; if I had taken up the revolver the man would be dead. I took up the wrong, and that man will be my death. The cards never forgive! I had the odd trick, and didn't take it, I shall lose the game.'

'No ye shan't,' cried Jem hastily. 'What if the man got clear for the moment, we will hunt him out for you. You give me his description.'

'I couldn't,' said Robinson despondingly. It was so dark! Here is his pistol, but that is no use; if I had but a clue, ay ever so slight, I'd follow it up : but no there is none. Hallo, what is the matter! A\niat is it? what on earth is the man looking at like that!'

'What was you asking for' stammered Jem. 'Wasn't it a clue!'

'Yes.'

Robinson got up and came to Jem, who was standing with dilated eyes looking at the ground in the very comer of the tent. He followed the direction of Jem's eyes, and was instantly transfixed with curiosity and rising horror.

'Take it up Jem' he gasped.

'No, you take it up! it was you who'—

'No yes! there is George's voice, I wouldn't let him see such a thing for the world. Oh God! here is another.'

'Another?'

'Yes, in the long grass! and there is George's voice.'

'Come out, Jem. Not a word to George for the world. I want to talk to you. If it hasn't turned me sick! I should make a poor hangman. But it was in self defence, thank heaven for that!'

'Where are you going in such a hurry, Tom?'

'Oh, only a little way with Jem.'

'Don't be long, it is getting late.'

'No, George!'

'Jem, this is an ugly job 1'

'An ugly job, no I him, I wish it was his head. Give them me, captain.'

'What, will you take charge of them?'

'That I will, captain, and what is more I'll find your enemy out by them, and when you come back he shall be in custody waiting your orders. Give them me.'

'Yes, take them. Oh, but I am glad to be rid of them. Wliat a ghastly look they have.'

'I don't care a button for their looks. I am right glad to see them, they are a clue and no mistake. Keep dark to-night. Don't tell this to Ede, he is a good fellow but chatters too much—let me work it out. I'll find the late owner double quick' said Jem, with a somewhat brutal laugh.

'Your orders about the prisoners captain,' cried Ede, coming up.

Robinson reflected.

'Turn them all loose—but one.'

'And what shall I do with him?'

'Himi!—Put a post up in your own tent.' . •

'Yes.'

'Tie him to it in his hand-cufFs. Give him food enough.'

'And when shall we loose him?' 'At noon to-morrow/

'It shall be done! but you must come and show me which of the four it is.'

Eobinson went with Ede and his men.

'Turn this one loose,' said he; it was done on the instant.

'And this.'

'And this.'

'And (laying his finger on brutus) keep this one prisoner in your tent hand-cuffed and chained till noon to-morrow.'

At the touch brutus trembled with hate; at the order his countenance fell like Cain's.

Full two hours before sun-rise the patrol called Eobinson by his own order, and the friends made for the bush with a day's provision and their blankets their picks, and their revolvers. "When they arrived at the edge of the bush Eobinson halted and looked round to see if they were followed. The night was pretty clear; no one was in sight. The men struck rapidly into the bush, which at this part had been cut and cleared in places, lying as it did so near a mine.

'What, are we to run, Tom?'

'Yes! I want to get to the river of quartz as soon as possible' was the dry answer.

'With all my heart.'

After running about half a mile Greorge pulled up, and they walked.

'What do you keep looking behind for Tom?'

'Oh, nothing.'

'You fidget me, Tom!'

'Can't help it. I shall be like that till day-light. They have shaken my nerves among them.'

'Don't give way to such nonsense. What are you afraid of?'

'I am not afraid of anything. Come, George, another run.'

'Oh, as you like: this beats all.'

This run brought them to the end of the broad road, and they found two smaller paths; after some hesitation Eobinson took the left-hand one, and it landed them in such a tremendous thick scrub they could hardly move. They forced their way through it, getting some frightful scratches, but after struggling with it for a good half-hour began to fear it was impenetrable and interminable, when the sun rising showed them a clear space some yards ahead. They burst through the remainder of the scrub and came out upon an old clearing full a mile long and a quarter of a mile broad. They gave a hurrah at the sight of it, but when they came to walk on it the ground was clay and so sticky with a late shower that they were like flies moving upon varnish, and at last were fain to take off their shoes and stockings and run over it on the tips of their toes. At the end of this opening they came to a place like the "Seven-Dials"—no end of little paths into the wood.

and none very promising. After a natural hesitation they took the one that seemed to be most on their line of march and followed it briskly till it brought them plmnp upon a brook, and there it ended. Eobinson groaned.

,'Confound the bush/ cried he. 'You were wrong not to let me bring Jacky. What is to be done?'

'Go back.'

'I hate going back. I would rather go thirty miles ahead than one back. I've got an idea: off shoes and paddle up the stream; perhaps we shall find a path that comes to it from the other side.'

They paddled up the stream a long way, and at last sure enough they found a path that came down to tlie stream from the opposite side. They now took a hasty breakfast, washing it down with water from the brook, then dived into the wood.

The sun was high in heaven, yet still they had not got out of the bush.

' I can't make it out George, there is nothing to steer by, and these paths twist and turn so. I don't think we shall do any good till night. When I see the southern cross in the sky I shall be able to steer northeast. That is our line.'

' Don't give in' said George, * I think it looks clearer ahead. I believe we are at the end of it.'

' No such luck I am afraid' was the despondent reply.

For all that in a few yards more they came upon an open place.

They could not help cheering. ' At last!' cried they. But this triumph gave way to doubts.

' I am afraid we are not clear yet,' said Robinson. ' See there is wood again on the other side. Why it is that sticky clay again. Why Greorge it is the clearing we crossed before breakfast.'

* You are talking nonsense Tom/ cried Greorge angrily.

' No I am not,' said the other sadly. ' Come across ? We shall soon know by our footsteps in the clay.'

Sure enough half way across they found a track of footsteps. George was staggered. ' It is the place I really think,' said he. * But Tom, when you talk of the footsteps, look here ? You and I never made all these tracks. This is the track of a party.'

Eobinson examined the ground.

' Tracks of three men: two barefoot, one in nailed boots.'

' Well, is that us ?'

' Look at the clearing Greorge, you have got eyes. It is the same.'

* So 'tis, but I can't make out the three tracks.' Robinson groaned. ' I can. This tliird track has

come since we went by.'

' No doubt of that Tom. Well ?'

' Well, don't you see ?'

' No. What?'

' You and I are being hunted.'

George looked blank a moment. ' Can't we be followed without being hunted ?'

* No; others might, but not me. We are being hunted,' said Eobinson sternly. * Curse them! George 1 am sick of this, let us end it. Let us show these fellows they are hunting lions and not sheep. Is your revolver loaded ?'

* Yes.'

* Then come on!' And he set off to run, following the old tracks. George ran by his side, his eyes flashing with excitement. They came to the brook. Robinson showed George that their pursuer had taken some steps down the stream. ' No matter,' said he ' don't lose time George, go right up the bank to our path. He will have puzzled it out you may take your oath.'

Sure enough they foimd another set of footsteps added to their own. Robinson paused before entering the wood. He put fresh caps on his revolver. * Now George,' said he in a low voice, ' we couldn't sleep in this wood without having our throats cut, but before night I'll be out of danger or in my grave, for life is not worth having in the midst of enemies. Hush ! hus-s-sh!

You must not speak to me but in a whisper.'

' No !' whispered George.

' Nor rustle against the boughs.'

' No, I won't,' whispered George. ' But make me sensible Tom. Tell me what all this caution is to lead to. What are you doing ?'

' I AM HUNTING THE HUNTER!' hissed Robinson with concentrated fury. And he glided rapidly down the trodden path, his revolver cocked, his ears pricked, his eye on fire, and his teeth clenched.

George followed silent and cautious, his revolver ready cocked in his hand.

As they glided thus following their own footsteps and hunting their hunter with gloomy brows and nerves quivering and hearts darkening with anger and bitterness, sudden a gloom fell upon the wood—it darkened and darkened. Meantime a breeze chill as ice disturbed its tepid and close air, forerunner of a great wind which was soon heard first moaning in the distance, then howling and rushing up and sweeping over the tall trees and rocking them like so many bull-ruslies. A storm was coming.

(166)

CHAPTER XV.

This very afternoon Mr. Levi came to inquire for George Fielding. Unable to find him he asked of several diggers where the young man was; he could get no information till Jem saw him and came and told him.

Now when he heard they were gone, and not expected back for some days, Isaac gave quite a start, and showed a degree of regret and vexation that Jem was puzzled to account for.

On reflection he begged Jem to come to his tent; there he sat down and wrote a letter.

' Young man' said he ' I do entreat you to give this to George Fielding the moment he returns to the camp. Why did he go without coming to see me ; my old heart is full of misgivings.'

' You needn't have any sir,' said Jem, surprised at the depth of feeling in the old Jew's face and voice. ' He shall have the letter you may depend.'

Levi thanked him.

He then said to Nathan ' Strike the tents, collect our party and let us be gone.'

' What going to leave us, sir !'

' Yes ! young man this very hour.'

' Well now I am sorry for that, and so will the captain be and his pal that you think so much of.'

' We shall not be long parted' said the old man in his sweet musical Eastern accent, ' not very long if you are faithful to your trust and give the good young man my letter. May good angels hover round him, may the God of Abraham Isaac and Jacob guard him!'

' Amen!' said rough Jem; for the reverend face glowed with piety and the voice was the voice of prayer.

Suddenly an unpleasant reflection occurred to Jem.

' Well but if you go who is to buy our gold dust?'

' The Christian merchants,' said Isaac with an indifferent air.

' But they are such Jews,' cried Jem inadvertently. ' I mean—I mean—' and rough as he was he looked as if he could have bitten his tongue off.

' I know what you mean,' said Isaac sadly. He added, ' such as they are they are all you have now. The old Jew was hunted, and hooted, and insulted in this place yesterday; here then he trades no more; those who set no value on him can of course supply his place.'

' The blackguards,' cried Jem, * the ruffians—I wish I had seen them; come, Mr. Levi that was not the mine: that was only the riffraff, you might forgive us that.'

* I never forgive ' was the calm reply.

CHAPTER XVI.

A TREMENDOUS snow-storm fell upon the mine and drove Jem into his tent, where he was soon after joined by Jacky, a circumstance in itself sufficient to prove the violence of the storm, for Jacky loathed in-doors, it choked him a good deal.

The more was Jem surprised when he heard a lamentable howl coming nearer and nearer and a woman burst into his tent, a mere pillar of snow, for she was covered with a thousand flakes each as big as a lady's hand.

' Ochone ! ochone! ochone!' cried Mary M'Dogherty, and on being asked what was the matter, she sat down and rocked herself and moaned and cried—Ochone— och captain avick what will I do for you; an who will I find to save you; an oh it is the warm heart and the kind heart that ye had to poor Molly M'Dogherty that ud give her life to save yours this day.

* The captain,' cried Jem in great alarm. * What is wrong with the captain ?'

* He is lying could and stiff in the dark, bloody wood. Och the murthcring villains 1 och what will I do at all! och captain avich warm was your heart to

the poor Irish boys, but it is could now. Ochone! ochone 1'

'Woman!' cried Jem in great agitation, * leave off blubbering and tell me what is the matter.'

Thus blandly interrogated Mary told him a story (often interrupted with tears and sighs) of what had been heard and seen yester eve by one of the Irish boys, a story that turned him cold, for it left on him the same impression it had left on the warm-hearted Irish woman, that at this moment his good friend was lying dead in the bush hard by.

He rose and loaded Robinson's double-barrelled gun ; he loaded it with bullets, and as he rammed them fiercely down, he said angrily, * Leave off crying and wringing your hands; what on earth is the use of that ? here goes to save him or to revenge him.'

* An och James, take the wild Ingine wid ye; they know them bloody murthering woods better than our boys, glory be to God for taching them that same.'

* Of course I shall take him. You hear Jacky, will you show me how to find the poor dear captain and his mate if they are in life ?'

* If they are alive Jacky will find them a good deal soon—if they are dead still Jacky will find them.'

The Irishwoman's sorrow burst out afresh at these words. The savage then admitted the probability of that she dreaded.

* And their enemies the cowardly villains, what will you do to them ?' asked Jem black with rage.

Jacky's answer made Mary scream with afright, and VOL. in. I

Startled even Jem's iron nerves for a moment. At the very first word of the Irishwoman's story the savage had seated himself on the ground with his back turned to the others, and unnoticed by them had rapidly painted his face with the war paint of his tribe. Words cannot describe the ghastly terrors the fiendish ferocity these traditional lines and colours gave his countenance. This creature that looked so like a fiend came erect into the middle of the tent with a single bound as if that moment vomited forth by hell, and yet with a grander carriage and princelier presence than he had worn in time of peace; and even as he bounded he crossed his tomahawk and narrow wooden shield, to signify that his answer was no vulgar asseveration but a vow c f sacred war. ' Kalingalunga will kill them and drink their

BLOOD.'

Kalingalunga glided from the tent. Jem followed him. The snow fell in flakes as large as a lady's hand and the air was dark; Jem could not see where the himter was taking him, but he strode after him and trusted to his sagacity.

Five hours' hard walking and then the snow left off. The air became clear, and to Jem's surprise the bush instead of being on his right hand was now on his left; and there on its skirts about a mile off was the native camp. They had hardly come in sight of it when it was seen to break from quietude into extraordinary bustle.

' What is up ?' asked Jem.

The hunter smiled and pointed to his own face— ' Kalingalunga painted war.'

* What eyes the beggars must have ' said Jem.

The next minute a score of black figures came tearing up in such excitement that their long rows of white teeth and the whites of their eyes flashed like Bude-lights in their black heads.

Kalingalimga soon calmed them down by letting them know that he was painted for a private not a national feud. He gave them no further information. I suspect he was too keen a sportsman to put others on the scent of his game. He went all through the camp and ascertained from the stragglers that no men answering the description of George and Robinson had passed out of the wood.

* They are in the wood' said he.

He then ordered a great fire, bade Jem dry his clothes and eat; he collected two of his wives and committed Jem to their care, and glided like a panther into the wood.

What with the great heat succeeding to the great cold and the great supper the gins gave him Jem fell fast asleep. It was near daylight when a hand was laid on his shoulder, and there was Kalingaltinga.

* Not a track on the snow.'

' No ? then let us hope they are not in the wood.' The hunter hung his head.

* Me tink they are in the wood' said he gravely. Jem groaned, ' Then they are lying under the soil of

it or in some dark pit.'

i2

Kalingalunga reflected; he replied to this effect—

' That there were no more traces of an assassin than of victims, consequently that it was impossible to know anything, and that it was a good deal too stupid to speak a good deal knowing nothing.'

All this time Jem's fear and rage and impatience contrasted greatly with the philosophic phlegm of the Pict, who looked so fierce and took it all so cool ending with an announcement that now Kalingaliinga would sleep a good deal.

The chief was soon asleep, but not till he had ordered his gins to wake him the moment the snow should be melted. This occurred at noon the next day, and after snatching a hasty meal he put a tomahawk into Jem's hands and darted into the bush.

All the savage's coldness disappeared now he was at work. He took Jem right across the wood from south-east to north-west. Nothing stopped him. When the scrub was thick above but hollow below he threw himself on his belly and wriggled along like a snake. When it was all thick he hacked into it with fury and forced a path. When it was impenetrable he went round it, and by some wonderful instinct got into the same line again. Thus they cut clean across the wood but found no tracks. Then the savage being out in the open trotted easily down the woodside to the south-west point, here he entered and took a line straight as an arrow to the north-east.

It was about five in the afternoon. Kalingalunga was bleeding all over with scratches, and Jem was torn to pieces and done up. He was just about to tell the other that he must give in when Kalingaltinga suddenly stopped, and pointed to the ground—

'Track!'

'What of?'

* A white man's shoe.'

' How many are there ? ' One.' Jem sighed.

* I doubt it is a bad job Jacky,' said he.

* Follow—not too close,' was the low reply.

And the panther became a serpent, so smooth and imdulating were the motions with which he glided upon the track he had now discovered.

Jem, well aware that he could not move noiselessly like the savage, obeyed him and crept after at some distance.

The savage had followed the man's footsteps about half a mile and the white man the savage when suddenly both were diverted from their purpose. Kalin-galiinga stood still and beckoned Jem. Jem ran to him, and found him standing snuffing the air with his great broad nostrils like a stag.

'What is it?'

' White fellow burn wambiloa wood.'

' How d'ye know ? how d'ye know ?'

'Wambiloa wood smell a good way off when him burn.'

' And how do you know it is a white man ?'

' Black fellow never burn wambiloa wood : not s^ood to burn that. Keep it for milmeridien.'

The chief now cut off a few of his long hairs and held them up to ascertain the exact direction of the wind. This done, he barked a tree to mark the spot to which he had followed the trail, and striking out into quite a different direction he hunted by scent.

Jem expected to come on the burning wambiloa very soon, but he imderrated either the savage's keen scent or the acrid odour of the sacred wood—perhaps both. They had gone half a-mile at least before his companion thought it necessary to show any caution. At last he stopped short, and then Jem smelled a smell as if * cinnamon and ginger, nutmegs and cloves' were all blazing in one bonfire. With some difficulty he was prevailed on to stand still and let the subtle native creep on, nor would he consent to be inactive until the other solemnly vowed to come back for him and give him his full share of the fighting. Then Kalingalimga went gliding like a shadow and flitted from tree to tree.

Woe be to the enemy the subtle noiseless pitiless remorseless savage surprises; he has not put on his war-paint in sport or for barren show.

CHAPTER XVII

A MAN was hunting Robinson and Greorge Fielding, and they were hunting him. Both parties inflamed with rage and bitterness; both master of the other's fate they thought.

A change of wind brought a fall of snow, and the fall of snow baffled both parties in five minutes. Down came the Australian flakes large as a woman's hand (I am not romancing), and effaced the tracks of the pursuing and pursued and pursuers. So tremendous was the fall that the two friends thought of nothing but shelter. They threw their blankets over their heads and ran hither and thither looking for a friendly tree. At last they found an old tree with a prodigious stem that parted about ten feet up into two forks. With some effort they got up into this cleft, and then they were on a natural platform. Robinson always carried nails in his pocket, and he contrived to nail the two blankets to the forks so as to make a,

screen. They then took out their provisions and fortified themselves with a hearty supper.

As they were eating it they were suddenly startled by an explosion so tremendous that their tree seemed to have been struck by lightning. Out went Eobinson with his mouth full and was seated on a snowdrift four feet high. He looked up and saw the cause of the fracas. A large bough of a neighbouring tree had parted from the trunk with the enormous weight of the snow. Eobinson climbed back to George and told him. Supper recommenced, but all over the wood at intervals they now heard huge forks and boughs parting from their parent stems with a report like a thirty-two pounder ringing and echoing through the wood; others so distant that they were like crackers.

These sounds were very appalling in the ghostly wood. The men instinctively drew closer to each other; but they were no chickens: use soon hardened them even to this. They settled it that the forks they were sitting on would not give way because there were no leaves on them to hold a great burden of snow; and soon they yielded to nature and fell fast asleep in spite of all the dangers that hemmed them.

At his regular hour, just before sunrise, Robinson awoke and peeped from below the blanket. He shook George.

* Get up directly, George. We are wasting time when time is gold.'
* What is it?'
* What is it ? There is a pilot in the sky that will

take us out of this cursed trap if the sun does not come and spoil all.'

George's eye followed Robinson's finger, and in th(^ centre of the dark vault of heaven this glittered.

CHAPTER XVIII.

' I KNOW it, Tom. When I was sailing to this country we came to a part where the north star went down and down to the water's edge and this was all we got in exchange for it/

' George ' said Tom rather sternly, ' how do you know they don't hear us, and here we are suiTounded by enemies and would you run down our only friend ? That silver star will save our lives if they are to be saved at all. Come on; and George, if you were to take your revolver and blow out my brains it is no more than I deserve for sleeping away the precious hours of night when I ought to have been steering out of this cursed timber-net by that blessed star.'

With these words Robinson dived into the wood, steering due east by the Southern Cross. It was like going through a frozen river. The scrub was loaded with snow, which it discharged in masses on the travellers at every step.

'Keep your revolver dry in your hat and your lucifers too' cried Robinson. ' We shall have to use them both ten to one. As to our skins, that is hopeless.'

Then the men found how hard it is to take a line and keep it in the Australian bush. When the Southern Cross was lost in a cloud, though but for a minute, they were sure to go all wrong, as they found upon its reappearance; and sometimes the scrub was impenetrable and they were forced to go round it and walk four himdred yards, advancing eastward but twenty or thirty.

Thus they battled on till the sun rose.

' Now we shall be all in the dark again,' said poor Robinson, here comes a fog.'

' Stop Tom,' said George; ' oughn't we to make this good before we go on ?'

' What do you mean ?'

' We have come right by the star so far have we not?'

'Yes.'

' Then let us bark fifty of these trees for a mark. I have seen that varmint Jacky do that.'

' A capital idea, George; out with our knives—here goes.'

' No breakfast to-day, Tom.'

' No, George, nor dinner either till we are out of the wood.'

These two poor fellows walked and ran and crept and struggled all day, sometimes hoping, sometimes desponding. At last at five o'clock in the afternoon, their bellies gnawed with hunger, their clothes torn to rags, their skin bleeding, they came out upon some trees with the bark stripped. They gave one another a look that

words can hardly paint. They were the trees they had barked twelve hours ago!

The men stood silent—neither cared to tell the other all he felt, for now there crept over these two stout bosoms a terrible chill, the sense of a danger new to them in experience but not new in report. They had heard of settlers and others who had been lost in the fatal labyrinth of the Australian bush, and now they saw how easily it might be true.'

' We may as well sit down here and rest; we shall do no good till night. What, are you in pain, George ?' . ' Yes, Tom, a little.'

'Where?'

' Something gnaws my stomach like an adder.*

* Oh, that is the soldier's gripes' said Tom with a ghastly attempt at a jest. ' Poor George I' said he kindly, ' I dare say you never knew what it was to go twenty-four hours without food before ?'

' Never in my life Tom.'

' Well, I have, and I'll tell you the only thing to do : when you can't fill the bread-basket shut it. Go to sleep till the Southern Cross comes out again.'

' What, sleep in our dripping clothes ?'

' No, we will make a roaring fire with these strips of bark; they are dry as tinder by now.'

A pyre four feet high was raised, the strips being laid from north to south and east to west alternately, and they dried their blankets and warmed their smoking bodies.

* George, I have got two cigars; they must last us two days.'

'Oh, I'm no great smoker—keep them for your own comfort.'

Robinson wore a sad smile.

' We can't afford to smoke them ; this is to chew; it is not food George, but it keeps the stomach from eating itself. We must do the best for our lives we can for Susan's sake.'

* Give it me, Tom; I'll chew it, and thank you kindly. You are a wise companion in adversity, Tom ; it is a great grief to me that I have brought you into this trouble looking for what I know you think is a mare's nest as the saying is.'

* Don't talk so, George. True pals like you and me never reproach one another. They stand and fall together like men. The fire is warm, George—that is one comfort.'

' The fire is well enough, but there's nothing down at it. I'd give a hundred pounds for a mutton chop.'

The friends sat like sacrifices by the fire and chewed their cigars in silence, with foreboding hearts. After a while, as the heat laid hold of him, George began to dose. Robinson felt inclined to do the same, but the sense that perhaps a human enemy might be near caused him to fight against sleep in this exposed locality, so whenever his head bobbed down he lifted it sharply and forced his eyes open. It was on one of these occasions that, looking up, he saw set as it were in a frame

of leaves a hideous countenance glaring at him; it was painted in circular lines, red, blue and white.

' Gret up George ' roared Kobinson; ' they are upon us!'

And both men were on their feet, revolvers pointed. The leaves parted and out came this diabolical face which they had never seen before, but with it a figure they seemed to know and a harsh cackle they instantly recognised, and it sounded like music to them.

' Oh, my dear Jacky,' cried George, ' who'd have thought it was you! Well, you are a godsend! Good afternoon. Oh Jacky!—how d'ye do ?'

' Jacky not Jacky now, cos um a good deal angry and paint war. Kalingalilnga berywelltanku' (he always took these four words for one). Now 1 go fetch white fellow;' and he disappeared.

' Who is he going to fetch ? is it the one that was following us ?'

* No doubt. Then Tom, it was not an enemy after all!'

Jacky came back with Jem, who at sight of them alive and well burst into extravagances. He waved his hat round his head several times and then flung it into a tree; then danced a pas seul consisting of steps not one of them known at the opera-house, and chanted a song of triumph the words of which were Ei tol de riddy iddy dol, and the ditty naught; finally he shook hands with both.

' Never say die!'

* Well, that is hearty ! and how thoughtful of him to come after us, and above all to bring Jacky!'

' That it was ' replied George. ' Jem' said he with feeling, ' I don't know but what you have saved two men's lives.'

' If I don't it shan't be my fault, farmer.'

George. ' Oh, Jacky, I am so hungry ! I have been twenty-four hours without food.'

Kalingalunga. ' You stupid fellow to go widout food, always a good deal food in bush.'

Greorge, 'Is there? then for heaven's sake go and get us some of it.'

Kalingalunga. ' No need go, food here.'

He stepped up to the very tree against which George was standing, showed him an excrescence on the bark, made two clean cuts with his tomahawk, pulled out a huge white worm and offered it George. George turned from it in disgust; the wild chief grinned superior and ate it himself, and smacked his lips with infinite gusto.

Meantime his quick eye had caught sight of something else. ' A good deal dinner in dis tree,' said he, and he made the white men observe some slight scratches on the bark. * Possum claws go up tree.' Then he showed them that there were no marks with the claw reversed, a clear proof the animal had not come down. * Possum in tree.'

The white men looked up into the bare tree with a mixture of wonder and incredulity. Jacky cut steps with his tomahawk and went up the main stem, which

was short, and then up a fork, one out of about twelve, among all these he jumped about like a monkey till he found one that was hollow at the top.

' Throw Kalingalunga a stone, den he find possum a good deal quick.'

They could not find a stone for their lives, so being hungry Robinson threw a small nugget of gold he had in his pocket. Jacky caught it, placed it at the top of the hollow fork and let it drop. Listening keenly his fine ear heard the nugget go down the fork, striking the wood first one side then another, and then at a certain part sound no more. Down he slips to that silent part, makes a deep cut with his tomahawk just above the spot, thrusts in his hand and pulls out a large opossum, yelling and scratching and emitting a delicious scent in an agony of fear. The tomahawk soon silenced him and the carcass fell among the applauding whites. Now it was Robinson's turn, he carved the raw animal for greater expedition, and George helped him to wrap each limb and the carcass in a thin covering of clay. Thus prepared it was thrust into the great pile of burning ashes.

' Look yonder, do! look at that Jem! Why Jem what are you up to patrolling like a sentinel out there ?'

* Never you heed Jem,' was the dry reply; ' you mind the roast captain, and I'll mind—my business,' and Jem continued to parade up and down with his gun cocked and his eye piercing the wood.

To Robinson's repeated and uneasy enquiries what meant this pantomime Jem persisted in returning no

answer but this, * You want your dinner, captain; eat your dinner and then I'll hoiFer a hobservation : meantime as these woods are queer places a little hextra caution is no sin.'

The pie dishes were now drawn out of the ashes and broken, and the meat baked with all its juices was greedily devoured, * It tastes like a rabbit stuflfed with peppermint' said George, 'and uncomon nice it is. Now I am another man.'

* So am I; Jacky for ever!'

' Now Jem I have dined: your story if you please. Why are you here ? for you are a good fellow but you haven't got gumption enough to say to yourself, " These two will get lost in the bush, I'll take Jacky and pull them out."'

* You are right captain, that wasn't the way at all, and since your belly is full and your courage up, you will be able to enjoy my story better than you could afore.'

' Yes, so let us have it;' and Robinson leaned back luxuriously, being filled and warmed.

' First and foremost' commenced this artful narrator, ' there is a chap prowling in this wood at the present time with a double-barrelled gun to blow out your brains captain.'

* The devil' cried Robinson starting to his feet.

* And yours farmer.'

* How do you know ?' asked George without moving. ' That is what I am going to tell you. That Mary

M'Dogherty came crying to my tent all through the

snow. " What is up?" says I; says she, " Murder is up." Then she told me her cousin, an Irish boy, was at Bevan's store and he heard some queer talk, and he looked through a chink in the wall and saw two rascals putting their heads together, and he soon made out they were driving a bargain to rob you two. One was to do it, the other was a egging him on. " I must have fifty pounds first," says this one: *'Why?" says the other. " Because he has been and locked my pal up that was to be in it with me."'

' Ah !' cried Kobinson. ' Go on Jem, there is a clue any way.'

" I have got a thicker one behind." Says the other, '* Agreed ! when will you have it ?" " Why now," says t'other. Then this one gave him a note. Pat couldn't see that it was a fifty, but no doubt it was, but he saw the man take it and put it in a little tin box and shove it in his bosom.'

' That note was the price of blood' said Robinson. ' Oh the blaxjk-hearted villains. Tell me who they were that is all; tell me but who they were.'

' The boy didn't know.'

' There! it is always so. The fools! they never know.'

' Stop a bit captain, there is a clue (your own word).'

* Ay! and what is the clue ?'

* As soon as ever the note was safe in his bosom he says, " I sold you blind mate; I'd have given fifty sooner than not done this job. Look here!" says he, " I have sworn to have a life for each of these," and

captain,' said Jem suddenly lowering his voice, ' with that it seems he held up his right hand.' . ' Well, yes! yes! eh !'

* And there were two fingers a missing on it.' 'Ah!'

' Now those two fingers are the ones you chopped ofi" with your cutlass the night when the tent was attacked.'

'Why Tom, what is this? you never told me of' this' cried George.

* And which they are in my pocket.'

' In your pocket,' said George, drawing away fi:om him.

' Ay, farmer! wrapped up in silver paper, and they shall never leave my pocket till I have fitted them on the man and seen him hung or shot with them two pickers and stealers tied round his blood-thirsty, mer-cenairy, aass-aassinating neck, say that I said it.'

George. ' Jacky, show us the way out of this wood.'

Kalingalunga bowed assent, but he expressed a wish to take with him some of the ashes of the wambiloa. George helped him.

Robinson drew Jem aside, ' You shouldn't have mentioned that before George; you have disgusted him properly.'

* Oh, hang him! he needn't be so squeamish ; why, I've had 'em salt—'

* There, there! drop it Jem, do!'

* Captain! are you going to let them take us out of the wood before we have hunted it for that scoundrel ?'

' Yes I am. Look here, Jem, we are four and he is

one, but a double-barrelled gun is an awkward enemy in a dark wood. No Jem, we will out-wit him to the last. We will clear the wood and get back to the camp. He doesn't know we have got a clue to him. He will come back without fear, and we will nail him with the fifty poimd note upon him; and then Jack Ketch.

The whole party was now on the move, led by Ka-lingalunga bearing the sacred ashes.

' What on earth is he going to do with them ?'

The chief heard this query, and looking back said gravely, * He take them to " Milmeridien,"' and the party followed Jacky, who twisted and zig-zagged about the bush, till at last he brought them to a fairy spot, whose existence in that rugged wood none of them had dreamed possible. It was a long open glade, meandering like a river between two deep irregular fringes of the drooping acacia and another lovely tree which I only know by its uncouth, unmelodious, scientiuncular name—the eucalyptus. This tree as well as the drooping acacia leaned over the ground with long leaves like dishevelled hair.

Kalingalilnga paused at the brink and said to his companions in a low awe-struck voice— " Milmeridien."

The glade was full of graves, some of them fresh, glittering with bright red earth under the cool green acacias, others richly veiled with golden moss more or less according to their age; and in the recesses of the grove peeped smoother traces of mortality, mossy mounds a thousand years old, and others far more

ancient still now mere excrescences of green, known to be graves only by the light of that immense gradation of times and dates and epochs.

The floor of the open glade was laid out as a vast parterre, each grave a little flower-bed, round, square, oval, or rhomboid; and all round each bed flowed in fine and graceful curves little paths too narrow for a human foot. Primeval traditions had placed them there that spirits might have free passage to visit all the mighty dead. For here reposed no vulgar corpses. Here, their heads near the surface, but their feet deep in earth, sat the great hunters and warriors of every age of the race of Kalingaliinga once a great nation though now a failing tribe. They sat there this many a day, their weapons in their hands, ready to start up whenever the great signal should come, and hunt once more but without fatigue and in woods boundless as the sea, and with bodily frames no longer mortal to knock and be knocked on the head, ad infinitimi.

Simple and benign creed!

A cry of delight burst from the white men, and they were going to spread themselves over the garden of the dead.

The savage checked them with horror.

* No body walk there while him alive,* said he. ' Now you follow me and not speak any words at all, or Ka-lingalimga will leave you in the bush.—Hush!'

The savage paused, that even the echo of his remonstrance might die well away before he traversed the garden. He then bowed his head down upon his breast

in a set maimer, and so remained quiet a few seconds. In that same attitude he started and walked slowly by the verge of the glade, keeping carefully clear of the graves, and never raising his head. About half-way he stopped and reverently scattered the ashes of the wam-biloa upon three graves that lay near the edge, then forward silent downcast reverential.

* Mors omnibus est commimis!' The white men, even down to Jem understood and S3nnpathized with Kalingalunga. In this garden of the dead of all ages they felt their common humanity, and followed their black brother silent and awe-struck: melted too by the sweet and sacred sorrow of this calm scene: for here death seemed to relax his frown, and the dead but to rest from trouble and toil, mourned by gentle tender trees; and in truth it was a beautiful thought of these savage men to have given their dead for companions those rare and drooping acacias that bowed themselves and loosed their hair so like fair women abandoned to sorrow over the beloved and dead, and night and morning swept with their dewy eye-lashes the pillows of the brave. Eequiescant in pace: resurgant in pacem. For I wish them better than they wished themselves.

After Milmeridien came a thick scrub, through which Kalingaltmga tracked his way and then a loud hurrah burst from all, for they were free—the net was broken. There were the mountains before them and the gaunt wood behind them at last. The native camp was visible two miles distant, and thither the party ran and

found food and fires in abundance. Black sentinels were set at such distances as to render a surprise impossible, and the travellers were invited to sleep and forget all their troubles. Robinson and Jem did sleep, and George would have been glad to, and tried but was prevented by an unfortunate incident —les enfans terri-bles found out his weak point, viz. that nothing they could do would make him hit them. So half a dozen little rascals, potter bellied than you can conceive, climbed up and down Greorge, sticking in their twenty claws Hke squirrels, and feeling like cold slippery slugs. Thus was sleep averted until a merciful gin hearing the man's groans came and cracked two or three of these little black pots with a waddie or club, so then George got leave to sleep, and just as he was dozing off, ting, tong, ti tong, tong, tong, came a fearful drumming of parchment. A corroboree or native dance was beginning. No more sleep till that was over so all hands turned out. A space was cleared in the wood, women stood on both sides with flaming boughs and threw a bright red light upon a particular portion of that space, the rest was dark as pitch. Time, midnight. When the white men came up, the dancing had not began.

Kalingaltmga was singing a preliminary war song.

George had picked up some of the native language, and he explained to the other that Jacky was singing about some great battle, near the Wurra-Gurra River.

' The Wurra-Gurra! why that is where we first found gold.'

* Why, of course it is ! and—yes! I thought so!' ' Thought what?'

' It is our battle he is describing.'

* Which of 'em ?—we live in hot water.'

' The one before Jem was our friend. What is he singing ? Oh, come! that is over-doing it Jacky! Why, Jem 1 he is telling them he killed you on the spot.'

' I'll punch his head!'

' No! take it easy' said Robinson; * he is a poet; this is what they call poetical license.'

* Lie without sense I call it when here is the man.'

* Ting tong! ting tong ! tong !— I slew him—he fell—by the Wurra-Gurra River. I slew him !—ting tong! he fell—ting tong! By the Wurra-Gurra Eiver—ting ting tong !'

This line Jacky repeated at least forty times; but he evaded monotony by the following simple contrivance—

* I slew him; he felly by the Wurra-Gurra River—ting tong ! / slew him ; he fell, by the Wurra-Gurra River.

I slew him ; he fell, by the Wurra-Gurra River,*

with similar changes, and then back again.

One of our own savages saved a great poet from monotony by similar means :* very good of him.

* The elder Sheridan, who used to teach his pupils to thresh dead Dryden out thus :—
None but the brave, None but the brave^ None but the brave—deserve the fair.

And now the gins took up the tune without the words, and the dance began to it. First two figures ghastly with white paint came bounding like Jacks-in-the-box out of the gloom into the red light, and danced gracefully, then one more popped out, then another, at set intervals of time, then another, all painted differently, and swelled the dance by degrees; and still as the dance grew in numbers, the musicians sang and drummed louder and faster by well-planned gradations, and the motion rose in intensity, till they all warmed into the terrible savage corroboree jump legs striding wide head turned over one shoulder the eyes glaring with fiendish intensity in one direction the arms both raised and grasping waddies and boomerangs, till at last they worked up to such a gallop of fierce buck-like leaps that there was a jump for each beat of the music. Now they were in four lines, and as the figures in the front line jumped to the right, each keeping his distance to a hair, the second line jumped to the left, the third to the right, and the fourth to the left.

The twinkle and beauty and symmetry of this was admirable, and strange as it may appear, not only were the savages now wrought up to frenzy at this climax of the dance, but the wonderful magnetic influence these children of Nature have learned to create and launch in the corroboree so stirred the white men's blood, that they went half mad too, and laughed and shouted and danced, and could hardly help flinging themselves among the mad fiends, and jumping and yelling with VOL. III. K

them; and when the jump was at its fiercest and quickest and the great frenzy boiling over, these cunning artists brought it to a dead stop sharp upon the climax and all was still.

In another minute they were all snoring; but George and Robinson often started in their sliunbers dreaming they saw the horrid figures—the skeletons lizards snakes tartan shawls and whitened fiends, the whole lot blazing at the eyes and mouth like white bude-lights, come bounding one after another out of the black night into the red torchlight, and then go striding and jumping and lurid and raging and bucking and prancing and scattering battle and song and joy and rage and inspiration and stark-staring phrenzy all around.

They awoke at daylight rather cold, and found piles of snow upon their blankets, and the lizards and skeletons and imps and tartan shawls sadly deteriorated. The snow had melted on their bodies, and the colours Kad all run—some of them away. Quid multa? we all know how beauties look when the sun breaks on them after a ball.

They asked for Jacky; to their great chagrin he was not to be found. They waited getting crosser and Grosser till nine o'clock, and then out comes my lord from the wood, walking towards them with his head down on his bosom, the picture of woe—the milmeri-dian movement over again.

' There! don't let us scold him ' said George, ' I am afraid he has lost a relation, or maybe a dear friend,

anyway I hope it is not his sweetheart—poor Jacky. Well, Jacky! I am glad you have washed your face, now I know you again. You can't think how much better you look in your own face than painted up in that unreasonable way, like — like — like — I dono-what-all.'

* Like something between a devil and a rainbow,' suggested Robinson.

' But what is wrong?' asked George, kindly. * I am almost afraid to ask though!'

Encoiu-aged by the tone of sympathy the afflicted chief pointed to his face, sighed, and said—

* Kalingaliinga paint war, and now Kalingalunga wash um face and not kill anybody first. Kalingalunga Jacky again, and show you white place in um hill a good deal soon.'

_And the amiable heathen cleared up a little at the prospect of serving George, whom he loved—aboriginally.

Jem remained with the natives upon some frivolous pretence. His real hope was to catch the ruffian whom he secretly believed to be still in the wood. ' He is like enough to creep out this way ' thought Jem, ' and then—won't I nail him!'

In half an hour they were standing under the spot whose existence Robinson had so often doubted.

' Well George, you painted it true; it really is a river of quartz running between those two black rocks. And that you think is the home of the gold, eh?'

* Well, I do! Look here, Tom! look at this great

k2

large heap of quartz boulders, all of different sizes; they have all rolled down here out of that river of quartz.'

' Why of course they have! who doubts that?'

' Many is the time I have sat on that green mound, where Jacky is sitting now, and eaten my bread and cheese.'

' I dare say! but what has that to do with it? what are we to do? Are we to go up the rock, and peck into that mass of quartz?'

' Well, I think it is worth while.'

' Why, it would be like biting a piece out of the world! Look here. Master George, we can put your notion about the home of the gold to the test without all that trouble.'

' As how?'

* You own all these quartz stones rolled out of yon river; if so, they are samples of it.

Ten thousand quartz stones is quite sample enough, so begin and turn them all over, examine them break them if you like. If we find but a speck of gold in one of them I'll believe that quartz river is gold's home—if not, it is all humbug !*

George pulled a wry face; he found himself pinned to his own theory.

' Well,' said he, ' I own the sample tells us what is in the barn; so now I am vexed for bringing you here.'

' Now we are here give it a fair trial; let us set to and break every boulder in the thundering heap.'

They went to work and picked the quartz boulders ; full two hours they worked, and by this time they had

made a considerable heap of broken quartz; it glittered in the sun, but it glittered white, not a speck of yellow came to light.

George was vexed. Eobinson grinned, expecting-nothing he was not disappointed. Besides he was winning an argument, and we all like to turn out prophets. Presently a little cackle from Jacky.

' I find um !'

' Find what ? ' asked Robinson, without looking up.

' A good deal yellow stone' replied Jacky, with at least equal composure.

' Let me see that' said George with considerable curiosity and they both went to Jacky.

Now the fact is that this heap of quartz stones was in reality much larger than they thought, only the greater part of it had been overgrown with moss and patches of grass a few centuries of centuries ago.

Jacky seated on what seemed a grassy mound was in reality perched upon a part of the antique heap; his keen eye saw a little bit of yellow protruding through the moss, and he was amusing himself clipping it with his tomahawk, cutting away the moss and chipping the stone, which made the latter glitter more and yellower.

' Hallo!' cried George, ' this looks better.'

Robinson went on his knees without a word.

* It is all right' said he in a great flutter, 'it is a nugget and a good-sized one, a pound weight I think. Now then, my lad out you come,' and he dug his fingers imder it to jerk it out.

But the next moment he gave a screech and looked up amazed.

' Why this is the point of the nugget; it lies the 4)ther way, not flat. Greorge! I can't move it! The pick! Oh Lord ! oh Lord! The pick! the pick!'

' Stand clear' shouted Greorge, and he drove the point of the pick down close by the prize, then he pressed on the handle—' Why Tom, it is jammed some how.'

' No, it is not jammed—it is its own weight. Why, George!'

' Yes, Tom! it is an hundred weight if it is an ounce,'

* Don't be a fool,' cried the other trembling all over; ' there is no such thing in Nature.'

The nugget now yielded slowly to the pressure, and began to come up into the world again inch by inch after so many thousand years. Of course before it could come all out the soil must open first, and when Robinson glaring down saw a square foot of earth part and gape as the nugget came majestically up, he gave another cry and with trembling hands laid hold of the prize, and pulled and tugged and rolled it on to the clean moss—to lift it was not so easy. They fell down on their knees by the side of it like men in a dream. Such a thing had never been seen or heard of—a hundredweight of quartz and gold, and beautiful as it was great. It was like honeycomb, the cells of which had been sliced by a knife; the shining metal brimmed over in the delicate quartz cells.

They lifted it. Yes, full a hundredweight; half the mass was quartz, but four-fifths of the weight they knew must be gold. Then they jumped up and each put a foot on it, and shook hands over it.

' Oh! you beauty' cried George, and he went on his knees and kissed it; ' that is not because you are gold, but because you take me to Susan. Now, Tom, let us thank heaven for its goodness to us, and back to camp this very day.'

* Ay ! but stop we must wrap it in our wipes or we shall never get back alive. The very honest ones would turn villains at sight of it. It is the wonder of the world.

' I see my Susan's eyes in it,' cried Greorge in rapture. ' Oh! Tom, good kind honest Tom, shake hands over it once more.'

In the midst of all this rapture a horrible thought occurred.

' Why it is Jacky's' said George faintly ' he found it.'

* Nonsense ! nonsense !' cried Tom uneasily; he added, however, ' but I am afraid one-third of it is— pals share white or black.'

All their eyes now turned uneasily to the Aboriginal, who lay yawning on the grass.

' Jacky give him you George,' said this worthy savage with superb indifference: he added with a yawn, ' What for you dance corroboree when um not dark?—den you bite yellow-stone,' continued this original, ' den you red, den you white, den you red

again, all because we pull up yellow-stone—all dis a good deal dam ridiculous/

' So 'tis Jackj,' replied Robinson hastily, * don't you have anything to do with yellow-stone, it would make you as great a fool as we are. Now show us the shortest cut back home through the bush.'

At the native camp they fell in with Jem. The monstrous nugget was too heavy to conceal from his shrewd eye so they showed it him. The sight of it almost knocked him down. Robinson told him where they found it, and advised Jem to go and look for another. Alas! the great nugget already made him wish one friend away. But Jem said—

' No, I will see you safe through the bush first.'

(201)

CHAPTER XIX.

All this time two persons in the gold mine were upon thorns of expectation and doubt—brutus and Peter Crawley. George and Robinson did not retuin, but no more did Black Will. What had happened ? Had the parties come into collision? and if so with what result ? If the friends had escaped why had they never been heard of since. If on the other hand Will had come off conqueror why had he never re-appeared ? At last brutus arrived at a positive conviction that Black Will had robbed and probably murdered the men, and was skulking somewhere with their gold, thereby defrauding him his pal; however he kept this to himself, and told Crawley that he feared Will had come to grief, so he would go w^ell armed and see what was the matter, and whether he could help him. So he started for the bush well armed. Now his real object I blush to say was to murder Black Will, and rob him of the spoils of George and Robinson.

Wicked as these men of violence had been six months ago, gold and Crawley had made them worse, aye ! much worse. Crawley indeed had never openly

*

urged any of them to so deep a crime as murder, and it is worthy of note as a psychological fact that this reptile contrived to deceive itself into thinking that it had stopped short of crime's utmost limits; to be sure it had tempted and bribed and urged men to robbery under circumstances that were ahnost sure to lead to murder, but still murder might not occur; meantime it had openly discountenanced that crime and checked the natural proclivity of brutus and Black Will towards deeds of blood.

Self-deception will probably cease at the first blast of the archangel's trumpet: but what hmnan heart will part with it till then ? The circumstances under which a human being cannot excuse or delude or justify himself have never yet occurred in the huge annals of crime. Prejudice apart, Crawley's moral position behind brutus and Black Will seems to bear a strong family likeness to that which holy writ assigns to the great enemy of man. That personage knocks out nobody's brains, cuts nobody's throat—never was guilty of such brutality since the world was, but he finds some thorough egotist and whispers how the egotism of his passions or his interest may be gratified by the death of a fellow-creature. The egotist listens and blood flows.

Brutus and Black Will had. both suffered for their crimes. Brutus had been nailed by Carlo, twice gib-iDeted, and the bridge of his nose broken once. Black Will liad been mutilated and Walker nearly drowned, but " the close contriver of all harms " had kept out

of harm's way. Violence had never recoiled on him who set it moving. For all that Crawley, I must inform the reader, was not entirely prosperous. He had his little troubles too, whether warnings that he was on the wrong path, or punishments of his vices, oi-both, I can't say.

Thus it was. Mr. Crawley had a natural love of spirits without a stomach strong enough to deal with them. When he got away from Mr. Meadows he indulged more and more, and for some months past he had been subject to an unpleasant phenomenon that occasionally arises out of the fumes of liquor. At the festive board even as he raised the glass to his lips the face of Crawley would often be seen to writhe with a sort of horror, and his eyes to become fixed on unseen objects and perspiration to gather on his brow. Then such as were not in the secret would jump up and say, ' What on earth is the matter T and look fearfully round expecting to see some horrid sight to justify that look of horror and anguish, but Crawley, his glassy eyes still fixed, would whimper out his teeth chattering and clipping the words—' Oh, ne-ne-never mind, its o-o-only a trifling ap-pa-rition!' He had got to try and make light of it, because at first he used to cry out and point, and then the miners ran out and left him alone with his phantoms, and this was terrible. He dreaded solitude; he schemed against it, and provided against it, and paid fellows to bear him company night and day, and at the festive board it was one thing to drink his phantoms neat and anotlier to

dilute them with figures of flesh and blood. He much preferred the latter.

At first his supernatural visitors were of an unfavourable but not a ghastly character.

No. 1 was a judge who used to rise through the floor and sit half in and half out of the wall, with a tremendous flow of horse-hair, a furrowed face, a vertical chasm between the temples, and a strike-me-off-the-roUs eye gleaming with diabolical fire from under a grey shaggy eyebrow.

No. 2 was a policeman who came in through the window and stood imperturbable all in blue, with a pair of handcufis, and a calm eye and a disagreeable absence of effort or emotion—an inevitable looking policeman.

But as Crawley went deeper in crime and brandy, blood-boltered figures, erect corpses with the sickening signs of violence in every conceivable form, used to come and blast his sight and arrest the glass on its way to his lips, and make his songs and the boisterous attempts at mirth of his withered heart die in a quaver and a shiver of fear and despair. And at this period of our tale these horrors had made room for a phantom more horrible still to such a creature as Crawley.

The air would seem to thicken into sulphureous smoke and then to clear, and then would come out clearer and clearer, more and more awful, a black figure with hoofs and horns and tail, eyes like red-hot carbuncles, teeth like a chevaux-de-frise of white-hot iron, and an appalling grin."*

* The god Pan coloured black by the early Christians.

CHAPTER XX.

The party, consisting of Jacky, Jem, Robinson, and George, had traversed about one-half the bush when a great heavy crow came wheeling and cackling over their heads and then joined a number more who were now seen circling over a gum-tree some hundred yards distant.

' Let us go and see what that is,' said Jem.

Jacky grinned and led the way. They had not gone very far when another great black bird rose so near their feet as to make them jump, and peering through the bushes they saw a man lying on his back. His arm was thrown in an easy natural way round his gun, but at a second glance it was plain the man was dead. The crows had ripped his clothes to ribands with their tremendous beaks and lacerated the flesh and picked out the eyes.

They stepped a few paces from this sight. There was no sign of violence on the body.

' Poor fellow!' said Jem. ' How did he come by his end I wonder ?' And he stretched forward and peered with pity and curiosity mingled.

' Lost in the bush!' said Robinson very solemnly. And he and Greorge exchanged a meaning look.

' What is that for?' said George angrily to Jacky —grinning in sight of a dead body ?"

^ White fellow stupid fellow,' was all Jacky's reply.

The men now stepped up to the body to examine it, not that they had much hope of discovering who it was, but still they knew it was their duty for the sake of his kindred to try and find out.

George overcoming a natural repugnance examined the pockets. He found no papers. He found a knife, but no name was cut in the handle. In the man's bosom he found a small metal box, but just as he was taking it out Jem gave a hallo!

' I think I know him' cried Jem. ' There is no mistaking that crop of black hair; it is my old captain, Black Will.'

' You don't say so. What could he be doing here without his party ?'

' Anything in the box George ?' asked Robinson.

' Nothing but a little money. Here is a sovereign— look. And here is a bank-note.'

' A five-pound note ?'

' Yes—no; it is more than that a good deal. It is for fifty pounds Tom.'

*What?'

* A fifty-pound note I tell you.'

*Jem!'

' Captain!'

A most expressive look was exchanged between these two, and by one impulse they both seized the stQck of the gun that was in the dead man's hand. They lifted it, and yes—two fingers were wanting on the right hand.

' Come away from that fellow,' cried Robinson to George. ' Let him lie.'

George looked up in some wonder. Robinson pointed sternly to the dead hand in silence. George by the light of the other men's faces saw it all—and recoiled with a natural movement of repugnance as from a dead snake. There was a breathless silence, and every eye bent upon this terrible enemy lying terrible no longer at their feet.

' How did he die ?' asked Robinson in a whisper.

' In the great snow-storm' replied George in a whisper.

' No,' said Jem in the same tone ' he was alive yesterday. I saw his foot-print after the snow was melted.

' There was snow again last night, Tom. Perhaps he went to sleep in that with his belly empty.'

' Starvation and fatigue would do it without the snow George. We brought a day's provisions out with us George. He never thought of that I will be bound.'

* Not he' said Jem. ' I'll answer for him he only thought of robbing and killing—never thought about dying hunself.'

' I can't believe he is dead so easy as this' said Robinson.

The feeling was natural. This man had come into the wood and had followed them burning to work them ill, and they to work him ill. Both were utterly baffled. He had never prevailed to hurt them, nor they him. He was dead, but by no mortal hand. The immediate cause of his death was unknown, and will never be known for certain while the world lasts.

L'homme propose mais Dieu dispose !

(209)

CHAPTER XXI.

' Don't keep staring at it so farmer, it is an ugly sight. You will see him in your sleep if you do that. Here is something better to look at—a letter. And there I carried it and never once thought of it till the sight of his hand made me feel in my pocket, and then my hand ran against it. 'Tis from Mr. Levi.'

' Thank you, Jem. Tom will you be so kind as read it me while 1 work.'

* Yes, give it me. Work ? Why what are we going to work at in the bush ?'

' I should think you might guess,' replied George quietly, while putting down his pickaxe and taking off his coat. ' Well, I am astonished at both of you. You ought to know what I am going to do. Humph ! Under this tree will be as good a place as any.'

* Jem, as I am a sinner he is going to bury him.'

* Bury what ? The nugget ?' ' No Jem, the Christian.'*

' A pretty Christian' sneered Robinson.

* In Berkshire among a certain class this word means ' a human being.'

* You know what I mean, Tom ?'

' I know it is not very kind of you to take all this trouble to bury my enemy ' said Robinson, hurt.

' Don't ye say that' replied George, hurt in his turn. ' He was as much my enemy as yours.*

' No such thing. He was here after me, and has been tormenting me this twelve months. You have no enemy, a great soft spoon like you.'

'Keep your temper, Tom,' answered George in a mollifying tone. * Let each man act according to his lights. I couldn't leave a corpse to the fowls of the air.'

* Gibbet a murderer I say—don't bury him; especially when he has just been hunting our very lives.'

' Tom' replied George doggedly, ' death settles all accounts. I liked the man as little as you could; and it is not to say I am in love with a man because I sprinkle a little earth over his dead bones. Ugh! This is the unkindest soil to work. It is full of roots, enough to break a fellow's heart.'

Wliile George was picking and grubbing out roots and fighting with the difficult soil, Robinson opened Levi's letter viciously, and read out,

' George Fielding, you have an enemy in the mine —a secret cowardly unscrupulous enemy, who lies in wait for your return. I have seen his face, and tremble for you. Therefore listen to my words. The old Jew whom twice you have saved from harm and insult is rich, his children are dead, the wife of his bosom is dead. He loves no creature now but you and Susannah; therefore run no more risks for gold, since much gold

awaits you without risk. Come home. Respect the words of age and experience—come home. Delay not an hour. Oh, say not " I will sleep yet one more night in my tent, and then I will depart," but ride speedily after me on the very instant. Two horses have I purchased for you and the young man your friend—two swift horses with their saddles. The voucher is inclosed. Ride speedily after me this very hour, lest evil befall you and yet more sorrow fall upon Susannah and upon—Isaac Levi.'

The reading of this letter was followed by a thoughtful silence broken only by the sound of George's pickaxe and the bursting roots.

' This is a very extraordinary letter. Mr. Levi knows more than he tells you, George.'

' I am of your opinion.'

'Why captain' said Jem *to go by that letter Fielding is the marked man, and not you after all. So it is his own enemy he is digging that grave for.'

' Do you think you will stop him by saying that ?' asked Robinson with a shrug.

' He was my enemy, Tom, and your's too; but now he is nobody's enemy; he is dead. Will you help me lay him in the earth or shall I do it by myself?'

' We will help,' said the others a little sullenly.

They brought the body to its grave under the tall gum-tree.

' Isot quite so rough, Tom^ \iyou please.'

' I didn't mean to be rough that I know of—there.'

They laid the dead villain gently and reverently in

his grave. George took a handful of soil and scattered it over him.

' Ashes to ashes, dust to dust,' said he solemnly.

The other two looked down and sprinkled soil too, and their anger and bitterness began to soften by the side of George and over the grave.

Then Jem felt in his pocket and produced something wrapped in silver paper.

* This belongs!' said he with a horrible simplicity.

* The farmer is too good for this world, but it is a good fault. There, farmer,' said he, looking to George for approbation as he dropped the little parcel into the grave. ' After all,' continued Jem good-naturedly, * it would have been very hard upon a poor fellow to wake up in the next world and not have what does belong to him to make an honest living with.'

The grave was filled in and a little mound made at the foot of the tree. Then George took out his knife and began to cut the smooth bark.

' What now ? Oh, I see. That is a good idea, George. Read them a lesson. Say in a few words how he came here to do a deed of violence and died himself—by the hand of heaven.

' Tom,' replied George, cutting away at the bark,

* he is gone where he is sure to be judged; so we have no call to judge him. God Almighty can do that I do suppose without us putting in our word.'

' Well, have it your own way. I never saw the toad so obstinate before, Jem. What is he cutting I wonder ?'

The inscription when finished ran thus— ' Please don't cut down this tree.

* It IS A TOMB-STONE. ' A WHITE MAN LIES BELOW.'

' Now Tom for England.'

They set out again with alacrity and battled with the bush about two hours more. George and Robinson carried the great nugget on a handkerchief stretched double across two sticks. Jem carried the picks. They were all in high spirits and made light of scratches and difficulties. At last, somewhat suddenly, they burst out of the thick part into the mere outskirts frequented by the miners, and there they came plimp upon brutus, with a gun in his hand and pistols peeping out of his pockets, come to murder Black Will and rob him of his spoils.

They were startled and brutus astounded, forj he was fully persuaded George and Robinson had ceased to exist. He was so dumb-foundered that Robinson walked up to him and took the gun out of his hands without any resistance on his part. The others came round him, and Robinson demanded his pistols.

* What for ?' said he.

Now at this very moment his eye fell upon that fabulous mass of gold they carried, and both his eyes opened and a sort of shiver passed over him. With ready cunning he looked another way, but it was too late. Robinson had caught that furtive glance, and a chill came over him that this villain should have seen the

prize; a thing to excite cupidity to frenzy. Nothing now would have induced Ex)binson to leave him armed.

He replied sternly, * Because we are four to one, and we will hang you on the nearest tree if you don't give them up. And now, what are you doing here ?'

' I was only looking for my pal' said brutus.

' Well, you won't want a gun and pistols to look for your pal. Which way are you going ?'

* Into the bush.'

* Then mizzle ! That is the road.' brutus moved gloomily away into the bush.

' There,' said Robinson, ' he has turned bushranger. I've disarmed him and saved some poor fellow's life and property. Cover up the nugget George.'

They went on, but presently Robinson had a thought.

' Jacky' said he, * you saw that man; should you know him again?'

' Yes.'

' Jacky, that man is our enemy. Could you track him by his footsteps without ever letting him see you?'

Ja<5ky smiled superior.

* Then follow him and see where he goes, and whom he joins, and come to the mine directly and tell me.'

Jacky's eyes gleamed at this intelligence. He sat down, and in a few turns of the hand painted his face war, and glided like a serpent on brutus's trail.

The rest cleared the wood, and brought the nugget

' IT IS NEVER TOO LATE TO MEND.' 215

safe hidden in their pocket-handkerchief to camp. They begged Jem to accept the fifty pounds if he did not mind handling the price of blood.

Jem assured them he had no such scruples, and took it with a burst of thanks.

Then they made him promise faithfully not to mention to a soul about the monster nugget. No more he did while he was sober, but alas! some hours later, having a drop in his head, he betrayed the secret to one or two—say forty.

Robinson pitched their tent and mounted guard over the nugget. George was observed to be in a strange flutter. He ran hither and thither. Ran to the post-office—ran to the stationer—got paper—drew up a paper—found McLauchlan—made him sign it—went to Mr. Moore—showed him Isaac's voucher: on which Moore produced the horses; a large black horse with both bone and blood, and a good cob.

George was very much pleased with them and asked what Levi had given for them.

' Two hundred and fifty pounds for the pair.'

' Good heavens' cried George ' what a price ! Mr. Levi was in earnest:' then he ran out and went to the tent and gave Robinson his letters. ' But there were none for me Tom,' sighed George. 'Never mind, I shall soon'—

Now these letters brought joy and triumph to Robinson ; one contained a free pardon, the other was a polite missive from the Colonial Government in answer to the miners' petition he had sent up.

216 ' rr IS never too LAra to mend/

' Secretary had the honour to inform Mr. Eobinson that police were on the road to the mine, and that soldiers would arrive as to-morrow to form an escort, so that the miners' gold might travel in safety down to Sydney/

' Hurrah! this is good news,' cried Robinson, ' and what a compliment to me. Do you hear George, an escort of soldiers coming to the camp to-morrow ; they will take the nugget safe to Sydney.'

' Not if we are robbed of it to-night' replied Greorge. At this moment in came Jacky with news of brutus :

that wily man had gone but a little way in the bush when he had made a circuit, and had slipped back into another part of the mine, and Jacky had followed him first by trail afterwards by sight, and had marked him down into a certain tent, on which he had straightway put a little red mark.

' Come back after our nugget Greorge.' Fools we were to carry it blazing in folks' eyes.'

' I dare say we can beat him.'

' I am game to try. Jacky I want to put a question to you.'

Wliile Jacky and Tom were conferring in animated whispers, George was fixing an old spur he had picked up into the heel of his boot.

' That is capital, Jacky. Well George we have hit upon a plan.'

' And so have I.'

'You?'

' Yes ! me! but tell me yours first Tom.

Robinson detailed him his scheme with all its ramifications, and a very ingenious stratagem it was.

For all that when George propounded his plan in less than six words, Robinson stared with surprise and then gave way to ludicrous admiration.

' Well' cried he, ' simplicity before cunning; look at that now. Where was my head ?—George, this is your day—carried nem. con.'

' And Tom you can do yours all the same.'

' Can I ? why yes to be sure I can. There, he saw that too before. Why George if you don't mind you will be No. 1 and I No. 2. What makes you so sharp all of a sudden ?'

' I have to think for Susan as well as us,' said the poor fellow tenderly, 'that is why I am sharp—for once in a way. And now Jacky you are a great anxiety to me, and the time is so short—come sit by me dear Jacky, and let me try and make you understand what I have been doing for you that you may be good and happy, and comfortable in your old age, when your poor old limbs turn stiff and you can hunt no longer. In grateful return for the nugget, and more than that for all your goodness and kindness to me in times of bitter trouble.'

Then George showed Jacky how he had given Abner one-third of all his sheep and cattle, and Jacky two-thirds, and how M'Lauchlan, a just man, would see the division made: 'And do leave the woods except for a hunt now and then Jacky, you are too good for them.

Above all Greorge explained with homely earnestness the nature of the sheep, her time of lambing, etc., and showed Jacky how the sheep and cattle would always keep him fed and clothed if he would but use them reasonably and not kill the breeders for dinner.

And Jacky listened with glistening eyes, for George's glistened, and the sweet tones of affection and gratitude pierced through this family talk, and it is sad that we must drop the curtain on this green spot in the great camp and go among our villains.

CHAPTER XXII.

Robinson did not overrate the fatal power of the fabulous mass of gold, a glimpse of which he had incautiously given to greedy eyes. It drew brutus like a magnet after it. He came all in a flutter to mephis-topheles and told him he had met the two men carrying a lump of solid gold between them so heavy that the sticks bent under it; * the sweat ran down me at the sight of it, but I managed to look another way directly.'

What with the blows and kicks and bruises and defeats he had received, and with the gold mass his lawless eye had rested on, brutus was now in a state of mind terrible to think of.

Lust and hate, terrible twins, stung that dark heart to frenzy. Could he have had his will he would have dispensed with cunning, would have gone out and fired bullets from his gun into the tent, and if his enemies came out alive have met them hand to hand to slay or be slain. But the watchful foe had disarmed him, and he was compelled to listen to the more reynard-like ferocity of his accomplice.

' Bill,' said the assassin of Carlo, ' keep cool, and you shall have the swag; and yet not lose your revenge neither/
' you, tell me how/
' Let the bottle alone then! you are hot enough without that. Come nearer me. What I have got to say is not the sort of thing for me to bawl about: we should not be alive half an hour if it was heard to come from our lips.'

The two heads came close together, and Crawley leaned over the other side of the table, and listened with senses keen as a razor.

' Suppose I show you how to make those two run out of their tent like two frightened women, and never once think about their swag ?'

' Ah !'

' And fall blinded for life or dead or dying while we walk off with the swag.'

* Blind, dead, dying! give me your hand. How ? how? how?'

' Hush! don't shout like that; come closer, and you Smith.'

Then a diabolical scheme hissed into the listeners' ears,—a scheme at once cowardly and savage,—a scheme of that terrible kind that robs courage, strength, and even skill of their natural advantages, and reduces their owners to the level of the weak and the timid,—a scheme worthy of the assassin of Carlo, and the name I have given this wretch, whose brain was so fertile and his heart so fiendish. Its effect on the hearers was great but very different. Crawley recoiled, not violently but like a serpent on which water had been poured; but brutus broke into a rapture of admiration, exultation, gratified hate.

* Bless you, bless you!' cried he, with a violence more horrible than his curses, ' you warm my heart, you are a pal. What a head-piece you have got! you Smith, have you nothing to say ? Isn't this a dodge out of the common ?'

Now for the last minute or two Crawley's eyes had been fixed with a haggard expression on a distant corner of the room. He did not move them: he appeared hardly to have the power, but he answered, dropping the words down on the table anywhere.

' Ye—Yes ! it is very inge-nious, ah !'

Mephisto. ' We must buy the turpentine directly; there is only one store sells it, and that shuts at nine.'

Brutus. ' Do you hear Smith, hand us out the blunt.'

Crawler/. ' Oh, ugh!' and his eyes seemed fascinated to that spot.

Brutus (following Crawley's eye uneasily). ' What is the matter ?'

Crawley. ' Lo-o-o-k the-r-e! No! on your right. Oh, his tail is in the fire!'

Brutus. ' Whose tail ? don't be a fool!'

Crawley. ' And it doesn't burn!! Oh, it bums blaxjker in the fire!—Ah, ah! now the eyes have caught fire—diamonds full of hell. They blast! Ah, now the teeth have caught light—red-hot nails. The mouth is as big as tlie table, gaping wider, wider, wider. Ah! ah! ah!'

Brutus. * him; I won't stay in the room with such a fellow, he makes my blood run cold. Has he cut his father's throat in a church, or what ?'

Crawley (shrieking). ' Oh, don't go; oh, my dear friends, don't leave me alone with IT.

My dear friends, you sit down right upon it—that sends it away.' And Crawley hid his face, and pointed wildly to whereabouts they were to sit upon the phantom.

BrutuB. ' Come, it is gone now; was forced nearly to squash it first though, haw ! haw ! haw !'

Crawley. ' Yes, it is gone. Thank heaven—I'll give up drinking.'

Brutus. ' So now fork out the blunt for the turps.'

Crawley. ' No! I will give no money towards murder—robbery is bad enough. Where shall we all go to ?' And he rose and went out, muttering something about ' a little brandy.'

Brutus. ' The sneak to fail us at the pinch, I'll wring his neck round. What is this ? five pounds.

MepTiisto. * Don't you see the move ? he won't give it us, conscience forbids, but if we are such rogues as take it no questions asked.'

' The tarnation hypocrite,' roared brutus with disgust,—hypocrisy was the one vice he was innocent of— out of gaol, Mephistopheles stole Crawley's money left for that purpose, and went and bought a four gallon cask of turpentine.

brutus remained and sharpened an old cutlass, the

only weapon he had got left. Crawley and mephistx)-pheles returned almost together. Crawley produced a bottle of brandy.

* Now,' said he to mephistopheles, ' I don't dispute your ingenuity, my friend, but suppose while we have been talking the men have struck their tent, and gone away nugget and all?'

The pair looked terribly blank—what fools we were not to think of that.

Crawley kept them in pain a moment or two.

* Well, they have not,' said he, ' I have been to look.'

* Well done ' cried mephistopheles.

* Well done ' cried brutus, gasping for breath.

* There is their tent all right.'

* How near did you go to it ?'

' Near enough to hear their voices muttering.'

* When does the moon rise to-night ?'

* She is rising now.'

' When does she go down ?'

' Soon after two o'clock.'

' Will you take a share of the work, Smith ?'

* Hcaven forbid!'

('224)

CHAPTER XXIII.

It was a gusty night. The moon had gone down. The tents gleamed indistinct in form, but white as snow. Robinson's tent stood a little apart, among a number of deserted claims, some of them dry, but most of them with three or four feet of water in them.

There was, however one large tent about twenty yards from Robinson's.

A man crept on his belly up to this tent and listened ; he then joined another man who stood at some distance, and whose form seemed gigantic in the dim star-light.

' All right,' said the spy, * they are all fast as dormice, snoring like hogs ; no fear from them.'

' Go to work then,' whispered brutus. ' Do your part.'

Mephistopheles laid a deep iron dish upon the ground, and removed the bimg from the turpentine cask, and poured. ' Confound the wind, how it wastes the stuff,' cried he.

He now walked on tip-toe past Robinson's tent, and scattered the turpentine with a bold sweep, so that it

fell light as rain over a considerable surface. A moment of anxiety succeeded, would their keen antagonists heai' even that slight noise ? No! no one stirred in the tent.

Mephistophiles returned to the cask, and emboldened by success brought it nearer the doomed tent. Six times he walked past the windward side of the tent, and scattered the turpentine over it. It was at the other side his difficulties began.

The first time he launched the liquid, the wind took it and returned it nearly all in his face, and over his clothes. Scarce a drop reached the tent.

The next time he went up closer with a beatmg heart, and flung it sharper. This time full two-thirds went upon the tent, and only a small quantity came back like spray. By the time the cask was emptied, the tent was saturated. Then this wretch passed the tent yet once more, and scattered a small quantity of oil to make the flame more durable and deadly.

' Now it is my turn ' whispered brutus. ' I thought it would never come.'

What is that figure crouching and crawling about a hundred yards to windward. It is the caitiff Crawley, who after peremptorily declining to have anything to do with this hellish act, has crept furtively after them, partly to play the spy on them, for he suspects they will lie to him about the gold, partly urged by curiosity. He could see nothing at that distance but the dark body of mephistopheles passing at intervals between him and the white tent.

He shivered with cold and terror at the crime about to be done, and quivered with impatience that it was so long a doing.

The assassins now divided their force, mephisto-pheles took his station to leeward of the tent.

brutus to windward.

Crawley saw a sudden spark upon the ground, it was brutus striking a lucifer nuatch against his heel. With this he lighted a piece of tow, and running along the tent he left a line of fire behind him and awaited the result, his cutlass griped in his hand and his teeth clinched.

Crawley saw that line of fire come and then creep and then rise and then roar, and shoot up into a great column of fire thirty feet high, roaring and blazing and turning night into day all around. Simultaneously with this tremendous burst of fire and light, which started Crawley by bringing him in a moment into broad daylight, he saw rise from the earth a black figure with a fiendish face.

At this awful sight the conscience-stricken wretch fell flat and tried to work into the soil like a worm. Nor did he recover any portion of his presence of mind till he heard a shrill whoop savage and soul-chilling but mortal; and looking up, saw Kalingalunga go bounding down upon brutus with gigantic leaps, his tomahawk whirling.

Crawley cowered like a hare, and watched. Brutus, surprised but not dismayed, wheeled round and faced the savage cutlass in hand. He parried a fierce blow of

the tomahawk, and with his left fist struck Kalingaliinga on the temple, and knocked him backwards half a dozen yards. The elastic savage recovered himself, and danced like a fiend Tound brutus in the red light of the blazing tent.

Warned by that strange blow straight from the armpit, a blow entirely new to him, he came on with more deadly caution, eyes and teeth bude-lights, and brutus felt a chill for a moment, but it speedily turned to rage. Now as the combatants each prepared to strike again, screams suddenly issued firom the other side the tent, so wild, despairing and unnatural, as to suspend their arms for a moment. They heard but saw nothing, only the savage heart of brutus found time to exult,—his enemies were perishing. But Crawley saw as well as heard. A pillar of flame eight feet high burst out from behind the tent, and ran along the ground. From that conical flame issued those appalling shrieks, it was a man on fire. The living flame ran but a few steps, then disappeared from the earth, and the screams ceased. Apparently the fire had not only killed, but annihilated its prey and so itself Crawley sickened with horrcfl:, and for a moment with remorse.

But already brutus and Kalingalunga were fighting again by the light of the burning tent. They closed, and this time blood flowed on both sides, the savage, by a skilful feint, cut brutus on the flesh of the left shoulder but not deep, and brutus once more surprised the savage by delivering point with his cutlass, and inflicted a severe graze on the ribs.

At the sight of his enemy's blood brutus followed up and aimed a fierce blow at Kalingaltinga's head; he could not have made a more useless attack. The savage bore on his left arm a shield so called ; it was but three mches broad and two feet long but skill and practice had made it an impenetrable defence. He received the cutlass on this shield as a matter of course, and simultaneously delivered his tomahawk on brutus' unguarded head, brutus went down under the blow and rolled over on his face.

The crouching spectator of this terrible combat by the decaying light of the tent heard the hard blow and saw the white man roll upon the ground. Then he saw the tomahawk twice lifted and twice descend upon the man's back as he lay. The next moment the savage came running from the tent at his utmost speed.

Crawley's first thought was that assistance had come to brutus; his next was a terrible one. The savage had first risen from the earth at a spot between the tent and him. Perhaps he had been watching both him and the tent. A moment of horrible uncertainty, and then Crawley yielded to his instinct and ran. A terrible whoop behind told him he was indeed to be the next victim. He ran for the dear life ; no one would have believed he could shamble along at the rate he did. His tent was half a mile off; he would be a dead man long ere he could reach it. He turned his yelling head as he ran to see. The fleet savage had already diminished the distance between them by half. Crawley now filled the air with despairing cries for help. A large tent was before him; he knew not whose, but certain death was behind him. He made for the tent. If he could but reach it before thc death-stroke was given him! Yes, it is near! No, it is white and looks closer than it is. A whoop sounded in his ears; it seemed to ring inside his head, it was so near. He flung himself yelling with terror at the wall of the tent. An aperture gave way. A sharp cut as with a whip seemed to sting him, and he was on his knees in the middle of the tent howling for mercy, first to the savage, who he made sure was standing over him with his tomahawk: then to a man who got him by the throat and pressed a pistol barrel cold as an icicle to his cheek.

' Mercy! mercy! the savage! he is killing me ! murder! murder ! help !'

' Who are you ?' roared the man shaking him.

' Oh, stop him 1 he will kill me ! Shoot him ! Don't shoot me ! I am a respectable man. It is the savage ! kill him 1 He is at the door—please kill him! I'll give you a hundred pounds to kill him 1'

' What is to do ? The critter is mad !'

' There! there ! you will see a savage ! Shoot him ! kill him! For pity's sake kill him, and I'll tell you all! I am respectable. I'll give you a hundred pounds to kill him!'

' Why, it is Smith, that gives us all a treat at times.'

' Don't I! Oh, my dear good friend, he has killed me ! He came after me with his tomahawk. Have pity on a respectable man and kill him 1'

The man went to the door of his tent and sure

enough there was Jacky, who had retired to some distance. The man fired at him with as little ceremony as he would at a glass bottle, and as was to be expected missed him; but Jacky, who had a wholesome horror of the make-thunders, ran oiF directly, and went to hack the last vestiges of life out of brutus.

Crawley remained on his knees howling and whimpering so piteously that the man took pity on this abject personage.

' Have a drop, Mr. Smith; you have often given me one—there. I'll strike a light.'

The man struck a light and fixed a candle in a socket. He fumbled in a corner for the bottle and was about to ofier it to Crawley when he was arrested by a look of silent horror on his visitor's face.

' Why, what is wrong now ?'

* Look! look! look !' cried Crawley trembling from head to foot. * Here it comes ! there is its tail 1 Soon its eyes and teeth will catch light! It knows the work we have been at. Ah! ah ! ah!'

The man looked round very uneasily. Crawley's way of pointing and glaring over one's head at some object behind one was anything but encouraging.

^What? where?'

* There ! there! coming through the side of the tent It can come through a wall!' and Crawley shook from head to foot.

*Why, that is your own shadow,' said the man. ' Why, what a faint-hearted one to shake at your own shadow!'

* My shadow!' cried Crawley; * heaven forbid! Have I got a tail ?' screeched Crawley reproachfully.

' That you have ' said the man * now I look at you full'

Crawley clapped his hand behind him, and to his horror he had a tail!

(232)

CHAPTER XXIV.

Crawley who, what with the habit of cerebral hallucination due to brandy and the present flutter of his spirits and his conscience, had for a moment or two lost all the landmarks of probability, no sooner felt his hand encounter a tail—slight in size, but stiff as a pug's, and straight as a pointer's—than he uttered a dismal howl, and it is said that for a single moment he really suspected premature caudation had been inflicted on him for his crimes. But such delusions are short-lived. He slewed himself round after this tail in his efforts to see it, and squinting over his shoulder he did see it; and a warm liquid which he now felt stealing down his legs and turning cold as it went opened his eyes still farther. It was a reed spear sticking in his person, sticking tight. Jacky, who had never got so near him as he fancied, saw him about to get into a tent, and unable to tomahawk him, did the best he could—flung a light javelin with such force and address that it pierced his coat and trowsers and buried half its head in his flesh.

This spear-head made of jagged fish-bones had to be cut out by the simple and agreeable process of making all round it a hole larger than itself. The operation served to occupy Crawley for the remaining part of the night, and exercised his vocal powers. This was the first time he had smarted in his penetrable part—the skin, and it made him very spiteful. Away went his compunction, and at peep of day he shambled out very stiff, no longer dreading but longing to hear which of his enemies it was he had seen wrapped in flame, shrieking, and annihilated like the snuff of a candle. He came to the scene of action just as the sun rose.

But others were there before him. A knot of men stood round a black patch of scorched soil, round which were scattered little fragments of canvas burnt to tinder, talking over a most mysterious affair of the night past.

It came out that the patrol, some of whom were present, had been ordered by Captain Robinson not to go their rounds as usual, but to watch in a tent near his own; since he expected an attack. Accustomed to keep awake on the move, but not in a recumbent posture, they had slept the sleep of infancy till suddenly awakened by the sound of a pistol. Then they had run out and had found the captain's tent in ashes, and a man lying near it sore hacked and insensible, but still breathing. They had taken him to their tent, but he had never spoken, and the affair was incomprehensible. While each was giving some wild opinion or another, a faint voice issued from the bowels of the earth, invoking aid. .

Several ran to the spot, and at the bottom of an old
claim full thirty feet deep, they discovered on looking intently down the face of a man rising out of the clayey water. They lowered ropes and hauled him up.

' How did you come there, mate ?'

' He had come into the camp in the dark, and not knowing the ground, and having (to tell the truth) had a drop, he had fallen into the claim.'

He was asked with an air of suspicion how long ago this had happened.

' More than an hour' replied the wily one.

Crawley looked at him, and being, unlike the others, acquainted with the man's features, saw spite of the clay-cake he was enveloped in that his whiskers were fiizzled to nothing and his fiendish eyebrows gone. Then a sickening suspicion crept over him; he communicated it by a look to mephistopheles.

Acting on it he asked, with an artful appearance of friendly interest—

' But the men ? the poor men that were in the tent?'

' What! the captain and his mate ?'

^ Yes!'

* Wliy, ye fool! they are half way to Sydney by now.'

* Half way to Sydney ?' and a ghastly look passed between the speaker and mephistopheles.

' Ay, lad! they rode off on Moore's two best nags at midnight.'

' The captain had a belt round his waist crammed with dust and bank-notes,' cried another, ' and the
farmer a nugget as big as a pumpkin on the pommel of his saddle.'

Four hours had not elapsed ere Crawley and mephis-topheles were on the road to Sydney, but not on horseback. Crawley had no longer funds to buy two horses, and even if he had he could not have borne the saddle after the barbarous surgery of last night—the lance-head was cut out with a cheese-knife. But he and mephistopheles joined a company of successful diggers going down with their swag. On the road they constantly passed smaller parties of unfortunate diggers, who had left the mine in despair when the weather broke and the claims filled with water ; and the farther they went the more wretched was the condition of those they overtook. Ragged, shoeless, hungry, foot-sore, heart-sore, poor broken pilgrims from the shrine of mammon.

Now it befell, that forty miles on this side Sydney, they fell in with seven such ragged spectres ; and while they were giving these a little food, up came from the city a large joyful party,—the eagerness of hope and cupidity on their faces.

' Hallo! are they mad, going up to the diggings in the wet weather!'

They were questioned.

A hundred-weight of gold had been found at the diggings, and all the town was turning out to find some more such prizes; and in fact, every mile after this they met a -party, great or small, ardent sanguine on an almost hopeless errand.

Such is the strange and fatal no-logic of speculation. For us the rare is to turn common, and when we have got it be rare as ever.

Mephistophiles and Crawley parted at the suburb, the former was to go to certain haunts and form a gang to seize the rich prize. Meantime Crawley would enter the town and discover where the men were lodging. If in an inn, one of the gang must go there as a well-dressed traveller and watch his opportunity. If in a lodging, other means.

Crawley foimd the whole city ringing with the great nugget. Crawley put eager questions and received ready answers. He was shown the bank up to wliich the men had ridden in broad day-light, the one on the big horse had the nugget on his saddle; they had taken it and broken it and weighed it and sold it in the bank parlour for three thousand eight hundred pounds.

Crawley did not like this, he had rather they had not converted it into paper. His next question was whether it was known where the men lodged ?

' Known, I believe you ! why they are more thought of than the governor. Everybody runs to get a word with them gentle or simple. You will find them at the *' Ship " inn.'

To the " Ship " went Crawley. He dared not be too direct in his queries, so he put them in form of a statement.

' You have got some lucky ones here that found the great nugget ?'

' Well, we had! but they are gone—been gone this two hours. Do you know them ?'

' Yes,' said Crawley, without fear as they were gone. ' Where are they gone, do you know ?'

' Why home I suppose; you chaps make your money out of us, but you all run home to spend it.'

' What gone to England !' gasped Crawley.

' Aye, look! there is the ship just being towed out of the harbour.'

Crawley shambled and tore and ran, and was just in time to see the two friends standing with beaming faces on the vessel's deck as she glided out on her voyage home.

He sat down half stupid; mephistophiles went on collecting his gang in the suburbs. Collect them !!

The steamer cast off, and came wheeling back; the ship spread her huge white plumage, and went proudly off to sea, the blue waves breaking white under her bows.

Crawley sat glaring at all this in a state of mental collapse.

CHAPTER XXV.

Thus have I told in long and tedious strains how George Fielding went to Australia to make a thousand pounds, and how by industry sobriety and cattle he did not make a thousand pounds, and how aided with ijie help of a converted thief, this honest fellow did by gold digging industry and sobriety make several thousand pounds, and take them safe away home spite of many wicked devices and wicked men.

Thus have I told how Mr. Meadows flung out his left hand into Australia to keep George from coming back to Susan with a thousand pounds, and how spite of one stroke of success his left-hand eventually failed, and failed completely.

But his right ?

CHAPTEE XXYI.

Joyous as the first burst of summer were the months Susan passed after the receipt of George's happy letter. Many warm feelings combined in one stream of happiness in Susan's heart. Perhaps the keenest of all was pride at Greorge's success. Nobody could laugh at George now and insult her again there where she was most sensitive, by telling her that George was not good enough for her or any woman; and even those who set such store upon money-making would have to confess that George could do even that for love of her, as well as they could do it for love of themselves. Next to this her joy was greatest at the prospect of his speedy return.

And now she became joyfully impatient for further news, but not disappointed at his silence till two months had passed without another letter: then indeed anxiety mingled now and then with her happiness. Then it was that Meadows, slowly and hesitatingly to the last, raised his hand and struck the first direct blow at her heart. He struck in the dark—he winced for her both before and after.—Yet he struck.

One market-day a whisper passed through Fambo-rough that George Fielding had^met with wonderfiil luck. That he had made his fortune by gold, and was going

to marry a young lady out in Australia. Farmer Merton brought the whisper home, Meadows was sure he would.

Meadows did not come to the house for some days. He half feared to look upon his work: to see Susan's face agonized under his blow. At last he came : he watched her by stealth. He found he might have spared his qualms. She chatted as usual in very good spirits, and just before he went she told him the report with a smile of ineffable scorn.

She was simple, unsuspicious, and every way without a shield against a Meadows, but the loyal heart by its own virtue had turned the dagger's edge.

A week after this Jeffries brought Meadows a letter; it was from Susan to George. Meadows read it, writhing : it breathed kind affection, with one or two demi-maternal cautions about his health, and to be very prudent for her sake : not a word of doubt; there was, however, a postscript of which the following is the exact wording;—

' P.S. It is all over Famborough that you are going to be married to some one in Australia.'

Two months more passed and no letter from George. These two months told upon Susan; she fretted and became restless and irritable, and cold misgivings crept over her, and the anguish of suspense!

At last one day she unbosomed herself, though with hesitation, to a warm and disinterested friend; blushing all over with tearful eyes she confessed her grief to Mr. Meadows. ' Don't tell father, sir; I hide my trouble from him as well as I can, but what does it mean

George not writing to me this four months and three days. Do pray tell me what does it mean !' and Susan cried so piteously that Meadows winced at his success.

* Oh, Mr. Meadows! don't flatter me; tell me the truth.' While he was exulting in her firmness, who demanded the truth, bitter or not, she continued, * Only don't tell me that I am forgotten.' And she looked so piteously in the oracle's face that he forgot everything in the desire

to say something she Avould like him the better for saying; he muttered, ' Perhaps he has sailed for home.' He expected her to say ' and if he has he would have written to me before sailing.' But instead of this Susan gave a little cry of joy.

* Ah! how fullish I have been. Mr. Meadows, you are a friend out of a thousand; you are as wise as I am fullish. Poor George ! you will never let him know I was so wicked as to doubt him.' And Susan brightened with joy and hope. The heart believes so readily the thing it longs should be true. She was happy all the rest of the evening.

Meadows went away mad with her for her folly, and with himself for his feebleness of purpose, and next market-day again the whisper went round the market that George Fielding was going to marry out there. This time a detail was sketched in; 'it was a lady in the town of Bathurst'

Old Merton brought this home and twitted his daughter. She answered haughtily that it was a falsehood. She would stake her life on George's fidelity.

' See, Mr. Meadows, they are all against poor George,

VOL. III. M

all except you. But what does it mean ? if he does not write or come soon I think I shall go mad.'

' Eeport is a common liar; I would not believe anything till I saw it in black and white' said Meadows doggedly.

* No more I will.'

Soon after this William Fielding had a talk with Susan.

* Have you heard a report about George ?'

* Yes ! I have heard a rumour.'

* You don't believe it I hope.' ' Why should I believe it ?'

' I am going to trace it up to the liar that forged it if I can.'

Susan suppressed her satisfaction at this resolution of Will Fielding's.

' Is it worth while ?' asked she coldly.

' If I didn't think so I shouldn't take that much trouble, not expecting any thanks.'

* Have I said anything to offend you ?' asked Susan with a still more frigid tone.

The other did not trust himself to answer. But two days after he came again and told her he had written a letter to George, telling him what reports were about, and begging for an answer whether or not there was any truth in them.

A gleam of satisfaction from Susan's eyes but not a word. This man who had once been George's rival at heart was the last to whom she would openly acknowledge her doubts. Then Will went on to tell her that he had traced the rumour from one to another up to a

stranger whose name nobody knew, ' but I dare say Mr. Meadows has a notion.' 'No!'

* Are you sure ?'

* Yes ! he would have told me if he had.' William gave a snort of incredulity, and hinted that

probably Mr. Meadows himself was at the bottom of the scandal.

Now Meadows's artful conduct had fortified Susan against such a suspicion, and being by nature a warmhearted friend she fired up for him, as she would have for Mr. Eden or even for poor Will in his absence. She did it too in the most womanish way. She did not tell the young man that she had consulted Mr. Meadows, and that he had constantly discredited the report and set her against believing it. Had she done this she would have staggered the simple-minded Will: but no, she said to herself, * He has attacked a good friend of mine, I won't satisfy him so far as to give him reasons,' so she merely snubbed him.

' Oh ! I know you are set against poor Mr. Meadows, he is a good friend of ours, of my father and me and of George too.'

*I wish you may not have to alter your mind,' sneered William.

' I will not without a reason.'

' I will give you a reason: do you remember that day—'

' When you insulted him in his own house, and me into the bargain. Will ?'

' Not you Susan, leastways I hope not, but him I

M 2

did, and am just as like to do it again; well, when you were gone I took a thought and I said appearances deceive the wisest, I may be mistaken—'

' He! he!'

' I don't know what you are laughing at; and then says I, it is his own house alter all, so I said " If I am wrong and you don't mean to undermine my brother take my hand," and I gave it him.'

* And he refused it ?' ' Ko Susan!' 'Well then—

* But Susan,' said William solemnly * his hand lay in mine like a stone.'

' Really

now

' A lump of ice would be as near the mark.'

' Well! is that the reason you promised me ?'

William nodded.

* William you are a fool.'

' Oh ! I am a fool now ?'

' You go and insult a man, your superior in every respect, and the very next moment he is to give you his hand as warmly as to a friend and an equal; you really are too fullish to go about without a keeper, and if it was in any man's power to set me against poor George altogether you have gone the way to do it this twelvemonths past;' and Susan closed the conference abruptly.

It was William's fate to rivet Meadows's influence by every blow he aimed at it. For all that, the prudent Meadows thought it worth his while to rid himself of this honest and determined foe, and he had already

* IT IS NEVER TOO LATE TO MEND.' 245

taken steps. He had discovered that this last month William Fielding, returning from market, had been seen more than once to stop and chat at one Mts. Holiday's, a retired small tradeswoman in Famborough. Now Mrs. Holiday was an old acquaintance of Mea-dows's, and had given him sugar-plums thirty years ago. It suited his purpose to remember all of a sudden these old sugar-plums, and that Mrs. Holiday had lately told him she wanted to get out of the town and end her days upon turf.

There was a cottage, paddock, and garden for sale within a hundred yards of " The Grove." Meadows bought them a good bargain, and offered them to the widow at a very moderate rent.

The widow was charmed. ' Why we can keep a cow Mr. Meadows.'

' Well, there is grass enough.'

The widow took the cottage with enthusiasm.

Mrs. Holiday had a daughter, a handsome—a downright handsome girl, and a good girl into the bargain.

Meadows had said to himself, ' It is not the old woman Will Fielding goes there for. Well, she will want some one to teach her how to farm that half-acre of grass, and buy the cow and milk her. Friendly offices—chat coming and going—come in Mr. Fielding and taste your cow's cream; and when he has got a lass of his own his eye won't be for ever on mine.'

William's letter to George went to the post-office, and from the post-office to a little pile of intercepted letters in Meadows's desk.

CHAPTER XXVII.

Nearly eight months had now elapsed without a letter from Greorge. Susan could no longer deceive herself with hopes. George was either false to her or dead. She said as much to her false friend. This inspired him with an artifice as subtle as unscrupulous. A letter had been brought to him by Jeffries, which he at once recognized as the planned letter from Crawley to another tool of his in Famborough. This very day he set about a report that Greorge was dead. It did not reach Susan so soon as he thought it would, for old Merton hesitated to tell her, but on the Sunday evening with considerable reluctance and misgivings he tried in a very clumsy way to prepare her for sad news.

But her mind had long been prepared for bitter tidings. Fancy eight weary months spent in passing every possible calamity before her imagination, death as often as any.

She fixed her eyes on the old man. ' Father, George is dead!'

Old Merton himg his head, and made no reply.

That was enough. Susan crept from the room pale as ashes. She tottered, but she did not fall. She reached her room and locked herself in.

CHAPTER XXVIII.

Mr. Meadows did not visit Grassmere for some days: the cruel one distrusted his own firmness. When he did come he came with a distinct purpose. He found Merton alone.

' Susan sees no one. You have heard ?'

' What?'

' Her sweetheart. He is dead.'

' Why how can that be ? And who says so ?'

* That is the news.'

' Well, it is a falsehood !' said Mr. Meadows coolly.

* I wish to heaven it might,' whispered old Merton, * for she won't live long after him.'

Mr. Meadows then told Merton that he had spoken with a man who had got news of George Fielding not four months old, and he was in very good health.

' Will you tell Susan this?'

' Certainly.'

Susan was called down. Meadows started at the sight of her. She was pale and hollow-eyed, and in these few days seemed ten years older. She was dressed all in black. ' I am a murderer !' thought he. And

remorse without one grain of honest repentance pierced his heart.

* Speak out John,' said the father, * the girl is not a fool. She has borne ill news, she can bear good. Can't you Susan?'

' Yes, dear father, if it is God's will any good news should come to me.' And she never took her eyes off Mr. Meadows, but belied her assumed firmness by quivering like an aspen-leaf.

' Do you know Mr. Grriffin ?' asked Meadows,

' Yes!' replied Susan, still trembling gently, but all over.

' He has got a letter from Sydney from a little roguish attorney called Crawley. I heard him say with my own ears that Crawley tells him he had just seen George Fielding in the streets of Sydney well and hearty.'

' You are deceiving me out of kindness.' Her eyes fixed on his.

' I am not. I wish I may die if the man is not as well as I am !'

Her eyes were never off liis face, and at this moment she read for certain that it was true.

She uttered a cry of joy so keen it was painful to hear, and then she laughed and cried and sank into a chair laughing and crying in strong hysterics that lasted till the poor girl almost fainted from exhaustion. Her joy was more violent and even terrible than her grief had been.

The female servants were called to assist her, and old Merton and Meadows left her in their hands, feeble but

calm and thankful. She even smiled her adieu to Meadows.

The next day Meadows called upon Griffin. ' Let me look at that letter?' said he. ' I want to copy a part of it.'

* There has been one here before you/ said Griffin. MVho?'

She did not give her name, but I think it must have been Miss Merton. She begged me hard to let her see the letter. I told her she might take it home with her. Poor thing I she gave me a look as if she could have eaten me.'

* What else ?' asked Meadows anxiously, his success had run a-head of his plot.

' She put it in her bosom.'

* In her bosom ?'

' Ay ! and pressed her little white hands upon it as if she had got a treasure. I doubt it will be more like the asp in the Bible story, eh! sir ?'

' There ! I don't want your reflections,' said Meadows fiercely, but his voice quavered. The myrmidon was silenced.

Susan made her escape into a field called the Kyne-croft belonging to the citizens, and there she read the letter. It was a long tiresome one all about matters of business which she did not understand; it was only at the last page that she caught sight of the name she longed to see. She hurried down to it, and when she got to it with beating heart it was the fate of this innocent loving woman to read these words—

M 3

* What luck some have. There is George Fielding, of the Grove Farm, has made his fortune at the gold, and married yesterday to one of the prettiest girls in Sydney. I met them walking in the street to-day. She would not have looked at him but for the gold.'

Susan uttered a faint moan and sank down slowly on her knees like some tender tree felled by a rude stroke; her eyes seemed to swim in a mist, she tried to read the cruel words again but could not; she put her hands before her eyes.

' He is alive' she said, ' thank God he is alive,' and at last tears forced their way through her fingers. She took her handkerchief and dried her eyes, ' Why do I cry for another woman's husband ?' and the hot colour of shame and of wounded pride burst even through her tears.

* I will not cry,' said she proudly, ' he is alive, I will not cry, he has forgotten me; from this moment I will never shed another tear for one that is alive and mi worthy of a tear. I will go home.'

She went home: crying all the way.

And now a partial success attended the deep Meadows's policy. It was no common stroke of unscrupulous cunning to plunge her into the very depths of woe in order to take her out of them. The effects were manifold and all tended his way.

First she was less sorrowful than she had been before that deadly blow, for now the heart had realised a greater woe, and had the miserable comfort of the comparison; but above all new and strong passions had

risen and battled fiercely with grief—anger and wounded pride.

Susan had self-respect and pride too, perhaps a shade too much, though less small vanity than have most persons of her moderate calibre.

What! had she wept and sighed all these months for a man who did not care for her.

What! had she defied sneers and despised affectionate hints and gloried openly in her love to be openly insulted and betrayed.

What! had she shut herself from the world, and put on mourning and been seen in mourning for one who was not dead, but well and happy and married to another.

An agony of shame rushed over the wronged, insulted, humiliated beauty. She longed to fly from the world. She asked her father to leave Grassmere and go to some other farm a hundred miles away. She asked him suddenly, nervously, and so impetuously that the old man looked up in dismay.

' What! leave the farm where your mother lived with me, and where you were born. I should feel strange, girl, but'—and he gave a strange sigh—' mayhap I shall have to leave it whether I will or no.'

Susan misunderstood him and coloured with self-reproach. She said hastily—' No ! no ! Father you shan't leave it for me. Forgive me, I am a wayward girl.'

And the strung nerves gave way and tears gushed over the hot cheeks as she clung to her father, and tiied

252 ' IT IS NEVER TOO LATE TO MEND.'

to turn the current of her despised love and bestow it all on that selfish old noodle. A great treasure went a begging in Grrassmere farmhouse.

Mr. Meadows called, but much to his chagrin Susan was never visible. ' Would he excuse her ? she was indisposed.'

The next evening he came he found her entertaining four or five other farmer's daughters and a couple of young men. She was playing the piano to them, and talking and laughing louder and faster than ever he had heard her in his life. He sat moody a little while and watched her uneasily, but soon took his line, and exerting his excellent social powers became the life of the party. But as he warmed Susan froze, as much as to say—' Somebody must play the fool to amuse these triflers, if you undertake it I need not.' For all that the very attempt at society indicated what was passing in Susan's mind, and the deep Meadows invited all present to meet at his house in two days' time.

Meadows was now living in Isaac Levi's old house. He had examined it, found it a much nicer house for him than his new one—it was like himself, full of ins and outs, and it was more in the heart of business and yet quiet; for though it stood in a row yet it was as good as detached, because the houses on each side were unoccupied. They belonged to Jews, probably dependants on Isaac, for they had left the town about a twelvemonth after his departure and had never returned, though a large quantity of goods had been deposited in one of the houses.

Meadows contrived that this little party should lead to another. His game was to draw Susan into the world, and moreover have her seen in his company. She made no resistance, for her wounded pride said ' Don't let people know you are breaking your heart for one who does not care for you.' She used to come to these parties radiant and playing her part with consummate resolution and success, and go home and spend the night in tears.

Meadows did not see the tears that followed these unusual eiForts—perhaps he suspected them. Enough for him that Susan's pride and shame and indignation were set against her love, and above all against her grief, and that she was forming habits whose tendency at least was favourable to his views.

Another four months, and Susan, exhausted by conflicting passions, had settled down into a pensive languor, broken ^by gusts of bitter grief, which became rarer and rarer. Her health recovered itself all but its elasticity. Her pride would not let her pine away. But her heart scarcely beat at all, and perhaps it was a good thing for her that a trouble of another kind came to gently stir it. Her father, who had for some months been moody and depressed, confessed to her that he had been speculating and was on the verge of ruin. This dreadful disclosure gave little more pain to Susan than if he had told her his head ached; but she put down her work and came and kissed him, and tried to console him.

' I must work harder, that is all, father. I am often

asked to give a lesson on the pianoforte; I will do that for your sake, and don't you fret for me. What with the trifle my mother settled on me and my industry I am above poverty, and you shall never see me repine.'

In short poor Susan took her father for a woman— adopted a line of consolation addressed to his affection instead of his selfishness. It was not for her he was afflicted, it was for himself.

It was at this conjuncture that Meadows spoke out. There was no longer anything to be gained by delay. In fact, he could not but observe that since the fatal letter he appeared to be rather losing ground in his old character. There was nothing left him but to attack her in a new one. He removed the barrier from his patient impatience.

He found her alone one evening. He begged her to walk in the garden. She complied with an unsuspecting smile. Then he told her aU he had suffered for her sake : how he had loved her this three years with all his soul—how he never thought to tell her this— how hard he had struggled against it—how he had run away from it, and after that how he had subdued it, or thought he had subdued it to esteem—and how he liad been rewarded by seeing that his visits and his talk had done her some good. * But now,' said he, ' that you are free, I have no longer the force to hide my love; now that the man I dared not interfere with has thrown away the jewel, it is not in nature that I should not beg to be allowed to take it up and wear it in my heart.'

Susan listened; first with surprise, then with con-

fusion and pain, then with terror at the violence of the man's passion; for the long restraint removed, it overwhelmed him like a flood. Her bosom heaved with modest agitation, and soon the tears streamed down her cheeks at his picture of what he had gone through for her sake. She made shift to gasp out, ' My poor friend !' But she ended almost fiercely, ' Let no man ever hope for affection from me, for my heart is in the grave. Oh, that I was there too !' And she ran sobbing away from him in spite of his intreaties.

Another man and not George had made a confession of love to her. His voice had trembled, his heart quivered with love for her, and it was not George. So then another link was snapped. Others saw they had a right to love her now, and acted on it.

Meadows was at a loss, but he stayed away a week in silence and thought and thought, and then he wrote a line begging permission to visit her as usual:—' I have been so long used to hide my feelings, because they were unlawful, that I can surely hide them if I see they make you more unhappy than you would be without.'

Susan replied that her advice to him was to avoid her as he would a pestilence. He came as usual, and told her he would take her commands but could not take her advice. He would run all risks to his own heart. He was cheerful, chatty, and never said a word of love; and this relieved Susan, so that the evening passed pleasantly. Susan, listless and indifferent to' present events, and never accustomed like Meadows to

act upon a preconceived plan, did not even observe what Meadows had gained by this sacrifice of his topic for a single night, viz., that after declaring himself her lover he was still admitted to the house. The next visit he was not quite so forbearing, yet still forbearing; and so on by sly gradations. It was every way an unequal contest. A great man against an average woman —a man of forty against a woman of twenty-two—a man all love and selfishness against a woman all aifection and unselfishness. But I think his chief ally was a firm belief on Susan's part that he was the best of men; that from first to last of this affair his conduct had been perfection; that while George was true all his thought had been to console her grief at his absence ; that he never would have spoken but for the unexpected treason of George, and then seeing her insulted and despised he had taken that moment to show her she was loved and honoured. Oh what an ungrateful girl she was that she could not love such a man!

Then her father was on the same side. * John Meadows seems down like, Susan. Do try and cheer him up a bit, I am sure he has often cheered thee.*

' That he has, father.*

Susan pitied Meadows. Pitying him she forced herself at times to be gracious, and when she did he was so happy that she was alarmed at her power, and drew in.

Old Merton saw now how the land lay, and he clung 'to a marriage between these two as his only hope. * John Meadows will pull me through if he marries my Susan.'

I

' IT IS NEVER TOO LATE TO MEND.' 257

And SO the two selfish ones had got the unselfish one between them, one pulling gently the other pushing quietly, but both without intermission. Thus days and days rolled on.

Meadows now came four times a-week instead of two, and courted her openly, and beamed so with happiness that she had not always the heart to rob him of this satisfaction, and he overwhelmed her with kindness and attention of every sort, and if any one else was present, she was sure to see how much he was respected; and this man whom others courted was her slave. This soothed the pride another had wounded.

One day he poured out his love to her with such passion that he terrified her, and the next time he came she avoided him.

Her father remonstrated : * Girl you will break that man's heart if you are so unkind to him ; he could not say a word because you shunned him like. Why your heart must be made of stone.' A burst of tears was all the reply.

At last two things presented themselves to this poor girl's understanding; that for her there was no chance of earthly happiness, do what she would, and that, strangely enough she the wretched one had it in her power to make two other beings happy, her father and good Mr. Meadows.

Now a true woman lives to make others happy. She rarely takes the self-contained views of life men are apt to do.

It passed through Susan's mind—' If I refuse to make these happy why do I live, what am I on the earth for at all ?'

It seemed cruel to her to refuse happiness when she could bestow it without making herself two shades more miserable than she was.

Despair and unselfishness are evil counsellors in a scheming selfish world. The life blood had been drained out of her heart by so many cruel blows; by the long waiting, the misgivings, the deep woe when she believed George dead, the bitter grief and mortification and sense of wrong when she found he was married to another.

Many of us male and female treated as Susan imagined herself treated have taken another lover out of pique. Susan did not so. She was bitterly piqued, but she did not make that use of her pique.

Despair of happiness pity and pure unselfishness these stood John Meadows's friends with his unhappy dupe, and perhaps my male readers will be incredulous as well as shocked when I relate the manner in which at last this young creature, lovely as an angel, in the spring of life, loving another still and deluding herself to think she hated and despised him, was one afternoon surprised into giving her hand to a man for whom she did not really care a button.

It was as if she had said, ' Is it really true your happiness depends on me ? then take me—quick—before my courage fails—are you happy now my poor soul!' On the other side there were the passionate pleadings

of a lover; the deep manly voice broken with supplication, the male eyes glistening, the diabolical mixture of fraud and cunning with sincerity.

At the first symptom of yielding the man seized her as the hawk the dove; he did not wait for a second hint. He poured out gratitude and protestations. He thanked her and blessed her, and in his manly ardour caught her to his bosom.

She shut her eyes, and submitted to the caress as to an executioner.

* Pray let me go to my father' she whispered.

She came to her father and told him what she had done and kissed him, and when he kissed her in return that rare embrace seemed to her her reward.

Meadows went home on wings—he was in a whirlwind of joy and triumph.

' Aha ! what will not a strong will do ?' He had no fears, no misgivings. He saw she did not really like him even, but he would make her love him! Let him once get her into his house and into his arms, by degrees she should love him;—aye, she should adore him! He held that a young and virtuous woman cannot resist the husband who remains a lover unless he is a fool as well as a lover. She could resist a man, but hardly the hearth the marriage-bed the sacred domestic ties and a man whose love should be always present always ardent, yet his temper always cool and his determination to be loved unflinching.

With this conviction Meadows had committed crimes of the deepest dye to possess Susan. Villain as he was

it may be doubted whether he would have committed these felonies had he doubted for an instant her ultimate happiness. The unconquerable dog said to himself, ' The day will come that I will tell her how I have risked my soul for her; how I have played the villain for her; and she shall throw her arms round my neck and bless me for committing all those crimes to make her so happy against her will.'

It remained to clench the nail.

He came to Grassmere every day; and one night that the old man was telling Susan and him how badly things were going with him, he said with a cheerful laugh, ' I wonder at you, father-in-law taking on that way. Do you think Susan will let you be uncomfortable for want of a thousand pounds or two.'

Now this remark was slily made while Susan was at the other end of the room, so that she could hear it, but was not supposed to. He did not look at her for some time, and then her face was scarlet.

The next day he said privately to old Merton, * The day Susan and I go to church together you must let me take your engagements and do the best I can with them.'

' Ah, John, you are a friend! but it will take a pretty deal to set me straight again.'

' How much ? Two thousand ?'

* More I am afraid, and too much— '

* Too much for me to take out of my pocket for a stranger; but not for my wife's father— not if it was ten times that.'

« IT IS NEVER TOO LATE TO MEND.' 261

From that hour Meadows had an ally at Grassmere working heart and soul to hasten the wedding-day.

Meadows longed for this day ; for he could not hide from himself that as a lover he made no advances. Susan's heart was like a globe of ice; he could get no hold of it anywhere. He burned with rage when the bitter truth was forced on him that with the topic of George Fielding he had lost those bright, animated looks of affection she used to bestow on him, and now could only command her polite attention—not always that. Once he ventured on a remonstrance—only once. She answered coldly that she could not feign; indifferent she was to every thing on earth, indifferent she always should be. But for that indifference she should never have consented to marry him. Let him pause then, and think what he was doing, or better still, give up this folly, and not tie an icicle like her to an honest and warm heart like his.

The deep Meadows never ventured on that ground again. He feared she wanted to be off the marriage and he determined to hurry it on. He pressed her to name the day. She would not. ' Would she let him name it ?' ' No.'

Her father came to Meadows's assistance. ' I'll name it' said he. * Father! no ! no !'

Old Merton then made a pretence of selecting a day. Eejected one day for one reason, another for another, and pitched on a day only six weeks distant.

The next day Meadows bought the license.

* I thought you would like that better than being cried in church Susan.'

Susan thanked him and said ' Oh, yes.*

That evening he had a note from her, in which * She humbly asked his pardon, but she could not marry him; he must excuse her. She trusted to his generosity to let the matter drop, and forgive a poor broken-hearted girl, who had behaved ill from weakness of judgment not lightness of heart.'

Two days after this, which remained unanswered, her father came to her in great agitation and said to her, 'Have you a mind to have a man's death upon your conscience ?'

' Father!'

* I have seen John Meadows, and he is going to kill himself What sort of a letter was that to write to the poor man? Says he, "It has come on me like a thunderclap." I saw a pistol on his table, and he told me he wouldn't give a button to live. You ought to be ashamed of yourself trifling with folks' hearts so.'

* I trifle with folks' hearts! Oh! what shall I do!' cried Susan.

* Think of others as well as yourself replied the old man in a rage. ' Think of me.*

' Of you, dear father ? Does not your Susan think of you ?'

*No! What will become of me if the man kills himself? He is all I have to look to to save me from ruin.'

'IT IS NEVER TOO LATE TO MEND.* 263

'What then!' cried Susan, colouring scarlet, *it is not his life you care for? it is his means of being useful to us! Poor Mr. Meadows! He has no friend but me. I will give you a line to him.'

The line contained these words: * Forgive me.'

Half an-hour after receipt of it Meadows was at the farm. Susan was going to make some faint apology.

He stopped her, and said, ' I know you like to make folk happy. I have got a job for you. A gentleman, a friend of mine in Cheshire, wants a bailiif. He has written to me. A word from me will do the business. Now is there any one you would like to oblige? The place is worth five hundred a-year.'

Susan was grateful to him for waiving disagreeable topics. She reflected and said, *Ah! but he is no friend of yours?'

* What does that matter, if he is yours?'

' Will Fielding.'

' With all my heart. Only my name must not be mentioned. You are right. He can marry on this. They would both have starved in " The Grove." '

Thus he made the benevolent girl taste the sweets of power. ' You will be asked to do many a kind action like this when you are Mrs. Meadows.'

So he bribed father and daughter each after their kind.

The offer came in form from the gentleman to Will Fielding. He and Miss Holiday had already
been cried in church. They were married, and went off to Cheshire.

So Meadows got rid of Will Fielding at a crisis. When it suited his strategy he made his enemy's fortune with as little compunction as he would have ruined him. A man of iron! Cold iron, hot iron, whatever iron was wanted.

Mr. and Mrs. Fielding gone off to Cheshire, and Mrs. Holiday afiter them on a visit of domestic instruction, Meadows publicly announced his approaching marriage with Miss Merton. The coast being clear, he clinched the last nail. From this day there were gusts of repugnance, but not a shadow of resistance on Susan's side. It was to be.

The weather was fine, and every evening this man and woman walked together. The woman envied by all the women; the man by all the men. Yet they walked side by side, like the ghosts of lovers. And since he was her betrothed, one or two iron-grey hairs in the man's head had turned white, and lines deepened in his face. The victim had unwittingly revenged herself.

He had stabbed her heart again and again, and drained it. He had battered this poor heart till it had become more like leather than flesh and blood, and now he wanted to nestle in it and be warmed by it: to kill the affections and revive them at will, No!!!!

She tried to give happiness and to avoid giving pain, but her heart of hearts was inaccessible. The town had capitulated, but the citadel was empty yet
impregnable : and there were moments when flashes of hate mingled with the steady flame of this unhappy-man's love, and he was tempted to kill her and himself. But these weaknesses passed like air, the iron purpose stood firm. This day week they were to be married. Meadows counted the days and exulted ; he had faith in the magic ring. It was on this Monday evening then they walked arm-in-arm in the fields, and it so happened that Meadows was not speaking of love, but of a scheme for making all the poor people in Grass-mere comfortable,

especially of keeping the rain out of their roofs and the wind out of what they vulgarly but not unreasonably called their windys, and Susan's colour was rising and her eyes brightening at this the one interesting side marriage offered—to make people happy near her and round about her, and she cast a look of gratitude upon her companion. A look that coming from so lovely a face might very well pass for love. While thus pleasantly employed the pair suddenly encountered a form in a long bristling beard, who peered into their faces with a singular expression of strange and wild curiosity and anxiety, but did not stop: he was making towards Farnborough.

Susan was a little startled,
' Who is that?'
' I don't know.'
' He looked as if he knew us.'
' A traveller I think, dearest. The folk hereabouts have not got to wear those long beards yet.'
' Why did you. start when he passed us ?'
VOL. III. N
* Did I Start, Susan ?'
' Your arm twitched me/
' You must have fancied it,' replied Meadows with a sickly smile; * but come, Susan, the dew is falling, you had better make towards home.'

He saw her safe home, then instead of waiting to supper as usual, got his horse out and rode to the town full gallop.
' Any one been here for me ?'
' Yes! a stranger.'
' With a long beard ?'
' Why yes he had.'
' He will come again ?'
* In half an hour.'
' Show liim into my room when he comes, and admit no one else.'

Meadows was hardly seated in his study and his candles lighted, when the servant ushered in his visitor.
' Shut both the doors and you can go to bed. I will let Mr. Eichards out.'
'Well?'
* Well we have done the trick between us, eh ?'
* Yes! but what made you come home without orders?' asked Meadows somewhat sternly.
' Why you know as well as me, sir; you have seen them ?' 'Who?'
' George Fielding and his mate.' Meadows started. * How should I see them ?' ' Sir! Why they are come home. They gave me

the slip, and got away before me. I followed them. They are here. They must be here.'
Crawley not noticing Meadows's face went on.
' Sir, when I found they had slipped out of the camp on horseback, and down to Sydney, and saw them with my own eyes go out of the harbour for England, I thought I should have died on the spot. I thought I should never have the courage to face you, but when I met you arm-in-arm, her eye smiling on you, I knew it was all right then. When did the event come off?'
' Wliat event?'

' The marriage, sir,—you and the lady. She is worth all the trouble she has given us.'

' You fool,' roared Meadows, ' we are not married. The wedding is to be this day week!'

Crawley stared and gasped, ' We are ruined, we are imdone!'

' Hold your bawling' cried Meadows fiercely, * and let me think.'

He buried his face in his hands; when he removed them he was gloomy but self-possessed.

' They are not in England Crawley, or we should have seen them. They are on the road. You sailed faster than they; passed them at night perhaps. They will soon be here. My own heart tells me they will be here before Monday. Well, I will beat them still. I will be married Thursday next.'

The iron man then turned to Crawley and sternly demanded how he had let the man slip.

Crawley related all, and as he told his tale the tone of Meadows altered. He no longer doubted the zeal of his hireling. He laid his hand on his brow and more than once he groaned and muttered half articulate expressions of repugnance. At the conclusion he said moodily:

' Crawley, you have served me well—too well! All the women upon earth were not worth a murder, and we have been on the brink of several. You went beyond your instructions.'

* >To I did not,' replied Crawley ; ' I have got them in my pocket. I will read them to you. See! there is no discretion allowed me. I was to bribe them to rob.'

* Where do I countenance the use of deadly weapons?' ' Where is there a word against deadly weapons,' asked Crawley sharply. * Be just to me sir,' he added in a more whining tone. * You know you are a man that must and will be obeyed. You sent me to Australia to do a certain thing, and you would have flung me to perdition if I had stuck at any thing to do it. Well sir, I tried skill without force—look here,' and he placed a small substance like white sugar on the table. ' What is that?'

* Put that in a man's glass he will never taste it, and in half an hour he will sleep you might take the clothes off his back. Three of us watched months and months for a chance, but it was no go: those two were teetotal or next door to it.'

* I wish I had never sent you out.'

* Wliy' replied Crawley ' there is no harm done, no blood has been spilt except on our own side. George Fielding is coming home all right. Give him up the lady, and he will never know you were his enemy.'

' What!' cried Meadows, ' wade through all these crimes for nothing. Lie and feign, and intercept letters, and rob and all but assassinate—and fail. Wade in crime up to my middle, and then wade back again without the prize ! Do you see this pistol ? it has two barrels, if she and I are ever parted it shall be this way —I'll send her to heaven with one barrel, and myself to hell with the other.'

There was a dead silence ! Crawley returned to their old relation, and was cowed by the natural ascendency of the greater spirit.

* You need not look like a girl at me ' said Meadows, * most likely it won't come to that. It is not easy to beat me, and I shall try every move man's wit can devise. This last,' said he in a voice of iron, touching the pistol as it lay on the table.

There was another pause. Then Meadows rose and said calmly, ' You look tired, you shall have a bottle of my old port; and my own heart is staggered, but it is only for a moment. He struck his hand upon his breast, and walked slowly from the room. And Crawley heard his step descend to the hall, and then to the cellar; and the indomitable character of the man rang in his solid tread.

Crawley was uneasy. ' Mr. Meadows is getting wildish; it frightens me to see such a man as him burst

out like that. He is not to be trusted with a loaded pistol. Ah! and I am in his secrets, deep in his secrets : great men sweep away little folk that know too much. I never saw him with a pistol before.* All this passing rapidly through his head, Crawley pounced on the pistol, took off the caps, whipped out a little bottle, and poured some strong stuff into the caps that loosened the detonating powder directly; then with a steel pen he picked it all out and replaced the caps their virtue gone, before Mr. Meadows returned with two bottles: and the confederates sat in close conclave till the grey of morning broke into the room.

The great man gave but few orders to his subordinate, for this simple reason, that the game had fallen into his own hands.

Still there was something for Crawley to do. He was to have an officer watching to arrest Will Fielding on the old judgment should he, which was hardly to be expected, come to kick up a row and interrupt the wedding. And to-morrow he was to take out a writ against * father-in-law.' Mr. Meadows played a close game. He knew that things are not to be got when they are wanted. His plan was to have everything ready that might be wanted long before it was wanted.

But most of the night passed in relation of what had already taken place, and Crawley was the chief speaker, and magnified his services.

He related from his own point of view all that I have told, and Meadows listened with all his soul and intelligence.

At the attack on Mr. Levi Meadows chuckled: " The old heathen' said he contemptuously * I have beat him any way.'

' By the way sir have you seen anything of him ?' asked Crawley.

'No.'

* He is not come home then.'

' Not that I know of, have you any reason to think he has ?'

' No, only he left the mine directly after they pelted him, but he would not leave the country any the more for that and money to be made in it by handsful.'

' Now Crawley go and get some sleep.' A cold bath for me and then on horseback. I must breakfast at Grass-mere.'

' Great man, sir! great man! You will beat them yet, sir. You have beat Mr. Levi. Here we are in his house ; and he driven away to lay his sly old bones at the Antipodes. Ha ! ha! ha!'

The sun came in at the window, and the long conference broke up, and strange to say it broke into three.

Crawley home to sleep.

Meadows to Grassmere.

Isaac Levi to smoke an Eastern pipe, and so meditate with more tranquil pulse how to strike with deadliest effect these two his insolent enemies.

Siste viator, and guess that riddle.

CHAPTER XXIX.

Isaac Levi, rescued by George Fielding, reached his tent smarting with pain and bitter insult; he sat on the floor pale and dusty, and anathematized his adversaries in the Hebrew tongue. Wrath still boiling in his heart, he drew out his letters and read them. Then grief mingled with his anger. Old Cohen, his friend and agent and coeval was dead. Another self dead.

Besides the hint that this gave him to set his house in order, a distinct consideration drew Isaac now to England. He had trusted much larger interests to old Cohen than he was at all disposed to leave in the hands of Cohen's successors, men of another generation, " pro-geniem vitiosiorem " he sincerely believed.

Another letter gave him some information about Meadows that added another uneasiness to those he already felt on George's account. Hence his bitter disappointment when he found George gone from the mine, the date of his return uncertain. Hence too, the purchase of More's horses, and the imploring letter to George; measures that proved invaluable to that young man, whose primitive simplicity and wise humility led him not to question the advice of his elder but obey it.

And so it was, that although the old Jew sailed home upon his own interests, yet during the voyage George Fielding's assumed a great importance, direct and incidental. Direct, because the old man was warm with gratitude to him; indirect, because he boiled over with hate of George's most dangerous enemy. And as he neared the English coast, the thought that though he was coming to Farnborough he could not come home grew bitterer and bitterer, and then that he should find his enemy and his insulter in the very house sacred by the shadows of the beloved and dead !!

Finding in Nathan a youth of no common fidelity and shrewdness, Isaac confided in him; and Nathan proud beyond description of the confidence bestowed on him by one so honoured in his tribe, enlisted in his cause with all the ardour of youth tempered by Jewish address.

Often they sat together on the deck, and the young Jewish brain and the old Jewish brain mingled and digested a course of conduct to meet every imaginable contingency; for the facts they at present possessed were only general and vague.

The first result of all this was, that these two crept into the town of Farnborough at three o'clock one morning ; that Isaac took out a key and unlocked the house that stood next to Meadows' on the left hand; that Isaac took secret possession of the first-floor, and Nathan open but not ostentatious possession of the ground-floor, with a tale skilfully concocted to excite no suspicion wliatever that Isaac was in any way connected with his

Iv3

presence in the town. Nathan, it is to be observed, had never been in Famborough before.

The next morning they worked. Nathan went out locking the door after him to execute two commissions. He was to find out what the young Cohens were doing, and how far they were likely to prove worthy of the trust reposed in their father ; and what Susan Merton was doing, and whether Meadows was courting her or not. The latter part of Nathan's task was terribly easy.

The young man came home late at night, locked the door, made a concerted signal, and was admitted to the senior presence. He found him smoking his Eastern pipe. Nathan with dejected air told him that he had no good news ; that the Cohens not only thought themselves wiser than their father, which was permissible, but openly declared it, which he, though young, had observed to be a trait confined to very great fools.

' It is well said, my son,' quoth Isaac, smoking calmly—' and the other business ?'

* Oh, master!' said Nathan, * I bring still worse tidings of her* She is a true Nazarite, a creature without faith. She is betrothed to the man you hate, and whom I, for your sake, hate even to death.*

They spoke in an eastern dialect, which I am paraphrasing here and translating there according to the measure of my humble abilities.

Isaac sucked his pipe very fast; this news was a double blow to his feelings.

' If she be indeed a Nazarite without faith, let her

I

* IT IS NEVER TOO LATE TO MEND.' 275

go; but judge not the simple hastily. First let me know how far woman's frailty is to blame; how far man's guile—for not for nothing was Crawley sent out to the mine by Meadows. Let me consider '—and he smoked calmly again.

After a long silence, which Nathan was too respectful to break, the old man gave him his commission for to-morrow. He was to try and discover why Susan Merton had written no letters for many months to George; and why she had betrothed herself to the foe. * But reveal nothing in return,' said Isaac, * neither ask more than three questions of any one person, lest they say " who is this that being a Jew asks many questions about a Nazarite maiden, and why asks he them ?" '

At night Nathan returned full of intelligence. She loved the young man Fielding. She wrote letters to him and received letters from him, until gold was found in Australia. But after this he wrote to her no more letters, wherefore her heart was troubled.

' Ah! and did she write to him ?'

' Yes! but received no answer, nor any letter for many months.'

^ Ah!'—(puff!) (puff!)

' Then came a rumour that he was dead, and she mourned for him after the manner of her people many days. Verily master, I am vexed for the Nazarite maiden, for her tale is sad. Then came a letter from Australia, that said he is not dead, but married to a stranger. Then the maiden said " Behold now this twelve months he writes not to me, this then is true,"

and she bowed her head, and the colour left her cheek. Then this Meadows visited her, and consoled her day by day. And there are those who confidently affirm that her father said often to her, " Behold now I am a man stricken in years, and the man Meadows is rich;" so the maiden gave her hand to the man, but whether to please the old man her father, or out of the folly and weakness of females, thou 0 Isaac son of Shadrach shall determine; seeing that I am young, and little versed in the ways of women, knowing this only by universal report, that they are fair to the eye but often bitter to the taste.'

' Aha!' cried Isaac, ' but I am old, 0 Nathan son of Eli, and with the thorns of old age comes one good fruit " experience." No letters came to him, yet she wrote many—none came to her, yet he wrote many. All this is transparent as glass—here has been fraud as well as guile.'

Nathan's eye sparkled.

' What is the fraud, master ?'

* Nay, that I know not—but I will know!' ' But how, master?'

* By help of thine ears, or my own !'

Nathan looked puzzled. So long as Mr. Levi shut himself up a close prisoner on a first floor what could ne hear for himself.

Isaac read the look and smiled. He then rose and putting his finger to his lips led the way to his own apartments. At the staircase-door, which even Nathan liad not yet passed, he bade the yoimg man take off his

shoes; lie himself was in slippers. He took Nathan into a room, the floor of which was entirely covered with mattresses. A staircase, the steps of which was covered with horse-hair, went by a tolerably easy slope and spiral movement nearly up to the cornice. Of this cornice a portion about a foot square swung back on a well-oiled hinge, and Isaac drew out from the wall with the utmost caution a piece of gutta-percha piping, to this he screwed on another piece open at the end and applied it to his ear.

Nathan comprehended it all in a moment. His master could overhear every word uttered in Meadows's study.

Levi explained to him that ere he left his old house he had put a new cornice in the room he thought Meadows would sit in, a cornice so deeply ornamented that no one could see the ear he left in it, and had taken out bricks in the wall of the adjoining house and made the other arrangements they were inspecting together.

Mr. Levi farther explained that his object was simply to overhear and counteract every scheme Meadows should form. He added that he never intended to leave Farnborough for long. His intention had been to establish certain relations in that country, buy some land and return immediately; but the gold discovery had detained him.

' But master' said Nathan, ' suppose the man had taken his business to the other side of his house ?'

' Foolish youth,' replied Isaac, ' am I not on both sides of him ! ! !'

' Ah ! What is there another on the other ?'

Isaac nodded.

Thus, while Nathan was collecting facts, Isaac had been watching ' patient as a cat keen as a lynx,' at his ear-hole, and heard—nothing.

Now the next day Nathan came in hastily long before the usual hour.

* Master, another enemy is come—the man Crawley ! I saw him from a window; he saw not me. What shall I do?'

' Keep the house all day. I would not have him see you. He would say, " Aha! the old Jew is here too." '

Nathan's countenance fell. He was a prisoner now as well as his master.

The next morning rising early to prepare their food, he was surprised to find the old man smoking his pipe down below.

* All is well, my son. My turn has come. I have had great patience, and great is the reward.' He then told him with natural exultation the long conference he had been secretly present at between Crawley and Meadows—a conference in which the enemy had laid bare not his guilt only but the secret crevice in his coat of mail.

' She loves him not!' cried Levi with exultation. * She is his dupe! With a word I can separate them and confound him utterly.'

* Oh, master!' cried the youth eagerly, * speak that word to-day, and let me be there and hear it spoken if I have favour in your eyes ?'

' IT IS NEVER TOO LATE TO MEND.' 279

* Speak it to-day!' cried Levi with a look of intense surprise at Nathan's simplicity. ' Go to, foolish youth !' said he,' What! after I have waited months and months for vengeance would you have me fritter it away for want of waiting a day or two longer ? No, I will strike not the empty cup from his hand, but the full cup from his lips. Aha! you have seen the Jew insulted and despised in many lands; have patience now, and you shall see how he can give blow for blow ; aye ! old and feeble and without a weapon can strike his adversary to the heart.'

Nathan's black eye flashed. * You are the master I the scholar,' said he. ' All I ask is to be permitted to share the watching for your enemy's words since I may not go abroad while it is day.'

Thus the old and young lynx lay in ambush all day. And at night the young lynx prowled, but warily, lest Crawley should see him, and every night brought home some scrap of intelligence.

To change the metaphor, it was as though while the western spider wove his artful web round the innocent fly the oriental spider wove another web round him, the threads of which were so subtle as to be altogether invisible. Both East and West leaned with sublime faith on their respective gossamers, nor remembered that " Dieu dispose."

CHAPTER XXX.

Meadows rode to Grassmere, to try and prevail with Susan to be married on Thursday next instead of Monday. As he rode he revolved every argument he could think of to gain her compliance. He felt sure she was more inclined to postpone the day than to advance it, but something told him his fate himg on this:—* These two men will come home on Monday. I am sure of it. Aye! Monday morning, before we can wed. I will not throw a chance away; the game is too close.' Then he remembered with dismay that Susan had been irritable and snappish just before parting yester eve—a trait she had never exhibited to him before. When he arrived his heart almost failed him, but after some little circumlocution and excuse he revealed the favour, the great favour he was come to ask.

He asked it.

She granted it without the shade of a demur.

He was no less surprised than delighted, but the truth is that very irritation and snappishness of yesterday was the cause of her consenting; her conscience told her she had been unkind, and he had been too wise to snap in return. So now he benefited by the reaction and little bit of self-reproach. For do but abstain from reproaching a good girl who has been unjust or unkind to you, and ten to one if she does not make you the amende by word or deed—most likely the latter, for so she can soothe her tender conscience without grazing her equally sensitive pride. Poor Susan little knew the importance of the concession she made so easily.

Meadows galloped home triumphant. But two whole days now between him and his bliss! And that day passed and Tuesday passed. The man lived three days and nights in a state of tension that would have killed some of us or driven us mad; but his intrepid spirit rode the billows of hope and fear like a petrel. And the day before the wedding it did seem as if his adverse fate got suddenly alarmed and made a desperate effort and hurled against him every assailant that could be found. In the morning came his mother, and implored him ere it was too late to give up this marriage.

' I have kept silence, yea even from good words,' said the aged woman; ' but at last I must speak. John, she does not love you. I am a woman and can read a woman's heart; and you fancied her long before George Fielding was false to her, if false he ever was, John.'

The old woman said the whole of this last sentence with so much meaning that her son was stung to rage, and interrupted her fiercely :—

' I looked to find all the world against me, but not my own mother. No matter—so be it; the whole world shan't turn me, and those I don't care to fight I'll fly.'

And he turned savagely on his heel and left the old woman there shocked and terrified by his vehemence. She did not stay there long. Soon the scarlet cloak and black bonnet might have been seen wending their way slowly back to the little cottage, the poor old tidy bonnet drooping lower than it was wont. Meadows came back to dinner; he had a mutton-chop in his study, for it was a busy day. While thus employed there came almost bursting into the room a man struck with remorse—Jeffries the recreant postmaster.

' Mr. Meadows, I can carry on this game no longer, and I wont for any man living.'

He then in a wild, loud and excited way went on to say how the poor girl had come a hundred times for a letter, and looked in his face so wistfully, and once she had said, ' Oh, Mr. Jeffries, do have a letter for me!' and how he saw her pale face in his dreams, and little he thought when he became Meadows' tool the length the game was to be carried.

Meadows heard him out; then simply reminded him of his theft, and assured him with an oath that if he dared to confess his villainy—

* My villainy ?' shrieked the astonished postmaster.

' Whose else ? You have intercepted letters—not I. You have abused the public confidence—not I. So if you are such a fool and sneak as to cut your throat by peaching on yourself, I'll cry louder than you, and I'll show you have emptied letters as well as stopped them. Go home to your wife and keep quiet or I'll smash both you and her.'

' Oh! I know you are without mercy, and I dare not open my heart while I live; but I will beat you yet, you cruel monster. I will leave a note for Miss Merton confessing all, and blow out my brains to-night in the office.'

The man's manner was wild and despairing. Meadows eyed him sternly. He said with affected coolness :—

' Jeffries, you are not game to take your own life.'

' Aint I ?' was the reply.

* At least I think not.'

' To-night will show.'

' I must know that before night,' cried Meadows, and with the word he sprang on Jeffries and seized him in a grasp of iron, and put a pistol to his head.

' All! no 1 Mr. Meadows. Mercy ! mercy !' shrieked the man in an agony of fear.

' All right,' said Meadows, coolly putting up the pistol. ' You half imposed on me, and that is something for you to brag of. You won't kill yourself, Jeffries; you are not the stuff. Grive over shaking like an aspen and look and listen. You are in debt. I've bought up two drafts of yours—here they are. Come to me to-morrow after the wedding and I will give you them to light your pipe with.'

' Oh, Mr. Meadows, that would be one load off my mind!'

* You are short of cash too; come to me after the wedding and I'll give you fifty pounds cash.'

' You are very liberal, sir. I wish it was in a better cause.'

* Now go home and don't be a sneak and a fool—till after the wedding, or I will sell the bed from under your wife's back and send you to the stone-jug. Be off.'

Jeffries crept away paralysed in heart, and Meadows standing up called out in a rage—

' Are there any more of you that hope to turn John Meadows ? then come on, come a thousand strong with the devil at your back and then I'll beat you!'

And for a moment the respectable man was almost grand; a man-rock standing braving earth and heaven.

' Hist! Mr. Meadows.'

He turned and there was Crawley.

' A word sir. Will Fielding is in the town in such a passion.'

' Come to stop the wedding?'

' He was taking a glass of ale at the " Toad and Pickaxe," and you might hear him all over the yard.' -

' What is he going to do ?'

* Sir, he has bought an uncommon heavy whip; he was showing it in the yard. This is for Jolui Meadows's back,' said he, * and I'll give it him before the girl he has stolen from my brother. If she takes a dog instead of a man it shall be a beaten dog,' says he.

Meadows rang the bell.

' Harness the mare to the four-wheel chaise.'

I

' IT IS NEVER TOO LATE TO MEND.' 285

' You know what to, do Crawley.'

' Well I can guess.'

' But first get him told that I am always at Grass-mere at six o'clock.'

' But you won't go there this evening, of course.'

' Why not.'

' Aren't you afraid he—'

' Afiraid of Will Fielding ? Why you have never looked at me. I do notice your eyes are always on the ground. Crawley, when I was eighteen, one evening it was harvest home, and all the folk had drunk their wit and manners out. I found a farmer's wife in a lane hemmed in by three great ignorant brutes that were for kissing her, or some nonsense, and she crying help and murder and ready to faint with fright. It was a decent woman and a neighbour, so I interfered as thus. I knocked the first fellow senseless on his back with a blow before they knew of me, and then the three were two. I fought the two, giving and taking for full ten minutes, and then I got a chance and one went down. I put my foot on his neck and kept him down for all he could do, and over his body I fought the best man of the lot, and thrashed him so that his whole mug was like a ball of beet-root. When he was quite sick he ran one way, and t'other got up roaring and ran another, and they had to send a hurdle for No. 1. Dame Fielding gave me of her own accord what all the row was about, and more than one and hearty ones too, I assure you, and had me in to supper and told her man : and he shook my hand a good one.'

' Why sir, you don't mean to say the woman you fought for was Mrs. Fielding.'

' But I tell you it was, and I had those two boys on my knee, two chubby toads, pulling at my curly hair. Damnation! why do I talk of these things. Oh, I remember it was to show you I am not a man that can be bullied. I am a much better man than I was at eighteen. I won't be married in a black eye if I can help it. But when I am once married, here I stand against all comers, and if you hear them grumble or threaten you tell them that any Sunday afternoon when there is nothing better to be done, I'll throw my cap into the ring and fight all the Fieldings that ever were pupped one down another come on.' Then turning quite cool and contemptuous' all in a moment, he said, ' These are words, and we have work on hand,' and even as he spoke, he strode from the room pattered after by Crawley.

At six o'clock Meadows and Susan were walking arm-in-arm in the garden.

Presently they saw a man advancing towards them, with his right hand behind him.

' Why it is Will Fielding,' cried Susan, * come to thank you.'

' I think not by the look of liim,' replied Meadows, coolly.

' Susan, will you be so good as to take your hand from tliat man's arm. I have got a word to say to liim.'

Susan did more than requested, seeing at once that mischief was coming.. She clung to William's right arm, and while he ground his teeth with ineffectual rage, for she was strong, as her sex are strong, for half a minute and to throw her off he must have been much rougher with her than he chose to be, three men came behind imobserved by all but Meadows, and captured him on the old judgment. And Crawley having represented him as a violent man, they literally laid the grasp of the law on him.

' But I have got the money to pay it' remonstrated William.

* Pay it then.'

' But my money is at home, give me two days. I'll write to my wife and she will send it me.'

The officers with a coarse laugh told him he must come with them meantime.

Meadows whispered Susan ' I'll pay it for him tomorrow.'

They took off William Fielding in Meadow's four-wheeled chaise.

' Where are they taking him ? John.'

' To the county goal.'

* Oh! don't let them take him there. Can you not trust him ?'

' Yes.'

' Then why not pay it for him ?'

* But I don't carry money in my pocket, and the bank is closed.'

' How unfortunate!'

' Very ! but I'll send it over to-morrow early and we will have him out.'

* Oh, yes, poor fellow! the very first thing in the morning.'

* Yes ! the first thing—after we are married.'

Soon after this Meadows bade Susan affectionately farewell, and rode off to Newborough to buy his gloves and some presents for his bride. On the road he overtook William Fielding going to gaol, leaned over his saddle as he cantered by, and said, * Mrs. Meadows will send the money in to free you in the morning,' then on again cool as a cucumber and cantered into the town before sunset, put up black Kachel at the King's Head, made his purchases, and back to the inn. As he sat in the bar-parlour drinking a glass of ale and chatting with the landlady, two travellers came into the passage, they did not stop in it long, for one of them knew the house and led his companion into the coffee-room. But in that moment by a flash of recognition, spite of their bronzed colour and long beards. Meadows had seen who they were—George Fielding and Thomas Robinson.

Words could not paint in many pages what Meadows passed through in a few seconds. His very body was one moment cold as ice, the next burning.

The cofiee-room door was open, he dragged himself into the passage though each foot in turn seemed glued to the ground, and listened. He came back and sat down in the bar.

* Are they going to stay,' said the mistress to the waiter,

' Yes! to be called at five o'clock,'

The bell rang. The waiter went and immediately returned.

'Hot with,' demanded the waiter in a sharp, mechanical tone.

'Here take my keys for the lump sugar,' said the landlady, and she poured first the brandy then the hot water into a tumbler, then went up stairs to see about the travellers' beds.

Meadows was left alone a few moments with the liquor. A sudden flash came to Meadows's eye, he put his hand hastily to his waistcoat pocket, and then his eye brightened still more. Yes, it was there, he thought he had had the curiosity to keep it by him. He drew out the white lump Crawley had left on his table that night, and flung it into the glass just as the waiter returned with the sugar.

The waiter took the brandy and water into the cofiee-room.

Meadows sat still as a mouse, his brain boiling and bubbling awe-struck at what he had done yet meditating worse.

The next time the waiter came in, ' Waiter, said he, * one glass among two, that is short allowance.'

'Oh! the big one is teetotal,' replied the waiter.

'Mrs. White,' said Meadows, * if you have got a bed for me I'll sleep here, for my nag is tired and the night is darkish.'

* Always a bed for you, Mr. Meadows,' was the gracious reply.

Soon the two friends rang for bed-candles. Eobinson staggered with drowsiness. Meadows eyed them from behind a newspaper.

Half an hour later Mr. Meadows went to bed too— but not to sleep.

CHAPTER XXXI.

At seven o'clock in the morning Crawley was at Meadows's house by appointment. To his great surprise the servant told him master had not slept at home. While he was talking to her Meadows galloped up to the door, jumped off^ and almost pulled Crawley up stairs with him.

'Lock the door Crawley.'

Crawley obeyed but with some reluctance, for Meadows, the iron Meadows, was ghastly and shaken as he had never been shaken before. He sank into a chair. ' Perdition seize the hour I first saw her !'

As for Crawley he was paralysed by the terrible agitation of a spirit so much greater than his own.

'Crawley' said Meadows with a sudden unnatural calm * when the devil buys a soul for money how much does he give ? a good lump I hear. He values our souls high—we don't, some of us.'

* Mr. Meadows, sir !'

'Now count those,' yelled Meadows bursting out again, and he flung a roll of notes furiously on the ground at Crawley's feet, ' count and tell me what my soul has gone for. Oh ! oh!'

Crawley seized them and counted them as fast as his trembling fingers would let him. So now an eye all remorse, and another eye all greed, were bent upon the same thing.

'Why they are all hundred pound notes, bright as silver from the Bank of England. Oh dear ! how new and crimp they are—where do they come from, sir?'

* From Australia.'

* Ah! oh ! impossible ! No ! nothing is impossible to such a man as you. Twenty.'

' They are at Newborough—slept at " King's Head,"' whispered Meadows.

' Good heavens ! think of that. Thirty—' ' So did I.'

* Ah! forty—four thousand pounds.'

* The lump of stuff you left here—hocussed one—it was a toss up—luck was on my side—that one carried them—slept like death—long while hunting—found them imder his pillow at last.'

* Well done! and we fools were always beat at it. Sixty— one — two — five — seven. Seven thousand pounds.'

' Seven thousand pounds ! Who would have thought it ? This is a dear job to me.'

' Say a dear job to them and a glorious haul to you; but you deserve it all, ah!'

* Why, you fool,' cried Meadows, ' do you think I am going to keep the men's money ?'

' Keep it; why, of course ?'

*What! am I a thief? I, John Meadows, that never wronged a man of a penny. I take his sweetheart, I can't live without her; but I can live without his money. I have crimes enough on my head, but not theft, there I say halt.'

* Then why in the name of heaven did you take them at such a risk ?'

Crawley put this question roughly, for he was losing his respect for his idol.

' You are as blind as a mole, Crawley,' was the disdainful answer. ' Don't you see that I have made George Fielding penniless, and that now old Merton won't let him have his daughter. Why should he? He said—" If you come back with one thousand pounds." And don't you see that when the writ is served on old Merton he will be as strong as fire for me and against him. He can't marry her at all now. I shall soon or late, and the day I marry Susan that same afternoon seven thousand pounds will be put in George Fielding's hand, he won't know by whom but you and I shall know. I am a sinner but not a villain.'

Crawley gave a dissatisfied grunt.

Meadows struck a lucifer match and lighted a candle. He placed the candle in .the grate—it was warm weather.

' Come now,' said he coolly, ' burn them; then they will tell no tales.'

Crawley gave a shriek like a mother whose child is falling out of window, and threw himself on his knees, with the notes in his hand behind his back.

' No! no ! sir! Oh! don't think of it. Talk of crime, what are all the sins we have done together compared with this ? You would not bum a wheat-rick, no not your greatest enemy's; I know you would not, you are too good a man. This is as bad; the good money that the bountiful heaven has given us for —for the good of man.'

' Come,' said Meadows sternly,' no more of this folly,' and he laid his iron grasp on Crawley.

* Mercy! mercy! think of me—of your faithful servant, who has risked his life and stuck at nothing for you. How ungrateful great men are !'

' Ungrateful! Crawley. Can you look me in the face and say that ? '

' Never till now, but now I can ;' and Crawley rose to his feet and faced the great man: the prize he was fighting for gave him supernatural courage. * To whom do you owe them ? To me. You could never have had them but for my drug. And yet you would burn them before my eyes. A fortune to poor me.'

' To you ? '

* Yes! What does it matter to you what becomes of them so that he never sees them again? but it matters all to me. Give .them to me and in twelve hours I will be in France with

them. You won't missr me, sir. I have done my work. And it will be more prudent, for since I have left you 1 can't help drinking, and I might talk you know, sir, I might, and let out what we should both be sorry for. Send me away to foreign countries where I can keep travelling, and make it always summer. I hate the long nights when it is dark. I see such cu—^u—rious things. Pray ! pray let me go and take these with me, and never trouble you again.'

The words though half nonsense were the other half cunning, and the tones and looks were piteous. Meadows hesitated. Crawley knew too much, to get rid of him was a bait; and after all to annihilate the thing he had been all his life accumulating went against his heart. He rang the bell.

' Hide the notes, Crawley. Bring me two shirts, a r^^or, and a comb. Crawley these are the terms. That you don't go near that woman.'

Crawley with a brutal phrase expressed his delight at the idea of getting rid of her for ever.

* That you go at once to the railway. Station opens to-day. First train starts in an hour. Up to London, over to France tliis evening.'

' I will, sir. Hurrah! hurrah!' .Then Crawley burst into protestations of gratitude which Meadows cut short. He rang for breakfast, fed his accomplice, gave him a greatcoat for his journey, and took the precaution of going with him to the station. There he shook hands with him and returned to the principal street and entered the bank.

Crawley kept faith, he hugged his treasure to his bosom and sat down waiting for the train.

* Luck is on our side,' thought he; ' if this had been open yesterday those two would have come on from Newborough.'

He watched the preparations, they were decorating the locomotive with bouquets and branches. They did not start punctually, some soi-disant great people had not arrived.

* I will have a dram,' thought Crawley; he went and had three: then he came back and as he was standing inspecting the carriages a hand was laid on his shoulder; he looked roimd, it was Mr. Wood, a functionary with whom he had often done business.

' Ah, Wood! how d'ye do ? Going to make the first trip ?'

* No, sir! I have business detains me in the town.'

* What! a capias, eh ?' chuckled Crawley.

* Something of the sort. There is a friend of yours hard by wants to speak a word to you.'

' Come along then. Where is he ?'

' This way, sir.'

Crawley followed Wood to the waiting-room, and there on a bench sat Isaac Levi. Crawley stopped dead short and would have drawn back, but Levi beckoned to a seat near him. Crawley came walking like an automaton from whose joints the oil had suddenly dried. With infinite repugnance he took the seat, not liking to refuse before several persons who saw the invitation. Mr. Wood sat on the other side of him.

' What does it all mean,' thought Crawley, but his cue was to seem indifferent or flattered.

' You have shaved youi' beard, Mr. Crawley,' said Isaac in a low tone.

' My beard! I never had one/ replied Crawley in the same key.

* Yes, you had when last I saw you—in the gold mine; you set ruffians to abuse me, sir.'

* Don't you believe that Mr. Levi.'

* I saw it and felt it.'

The peculiarity of this situation was, that the room being full of people both parties wishing, each for his own reason, not to excite general attention, delivered scarce above a whisper the sort of matter that is generally uttered very loud and excitedly.

' It is my turn now,' whispered Levi; ' an eye for an eye, a tooth for a tooth.'

' You must look sharp then,' whispered Crawley; ' to-morrow perhaps you may not have the chance.' ' I never postpone vengeance when it is ripe.' ' Don't you, sir! dear me.'

' You have seven thousand pounds about you, Mr. Crawley.'

Crawley started and trembled.

' Stolen!' whispered Isaac in his very ear. ' Give it up to the officer.'

Crawley rose instinctively. A firm hand was laid on each of his arms; he sat down again.

' What—what—ever money I have is trusted to me by the wealthiest and most respectable man in the cou—nty, and—'

' Stolen by him, received by you ! Give it to Wood unless you prefer a public search.'

' You can't search me without a warrant.'

o3

' Here is a warrant from the mayor. Take tlie notes out of your left breast and give them to the officer, or we must do it by force and publicity.'

' I won't without Mr. Meadows's authority. Send for Mr. Meadows if you dare.'

Isaac reflected. ' Well! we will take you to Mr. Meadows. Keep the money till you see him, but we must secure you. Put his coat over his hands first.'

The greatcoat was put over his hands and the next moment under the coat was heard a little sharp click.

'Let us go to the carriage' said Levi in a brisk cheerful tone.

Those present heard the friendly invitation and saw a little string of acquaintances, three in number, break up a conversation and go and get into a fly, one carried a greatcoat and bundle before him with both hands.

(299)

CHAPTER XXXII.

Mr. Meadows went to the bank—into the parlour— and said he must draw seven thousand pounds of cash and securities. The partners look blank.

' I knew,' said Meadows, ' I should cripple you. Well I am not going to nor let any one else, it would not suit my book. Just hand me the securities and let me make over that sum to George Fielding and Thomas Robinson. There ! now for some months to come those two men are not to know how rich they are, in fact not till I tell them.'

A very ready consent to this was given by both partners; I am afraid I might say an eager consent.

' There ! now I feel another man, that is ofi' me any way,' and Meadows strode home double the man.

Soon his new top-boots were on, and his new dark blue coat with flat double-gilt buttons, and his hat broadish in the brim, and he looked the model of a British yeoman; he reached Grassmere before eleven o'clock. It was to be a very quiet wedding, but the bridesmaids, &c. were there and Susan all in white, pale but very lovely. Father-in-law cracking jokes, Susan writhing under them.

' Now then is it to be a wedding without bells, for 1 hear none ?'

' That it shall not,' cried one of the young men; and off they ran to the church.

Meantime Meadows was the life and soul of the mirthful scene. He was in a violent excitement that passed with the rustics for gaiety natural to the occasion. They did not notice his anxious glances up the hill that led to Newborough; his eager and repeated looks at his watch, the sigh of relief when the church bells pealed out, the tremours of impatience, the struggle to appear cool as he sent one to hurry the clerk, another to tell the clergyman the bride was ready; the stamp of the foot when one of the bridesmaids took ten minutes to tie on a bonnet. He walked arm-in-arm with Susan waiting for this girl; at last she was ready. Then came one running to say that the parson was not come home yet. What it cost him not to swear at the parson with Susan on his arm and the church in sight!

While he was thus fuming inwardly, a handsome dark-eyed youth came up and inquired which was the bride. She was pointed out to him.

' A letter for you. Miss Merton.'

' For me ? Who from ?'

She glanced at the handwriting, and Meadows looked keenly in the boy's face.

' A Jew,' said he to himself. ' Susan, you have got your gloves on.'

And in a moment he took the letter from her, but

quietly, and opened it as if to return it to her to read. He glanced down it, saw ' Jefferies, postmaster,' and at the bottom ' Isaac Levi.' With wonderful presence of mind he tore it in pieces.

' An insult, Susan,' he cried. ' A mean, malignant insult to set you against me—a wife against her husband.'

Ere the words were out of his mouth he seized the young Jew and whirled him like a feather into the hands of his friends.

' Duck him !' cried he.

And in a moment, spite of his remonstrances and attempts at explanation, he was flimg into the horse-pond. He struggled out on the other side and stood on the bank in a stupor of rage and terror, while the bridegroom menaced him with another dose should he venture to return.

' I will tell you all about it to-morrow, Susan.'

' Calm yourself,' replied Susan. ' I know you have enemies, but why punish a messenger for the letter he only carries ?'

' You are an angel, Susan. Boys, let him alone, do you hear ?' N.B. He had been ducked.

And now a loud hurrah was heard from behind the church.

' The parson at last,' cried Meadows exultingly.

Susan lowered her eyes, and hated herself for the shiver that passed through her. To her the parson was the executioner.

It was not the parson. The next moment two

figures came round in sight. Meadows turned away with a groan.

' George Fielding!' said he. The words dropped as it were out of his mouth.

Susan misunderstood this. She thought he read her heart, and ascribed her repugnance to her lingering attachment to Greorge. She was angry with herself for letting this worthy man see her want of pride.

' Why do you mention that name to me ? What do I care for him who has deceived me. I wish he stood at the church-door that he might see how I would look at him and pass him leaning on your faithful arm.'

' Susan!' cried a well-known voice behind her.

She trembled and almost crouched ere she turned; but the moment she turned round she gave a scream that brought all the company running, and the bride forgot everything at the sight of George's handsome honest face beaming truth and love, and threw herself into his arms.

George kissed the bride.

'Oh!' cried tiie bridesmaids, awaking from their stupor and remembering this was her old lover. 'Oh!' 'Oh!' 'Oh!' on an ascending scale.

These exclamations brought Susan to her senses. She sprang from George as though an adder had stung her; and red as fire, with eyes like basilisks, she turned on him at a safe distance.

'How dare you embrace me? How dare you come where I am? Father, ask this man why he comes here now to make me expose myself, and insult the honest man who honours me with his respect. Oh, father! come to me and take me away from here.'

'Susan—What on earth is this? what have I done?'

'What have you done? You are false to me! you never wrote me a letter for twelve months, and you are married to a lady in Bathurst! Oh, George!'

'If he is,' cried Eobinson, he must be slyer than I give him credit for, for I have never left his side night nor day, and I never saw him say three civil words to a woman.'

'Mr. Eobinson!'

'Yes, Mr. Robinson. Somebody has been making a fool of you, Miss Merton. Why, all his cry night and day has been "Susan! Susan!" When we found the great nugget he kisses it, and says he, "There, that is not because you are gold, but because you take me to Susan."'

'Hold your tongue Tom' said George sternly. 'Who puts me on my defence? Is there any man here who has been telling her I have ever had a thought of any girl but her? If there is let him stand out now, and say it to my face if he dares.'

There was a dead silence.

'There is a lie without a backer it seems;' and he looked round on all the company with his calm superior eye. 'And now, Susan, what were you doing on that man's arm?'

'Oh!'

'Miss Merton and I are to be married to-day,' said Meadows, 'that is why I gave her my arm.'

Greorge gasped for breath, but he controlled himself by a mighty effort. 'She thought me false, and now she knows I am true.'

'Susan,' faltered he, 'I say nothing about the promises that have passed between us two and the ring you gave. Here it is.'

'He has kept my ring!'

'I was there before you, Mr. Meadows, but I won't stand upon that; I don't believe there is a man in the world loves a woman in the world better than I love Susan, but still I would not give a snap of the finger to have her if her will was towards another. So please yourself, my lass, and don't cry like that: only this must end. I won't live in doubt a moment, no nor half a moment. Speak your pleasure and nothing else; choose between John Meadows and George Fielding.'

'That is fair,' cried one of the bridegrooms. The women secretly admired George. This is a man thought they—won't stand our nonsense.

Susan looked up in mute astonishment.

'What choice can there be? The moment I saw your face and truth still shining in it I forgot there was a John Meadows in the world!'

With these words Susan cast a terrified look all round, and losing every other feeling in a paroxysm of shame, hid her burning face in her hands, and made a sudden bolt into the house and up stairs to her room,

where she was followed and discovered by one of her bridesmaids tearing oiF her wedding clothes, and laughing and crying all in a breath,

1st Bridegroom. ' Well, Josh, what dye think ?' "

2nd Bridegroom. ' Why I think there wont be a wedding to-day.'

1st Bridegroom. ' No nor to-morrow neither. Sal, put on your bonnet and lets you and I go home. I came to Meadows's wedding; musn't stay to any body's else's.'

These remarks were delivered openly, pro bono, and dissolved the wedding party.

Four principal parties remained; Meadows, old Mer-ton, and the two friends.

* Well, uncle, Susan has spoken her mind, now you speak yours.'

' George, I have been an imprudent fool, I am on the brink of ruin. I owe more than two thousand pounds. We heard you had changed your mind, and Meadows came forward like a man and said he would—'

' Your word, uncle, your promise. I crossed the seas on the faith of it.'

An upper window was gently opened, and a blushing face listened, and the hand that they were all discussing and disposing of drew back a little curtain, and clutched it convulsively.

' You did, George,' said the old farmer.

' Says you, " Bring back a thousand pounds to show me you are not a fool, and you shall have my daughter,"

and she was to have your blessing. Am I right, Mr. Meadows ? you were present.'

' Those were the words' replied Meadows.

*Well! and have you brought back the thousand pounds ?'

' I have.'

' John, I must stand to my word; and I will—it is justice. Take the girl, and be as happy as you can with her; and her father in the workhouse.'

* I take her, and that is as much as to say that neither her father nor any one she respects shall go to the workhouse. How much is my share, Tom ?'

* Four thousand pounds.'

* No, not so much.'

* Yes it is. Jacky gave you his share of the great nugget, and you gave him sheep in return. Here they are, lads and lasses, seventy of them varying from one five six nought to one six two nine and all as crimp as a muslin gown new starched. Why ? I never put this,' and he took pieces of newspaper out of his pocket-book, and looked stupidly at each as it came out.

'Why, Tom?' *Eobbed!'

* Eobbed, Tom ?'

* Robbed! oh! I put the book under my pillow, and there I found it this morning. Robbed! robbed! Kill me George, I have ruined you.'

' I can't speak,' gasped George, ' Oh 1 what is the meaning of this ?'

' But I can speak! Don't tell me of a London thief being robbed I!! George Fielding if you are a man at all go and leave me and my daughter in peace. If you had come home with money to keep her, I was ready to give you Susan to my own ruin. Now it is your turn to show yourself the right stuff. My daughter has given her hand to a man who can make a lady of her, and set me on my legs again. You can only beggar us. Don't stand in the poor girl's light; for pity's sake, George, leave us in peace.'

You are right, old man; my head is confused, and George put his hand feebly to his brow. * But I seem to see it is my duty to go, and I'll go.'

George staggered. Eobinson made towards him to support him.

* There, don't make a fuss with me. There is nothing the matter with me, only my heart is

dead. Let me sit on this bench and draw my breath a minute, and then I'll go. Give me your hand, Tom. Never heed their jibes. I'd trust you with more gold than the best of them was ever worth.'

Eobinson began to blubber the moment George took his hand spite of the money lost.

' We worked hard for it too, good folks, and risked our lives as well as our toil;' and George and Robinson sat hand in hand upon the bench and turned their heads away—that it was pitiful to see.

But still the pair held one another by the hand, and George said, faltering, ' I have got this left me still.

308 ' IT IS NEVER TOO LATE TO MEND.'

Ay, I have heard say that friendship was better than love, and I dare say so it is.'

As if to plead against this verdict, Susan came timidly to her lover in his sorrow, and sat on his other side, and laid her head gently on his shoulder.

* What signifies money to us two ?' she murmured. * Oh, I have been robbed of what was dearer than life this bitter year, and now you are down-hearted at loss of money. How fuUish to grieve for such nonsense when I am so hap—hap—happy !' and again the lovely face rested light as down on George's shoulder, weeping deliciously.

* It is hard, Tom,' gasped George; ' it is bitter hard; but I shall find a little bit of manhood by-and-by to do my duty. Give me breath! only give me breath ! We will go back again where we came from, Tom ; only I shall have nothing to work for now. Where is William, if you please? Has he forgotten me too ?'

' William is in prison for debt,' said old Merton gravely.

* No, he is not,' put in Meadows, ' for I sent the money to let him out an hour ago.'

* You sent the money to let my brother out of gaol ? That sounds queer to me. I suppose I ought to thank you, but I can't.'

* I don't ask your thanks, young man.'

* You see, George,' said old Merton, ' ours is a poor family, and it will be a great thing for us all to have

such a man as Mr. Meadows in it if you will only let us.'

* Oh father, you make me blush,' cried Susan, beginning to get her first glimpse of his character.

' He doesn't make me blush,' cried Greorge; ^ but he makes me sick. This old man would make me walk out of heaven if he was in it. Come, let us go back to Australia.'

* Ay, that is the best thing you can do,' cried old Merton.

* If he does, I shall go with him,' said Susan with sudden calmness. She added, dropping her voice, ' If he thinks me worthy to go anywhere with him.'

' You are worthy of better than that, and better shall be your luck;' and Greorge sat down on the bench with one bitter sob that seemed to tear his manly heart in two.

There was a time Meadows would have melted at this sad sight, but now it enraged him. He whispered fiercely to old Merton, ' Toucji him on his pride; get rid of him, and your debts shall be all paid that hour: if not—'

He then turned to that heart-stricken trio, touched his hat, *Good day, all the company,' said he, and strode away with rage in his heart to set the law in motion against old Merton, and so drive matters to a point.

But before he had taken a dozen steps he was met by two men who planted themselves right before him.

' You can't pass, sir.'

Meadows looked at them with humorous surprise. They had hooked noses. He did not like that so well.

* Why not T said he quietly, but with a wicked look. One of the men whistled, a man popped out of the
churchyard and joined the two; he had a hooked nose. Another came through the gate from the lane; another from behind the house. The scene kept quietly filling with hooked noses till it seemed as if the ten tribes were reassembling from the four winds.

*Are they going to pitch into me?' thought Meadows, and he felt in his pocket to see if his pistol was there.

Meantime, George and Susan and Tom rose to their feet in some astonishment.

' There is a chentleman coming to put a question or two,' said the first speaker. And in fact an old acquaintance of ours, Mr. Williams, came riding up, and hooking his horse to the gate, came in, saying, * Oh, here you are Mr. Meadows. There is a ridiculous charge .brought against you, but I am obliged to hear it before dismissing it. Give me a seat. Oh, here is a bench. It is very hot. I am informed that two men belonging to this place have been robbed of seven thousand pounds at the " King's Head "—the ** King's Head " in Newborough.'

' It is true sir,' cried Eobinson, ' but how did you know ?'

* I am here to ash questions,' was the sharp answer. * Who are you ?'

* Thomas Eobinson.'

* Which is George Fielding ?'

* I am George Fielding, sir.'

* Have you been robbed ?'

* We have, sir.'

* Of how much ?'

* Seven thousand pounds.'

* Come, that tallies with the old gentleman's account. Hum ! where did you sleep last night, Mr. Meadows ?'

* At the "King's Head" in Newborough, sir,' replied Meadows without any visible hesitation.

* Well, that is curious, but I need not say I don't believe it is more than coincidence. Where is the old gentleman? Oh! give way there and let him come here.'

Now all this was inexplicable to Meadows, but still it brought a deadly chill of vague apprehension over him. He felt as if a huge gossamer net was closing round him. Another moment the only spider capable of spinning it stood in front of him.

* I thought so,' dropped from his lips as Isaac Levi and he stood once more face to face.

* I accuse that man of the theft. Nathan and I heard him tell Crawley that he had drugged the young man's liquor and stolen the notes. Then we heard Crawley beg for the notes, and after much entreaty he gave them him.'

* It is true!' cried Eobinson in violent agitation: * it must be true! You know what a light sleeper I am, and how often you had to shake me this morning. I was hocussed and no mistake!'

' Silence!'

* Yes, your worship."

* Where were you, Mr. Levi, to hear all this ?'

* In the east room of my house.' ' And where was he ?'

* In the west room of his house.' ' It is impossible.'

* Say not so, sir. I will show you it is true. Meantime I will explain it.'

He explained his contrivance at full. Meadows hung his head; he saw how terribly the subtle oriental had outwitted him; yet his presence of mind never for a moment deserted him.

' Sir,' said he, ' I have had the misfortune to offend Mr. Levi, and he is my sworn enemy. If you really mean to go into this ridiculous affair, allow me to bring witnesses and I will prove to you he has been threatening vengeance against me these two years—and you know a lie is not much to a Jew. Does this appear likely? I am worth sixty thousand pounds—why should I steal ?'

' Why indeed ?' said Mr. Williams.

' I stole these notes to give them away—that is your story is it?'

' Nay, you stole them to beggar your rival, whose letters to the maiden he loved you had intercepted by fraud at the post-office in Farnborough.'

Susan and George uttered an exclamation at the same moment.

' But having stole them, you gave them to Crawley.'

' How generous!' sneered Meadows. ' Well, when you find Crawley with seven thousand pounds and he says I gave them him, Mr. Williams will take your word against mine, and not till then I think.'

' Certainly not—the most respectable man for miles round 1'

' So be it' retorted Isaac coolly; ' Nathan bring Crawley.'

At that unexpected word Meadows looked round for a way to escape. The hooked-nose ones hemmed him in. Crawley was brought out of the fly quaking with fear.

' Sir,' said Levi, 'if in that man's bosom, on the left hand side, the missing notes are not found, let me sufier scorn; but if they be found give us justice on the evildoer.'

The constable searched Crawley amidst the intense anxiety of all present. He found a bundle of notes. There was a universal cry.

' Stop, sir!' said Robinson, ' to make sure I will describe our property—seventy notes of one hundred pounds each. Numbers one five six nought to one six two nine.'

Mr. Williams examined the bundle, and at once handed them over to Robinson, who shoved them hastily into George's hands and danced for joy*

Mr. Williams looked ruefully at Meadows, then he hesitated—then turning sharply to Crawley, he said—

' Where did you get these ?'

Meadows tried to catch his eye and prevail on him to VOL. III. p

say nothing; but Crawley who had not heard Levi's evidence, made sure of saving himself by means of Meadows's reputation.

' I had them from Mr. Meadows,' he cried; ' and what about it ? it is not the first time he has trusted me with much larger sums than that.'

' Oh! you had them from Mr. Meadows ?' ' Yes I had!'

' Mr. Meadows, I am sorry to say I must commit you ; but I still hope you will clear yourself elsewhere.'

' I have not the least uneasiness about that, sir, thank you. You will admit me to bail of course ?'

' Impossible! Wood, here is a warrant, I will sign it.'

While the magistrate was signing the warrant, Meadows's head fell upon his breast; he seemed to collapse standing.

Isaac Levi eyed him scornfully.

' You had no mercy on the old Jew. You took his house from him, not for your need but for hate. So he made that house a trap and caught you in your villainy.'

* Yes ! you have caught me,' cried Meadows, ' but you will never cage me !' and in a moment his pistol was at his own temple and he pulled the trigger—the cap failed ; he pulled the other trigger, the other cap failed. He gave a yell like a wounded tiger, and stood at bay gnashing his teeth with rage and despair. Half a dozen men threw themselves upon him, and a struggle ensued that almost baffles description. He

dragged those six men about up and down, some clinging to his legs, some to his body. He whirled nearly every one of them to the ground in turn; and when by pulling at his legs they got him down, he fought like a badger on his back, seized two by the throat, and putting his feet under another drove him into the air doubled up like a ball, and he fell on Levi and sent the old man into Mr, Williams's arms, who sat down with a Jew in his lap to the derangement of his magisterial dignity.

At last he was mastered, and his hands tied behind him with two handkerchiefs.

' Take the rascal to gaol T cried Williams in a passion. Meadows groaned.

' Ay! take me,' said he, * you can't make me live there. I've lived respected all these years, and now I shall be called a felon. Take me where I may hide my head and die!' and the wretched man moved away with feeble steps, his strength and spirit crushed now his hands were tied.

Then Crawley followed him, abusing and reviling him. ' So this is the end of all your manoeuvring! Oh! what a fool I was to side with such a bungler as you against Mr. Levi. Here am I, an innocent man, ruined through knowing a thief—ah ! you don't like that word, but what else are you but a thief?' and so he followed his late idol and heaped reproaches and insults on him, till at last Meadows turned round and cast a vague look of mute despair, as much as to say " How am I fallen, when this can trample me."

p2

One of the company saw this look and understood it. Yielding to an impulse he took three steps, and laid his hand on Crawley. ' Ye little snake,' said he, ' let the man alone!' and he sent Crawley spinning like a teetotum ; then turned on his own heel and came away, looking a little red and ashamed of what he had done.

My readers shall guess which of the company this was.

Half way to the county gaol Meadows and Crawley met William Fielding coming back.

It took hours and hours to realize all the happiness that had fallen on two loving hearts. First had to pass away many a spasm of terror at the wrongs they had suffered, the danger they had escaped, the long misery they had gi*azed.

They still rooted to the narrow spot of ground where such great and strange events had passed in a few minutes, and their destinies had fluctuated so violently, and all ended in joy unspeakable. And everybody put questions to everybody, and all compared notes, and the hours fled while they unravelled their own strange story. And Susan and George almost worshipped Isaac Levi; and Susan kissed him and called him her father, and hung upon his neck all gratitude. And he passed his hand over her chestnut hair, and said * Go to foolish child,' but his deep rich voice trembled a little, and wonderful tenderness and benevolence glistened in that fiery eye.

He would now have left them, but nobody there would part with him ; behoved him to stay and eat fish

and pudding with them, the meat they would excuse him if he would be good and not talk about going again. And after dinner George and Tom must tell their whole story, and as they told their eventful lives, it was observed that the hearers were far more agitated than the narrators. The latter had been in a gold-mine; had supped so full of adventures and crimes and horrors, that nothing astonished them, and they were made sensible of the tremendous scenes they had been through by the loud ejaculation, the pallor, the excitement of their hearers. As for Susan, again and again during the men's narratives, the tears streamed down her face, and once she was taken faint at George's peril, and the story had to be interrupted and water sprinkled on her, and the men in their innocence were for not going on with their part, but she peremptorily insisted, and sneered at them for being so fuUish as to take any notice of her fullishness: she would have every word; and after all was he not there alive and well, sent back to her safe after so many perils, never! never! to leave England again.

' Oh giomo felice !'

A day to be imagined; or described by a pen a thousand times greater and subtler than mine, but of this be sure it was a day such as neither to Susan nor George nor to you nor me nor to any man or woman upon earth, has ever come twice between the cradle and the grave.'

CHAPTER XXXIII.

A MONTH of Elysium. And then one day George asked Susan, plump, when it would be agreeable to her to marry him.

'Marry you, George,' replied Susan, opening her eyes ? * why never! I shall never marry any one after— you must be well aware of that.' Susan proceeded to inform George, that though fuUishness was a part of her character selfishness was not; recent events had destroyed an agreeable delusion under which she had imagined herself worthy to be Mrs. George Fielding; she therefore, though with some reluctance, intended to resign that situation to some wiser and better woman than she had turned out. In this agTee-able resolution she persisted, varying it occasionally with little showers of tears unaccompanied by the slightest convulsion of the muscles of the face. But as I am not like George Fielding, in love with Susan Merton, or with self-deception (another's), I spare the reader all the pretty things this young lady said and believed and did to postpone her inevitable happiness. Yes inevitable, for this sort of thing never yet kept lovers long

apart since the world was, except in a novel worse than common. I will but relate how that fine fellow George dried " these fullish drops " on one occasion.'

' Susan,' said he, ' if I had found you going to be married to another man with the roses on your cheek, I should have turned on my heel and back to Australia; but a look in your face was enough; you were miserable, and any fool could see your heart was dead against it; look at you now blooming like a rose, so what is the use of us two fighting against human nature, we can't be happy apart—let us come together.'

* Ah ! Greorge, if I thought your happiness depended on having—a fullish wife—'

* Why you know it does' replied the inadvertent Agricola.

' That alters the case; sooner than 7/ou should be unhappy—I think—I—'

' Name the day then.'

In short the bells rang a merry peal, and to reconcile Susan to her unavoidable happiness, Mr. Eden came down and gave an additional weight (in her way of viewing things) to the marriage ceremony by officiating. It must be owned that this favourable circumstance cost her a few tears too.

How so, Mr. Eeade ?

Marry sir thus:—

Mr. Eden was what they call eccentric; among his other deviations from usage he delivered the meaning of sentences in church along with the words.

This was a thmiderclap to poor Susan. She had

often heard a chaunting machine utter the marriage service all on one note, and heard it with a certain smile of imintelligent complacency her sex wear out of politeness; but when the man Eden told her at the altar with simple earnestness, what a high and deep and solemn contract she was making then and there with God and man, she began to cry and wept like April through the ceremony.

I have not quite done with this pair, but leave them a few minutes, for some words are due to other characters, and to none I think more than to this very Mr. Eden, whose zeal and wisdom brought our hero and unheroine happily together through the subtle sequence of causes I have related, the prime thread a converted thief.

Mr. Eden's strength broke down under the prodigious effort to defeat the effect of separate confinement on the bodies and souls of his prisoners. Dr. Gulson ordered him abroad. Having now since the removal of Hawes given the separate and silent system a long and impartial trial, his last public act was to write at the foot of his report a solemn protest against it, as an impious and mad attempt to defy God's will as written on the face of man's nature ; to crush too those very instincts from which rise communities, cities, laws, prisons, churches, civilization; and to wreck souls and bodies under pretence of curing souls, not by knowledge wisdom patience Christian love, or any great moral effort, but by the easy and physical expedient of turning one key on each prisoner instead of on a score.

' These,' said Mr. Eden, ' are the dreams of selfish, lazy, heartless dunces and reckless bigots, dwarf Robespierres with self-deceiving hearts that dream philanthropy, fluent lips that cant philanthropy, and hands swift to shed blood, which is not blood to them because they are mere sensual brutes so low in intelligence that although men are murdered and die before their eyes they cannot see it was murder because there was no knocking on the head or cutting of throats.'

The reverend gentleman then formally washed his hands of the bloodshed and reasonshed of the separate system and resigned his office, earnestly requesting at the same time that as soon as the government should come round to his opinion, they would permit him to co-operate in any enlightened experiment where God should no longer be defied by a knot of worms as in gaol.

Then he went abroad, but though professedly hunting health he visited and inspected half the principal prisons in Europe. After many months events justified his prediction, the government started a large prison on common sense and humanity, and Mr. Lacy's interest procured Mr. Eden the place of ite chaplain.

This prison was what every prison in the English provinces shall be in five years' time,— a well-ordered community, an epitome of the world at large, for which a prison is to prepare men, not unfit them as frenzied dunces would do; it was also a self-sustaining community, like the world.

The prisoners ate prisoner-grown com and meat,

p3

m

IT IS NEVER TOO LATE TO MEND.

wore prisoner-made clothes and bedding, were lighted by gas made in the prison, etc. etc. etc. etc. The agricultural labourers had out-door work suited to their future destiny, and mechanical trades were zealously ransacked for the city rogues. Anti-theft reigned triumphant. No idleness, no wicked waste of sweat. The members of this community sleep in separate cells, as men do in other well-ordered communities, but they do not pine and wither and die in cells for offences committed outside the prison walls.

Here if you see a man caged like a wild beast all day you may be sure he is there not so much for his own good as for that of the little community in which he has proved himself unworthy to mix pro tem.

Foul language and contamination are checkmated here not by the lazy, selfish, cruel expedient of universal solitude, but by Argus-like surveillance. Officers, sufficient in number, listen with sharp ears and look with keen eyes. The contaminator is sure to be seized and confined till prudence if not virtue ties his tongue: thus he is disarmed, and the better-disposed encourage one another. Compare this legitimate and necessary use of that most terrible of all tortures the cell, with the tigro-asinine use of it in seven English prisons out of nine at the present date.

It is just the diffijrence between arsenic as used by a good physician and by a poisoner. It is the difference between a razor-bladed needle-pointed knife in the hands of a Christian, a philosopher, a skilled surgeon,

and the same knife in the hands of a savage, a brute, a scoundrel, or a fanatical idiot.

Mr. Eden had returned from abroad but a fortnight when he was called on to imite Greorge and Susan.

I have little more to add than that he was very hard worked and supremely happy in his new situation, and that I have failed to do him justice in these pages. But he shall have justice one day, when pitiless asses will find themselves more foul in the eyes of the All-pure than the thieves they crushed under four walls, and * The just shall shine forth as the sun, and they that turn* many to righteousness as the stars for ever and ever.'

Thomas Robinson did not stay long at Grassmere. Things were said in the village that wounded him.

Ill-repute will not stop directly ill-conduct does.

He went to see Mr. Eden, sent his name in as Mr. Sinclair, was received with open arms, and gave the good man a glow of happiness such as most of us, I fear, go to the grave without feeling—or earning. He presented him a massive gold ring he had hammered out of a nugget. Mr. Eden had never worn a ring in his life, but he wore this with an innocent pride, and showed it people, and valued it more than he would the Pitt diamond, which a French king bought of an English subject, and the price was so heavy he paid for it by instalments spread over many years.

Robinson very wisely went back to Australia, and

* Not crush.

more wisely still married Jenny, with whom he had corresponded ever since he left her.

I have no fear he will ever break the eighth commandment again. His heart was touched long ago, and ever since then his understanding had received conviction upon conviction; for oh! the blaze of light that enters our souls when our fate puts us in his place— in her place—in their place whom we used to strike never realizing how it hurt them. He is respected for his intelligence and good nature; he is sober, industrious, pushing, and punctilious in business. One trait of the Bohemian remains: about every four months a restlessness comes over him; then the wise Jenny of her own accord proposes a trip. Poor Tom's eyes sparkle directly; off they go together. A foolish wife would have made him go alone. They come back, and my lord goes to his duties with fresh zest till the periodical fit comes again. No harm ever comes of it.

Servants are at a great premium, masters at a discount in the colony: hence a domestic phenomenon, which my English readers can hardly conceive, but I am told my American friends have a faint glimpse of it in the occasional deportment of their ' helps' in out of the way places.

Now Tom and especially Jenny had looked forward to reigning in their own house, it was therefore a disappointment when they found themselves snubbed and treated with hauteur, and Jenny revolted against servant after servant, who straightway abdicated and left her forlorn. At last their advertisement was answered

by a male candidate for menial authority, who proved to be Mr. Miles their late master. Tom and Jenny (joloured up and both agreed it was out of the question, they should feel too ashamed. Mr. Miles answered by offering to bet a crown he should make them the best servant in the street, and strange to say the bargain was struck, and he did turn out a model servant. He was civil and respectful, especially in public, and never abused his situation. Comparing his conduct with his predecessors it really appeared that a gentleman can beat snobs in various relations of life.

x\s Tom's master and Jenny's he had never descended to servility, nor was he betrayed into arrogance now that he had risen to be their servant.

A word about Jacky.

After the meal oif the scented rabbit in the bush, Robinson said slily to George, ' I thought you promised Jacky a hiding, well here he is.'

' Now, Tom,' replied the other colouring up, 'is it reasonable, and he has just saved our two lives; but if you think that I won't take him to task you are much mistaken.'

George then remonstrated with the chief for spoiling Abner with his tomahawk. Jacky opened his eyes with astonishment and admiration. Here was another instance of the white fellow's wonderful power of seeing things a good way behind him. He half closed his eyes and tried in humble imitation to peer back into the past. Yes! he could just manage to see himself very indistinctly giving Abner a crack; but stop! let him

see, it was impossible to be positive, but was not there also some small trifle of insolence, ingratitude, and above all bungality, on the part of this Abner. When the distance had become too great to see the whole of a transaction, why strain the eyes looking at a part. Finally Jacky submitted that these microscopic researches cost a good deal of trouble, and on the whole his tribe were wiser than the white fellows in this, that they revelled in the present, and looked on the past as a period that never had been, and the future as one that never would be. On this George resigned the moral culture of his friend.

' Soil is not altogether bad,' said Agricola, ' but bless your heart it isn't a quarter of an inch deep.'

On George's departure, Jacky being under the temporary impression of his words, collected together a mixed company of blacks, and marched them to his possessions. Arrived he harangued them on the cleverness of the white fellows, and invited them to play at Europeans.

' Behold this ingenious structure,' said he, in Australian ; ' this is called a house ; its use is to protect us from the weather at night; all you have to do is to notice which way the wind blows, and go and lie down on the opposite side of the house and there you are. Then again when you are cold, you will find a number of wooden articles in the house. You go in, you bring them out and bum them and are warm.' He then produced what he had always considered the chef d'oeuvre of the white races, a box of lucifer matches; this too was a present from Greorge. 'See what clever fellows they are,' said he, ' they carry about fire, which is fire or not fire at the fortunate possessor's will,' and he let off a lucifer. These the tribe admired, but doubted whether all those little sticks had the same marvellous property, and would become fire in the hour of need : Jacky sneered at their incredulity, and let them all off one by one in a series of preliminary experiments; this impaired their future usefulness. In short they settled there: one or two's heads had to be broken for killing the breeders for dinner, and that practice stopped; but the pot-bellied yoimgsters generally celebrated the birth of a lamb by spearing it.

They slept on the lee side of the house, warmed at night by the chairs and tables, etc., which they lighted. They got on very nicely, only one fine morning, without the slightest warning, whir-r-r-r they all went off to the woods, Jacky and all, and never returned. The remaining bullocks strayed devious, and the douce M'Lauchlan blandly absorbed the sheep.

Hasty and imperfect as my sketch of this Jacky is, give it a place in your note-book of sketches, for in a few years the Australian savage will breathe only in these pages, and the Saxon plough will erase his very grave, his milmeridien.

brutus lived; but the form and strength he had abused were gone, he is the shape of a note of interrogation, and by a coincidence is now an ' asker,' i. e. he begs, receives alms, and sets on a gang of burglars

with whom he is in league, to rob the good Christians that show him pity.

mephistopheles came suddenly to grief; when gold was found in Victoria he crossed over to that port and robbed. One day he robbed the tent of an old man, a native of the colony, who was digging there with his son a lad of fifteen. Now these currency lads are very sharp and determined : the yoimgster caught a glimpse of the retiring thief and followed him and saw him enter a tent. He watched at the entrance, and when mephistopheles came out again, he put a pistol to the man's breast and shot him dead without a word of remonstrance, accusation, or explanation.

A few diggers ran out of their claims.

' If our gold is not on him,' says the youngster, ' I have made a mistake.'

The gold was found on the carcass and the diggers went coolly back to their work.

The youngster went directly to the commissioner and told him what he had done.

' I don't see that I am called on to interfere,' replied that fimctionary, ' he was taken in the fact; you have buried him of course.'

' Not I. I let him lie for whoever chose to own him.'

' You let him lie ? What when there is a printed order from the government stuck over the whole mine that nobody is to leave carrion about. You go off directly and bury your carrion or you will get into trouble

young man.' And the official's manner became harsh, and threatening.

If ever a man was ' shot like a dog,' surely the assassin of Carlo was.

Mr. Meadows in the prison refused his food and fell into a deep depression; but the third day he revived and fell to scheming again. He sent to Mr. Levi and offered to give him a long lease of his old house if he would but be absent from the trial. This was a sore temptation to the old man. But meantime stronger measures were taken in his defence and without consulting him.

One evening that Susan and George were in the garden at Grassmere, suddenly an old woman came towards them with slow and hesitating steps. Susan fled at the sight of her, she hated the very name this old woman bore. George stood his ground, looking sheepish; the old woman stood before him trembling violently and fighting against her tears. She could not speak but held out a letter to him. He took it, the ink was rusty, it was written twenty years ago; it was from his mother to her neighbour Mrs. Meadows, then on a visit at Newborough, telling her how young John had fought for and protected her against a band of drunken ruiOfians and how grateful she was. ' And I do hope, dame, he will be as good friends with my lads when they are men as you and I have been this many a-day.'

George did not speak for a long time. 'He held the letter, and it trembled a little in his hand. He
looked at the old woman standing a piteous silent suppliant.

' Mrs. Meadows/ said he, scarce above a whisper, ' give me this letter if you will be so good. I have not got her handwriting except our names in the Bible.'

She gave him the letter half-reluctantly, and looked fearfully and inquiringly in his face. He smiled kindly, and a sort of proud curl came for a moment to his lip, and the woman read the man. This royal rustic would not have taken the letter if he had not granted the mother's unspoken prayer.

' God bless you both!' said she, and went on her way.

The assizes came, and Meadows' two plaintiffs both were absent; Robinson gone to Australia, and George forfeited his recognizances and had to pay a hundred pound for it. The defendants were freed. Then Isaac Levi said to himself, 'He will not keep faith with me.' But he did not know his man. Meadows had a conscience, though an oblique one. A promise from him was sacred in his own eyes. A man came to Grassmere and left a hundred poimd in a letter for George Fielding. Then he went on to Levi and gave him a parcel and a note. The parcel contained the title-deeds of the house; the note said, ' Take the house and the furniture, and pay me what you consider they are worth. And old man I think you might take your curse off me, for I have never known a heart at rest since you laid it on me, and you see now our case is altered— you have a home now and John Meadows has none.'

Then the old man was softened, and he wrote a line in reply, and said, ' Three just men shall value the house and furniture, and I will pay, etc., etc. Put now adversity to profit— repent and prosper. Isaac Levi wishes you no ill from this day, but rather good.' Thus died, as mortal feelings are apt to die, an enmity its owners once thought immortal.

A steam-vessel glided down the Thames bound for Port Philip. On the deck were to be seen a little girl crying bitterly—this was Hannah—a stalwart yeomanlike figure, who stood unmoved as the shores glided by,

Omne solum forti patria, and an old woman who held his arm as if she needed to feel him at the moment «bf leaving her native land. This old woman had hated and denounced his sins, and there was scarce a point of morality on which she thoroughly agreed with him. Yet at threescore years and ten she left her native land with two sole objects— to comfort this stout man and win him to repentance.

' He shall repent,' said she to herself. ' Even now his eyes are opening, his heart is softening. Three times he has said to me, " That George Fielding is a better man than I am." He will repent. Again he said to me, " I have thought too little of you, and too much where it was a sin for me even to look." He will repent—his voice is softer—^he bears no malice—he blames none but himself It is never too late to mend. He will repent, and I shall see him happy and lay my old bones to rest contented, though not where 1 thought to lay them—in Grassmere churchyard.'

IT IS NEVER TOO LATE TO MEND.

Ah, you do well to hold that quaint little old figure with that strong arm closer to you than you have done this many years, aye, since you were a curly-headed boy. It is a good sign, John; on neither side of the equator shall you ever find a friend like her.

* All other love is mockerj'- and deceit. 'Tis like the mirage of the desert that appears A cool refreshing water, and allures The thirsty traveller, but flies anon And leaves him disappointed wondering So fair a vision should so futile prove. A mother's love is like unto a well Sealed and kept secret, a deep-hidden fount That flows when every other spring is dry.'*

Peter Crawley, left to his own resources, practises at the County Courts in his old neighbourhood, and drinks with all his clients, who are of the lowest imaginable order. He complains that 'he can't peck,' yet continues the cause of this infirmity, living almost entirely upon cock-a-doodle broth or eggs beat up in brandy and a little water. Like Scipio, he is never less alone than when alone; with this difference, that the companions of P. C.'s solitude do not add to the pleasure of his existence. Unless somebody can make him see that it is never too late to mend. This little rogue, fool, and sot will ' shut up like a knife some day' (so says a medical friend), and then it will be too late.

A Royal Commission sat on gaol, and elicited

all the butchery I have related, and a good deal more.

The journals gave an able sketch of the horrors of that

* Sophia Woodrooffe.

hell, and a name or two out of the long list of the victims done to death by solitude, starvation, violence, and accumulated tortures of soul and body.

The nation cried ' Shame!' and then all good citizens waited in honest confidence that next month the sword of justice would fall on the man-slayer.

Well, months and months rolled away, and still, somehow, no justice came to poor little murdered Josephs and his fellow-martyrs.

Their sufferinors and the manner of their destruction had made all the flesh and blood in the nation thrill with pity and anger, but one little clique remained gutta-percha—the clerks that executed England.

Then " The Times " raised its lash, and threatened that band of heartless hirelings. ' You shall not leave us stained with all this blood shed lawlessly,' said " The Times." Then these hirelings began to do, for fear of the New Bailey in Printing House-yard, what they had not done for fear of God, or pity of the deceased, or love of justice, or respect for law and public morals, or for the honour of the nation and the credit of the human race.

They brought an indictment against Messrs. Hawes and Sawyer. But the mannikin who marches towards his duty because a man's toe is applied to his sense of honour may show fight, but he seldom fights. Our hirelings of Xerxes illustrated this trait of nature at every step. They indicted Messrs. Hawes and Sawyer for what, do you suppose ? He had starved men to death, which the law has, ere this, pronounced to be

334 ' IT IS NEVER TOO LATE TO MEND.'

murder. A gaoler was hanged in Paris for a single murder thus effected. Did they indict this man for murder? No! He had driven men to suicide by illegal bodily tortures and illegal mental tortures and felonious practices without number, which is manslaughter. Did they indict him for man-slaughter? No! they only indicted him for prisoner-slaughter; and they estimated this act at what? At a misdemeanor !

Coke and Blackstone and Camden had their just successors who came after them just as the Reverend Nullity Jones came after St. Paul and St. James. Unfortunately thjsse non-inheriting-success descendants from lawyers were the legal advisers of the crown in a case that required a legal intellect and a sense of public morality. This sham attack was a defence—the sword of the law in these hands shielded felony.

You can't hang a scoundrel for a misdemeanor; therefore the moment Mr. Hawes was indicted he was safe from justice. ,

The misdemeanor of man-slaughter in a prison was tried at last in open court at the county assize. The friendly prosecutor brought as few witnesses to Mr. Hawes's misdemeanors—or shall we say breaches of etiquette—as possible. I cannot find that any of the sufferers by his little misconduct were brought into court; yet they might have been; they were not all dead. Like soldiers in battle, there were nine wounded for every one killed. The prosecution seems to have been rested on the evidence of the prisoner's servants

' IT IS NEVER TOO LATE TO MEND.' 335

and confederates. Whether this arrangement was taken at the express request of the prisoner or originated with his friendly antagonists I don't know.

The move failed. The case was unburkable. On the evidence of servants and sympathising confederates, out came the man-slaughters and boy-slaughters and hellish cruelties of him who had forgotten propriety so far as to destroy the poor helpless powerless creatures whose sacred lives the sacred law had committed into his all-powerful all-responsible hand. Feebly attacked by the prosecution, he was defended with spirit by his own counsel, who addressed himself as in duty bound, to the old prejudices and anile confusion of ideas that had so often done good service in the cause of folly and falsehood.

' Prisoners are the scum of the earth. It was only human refuse the defendant had destroyed. Prisoners are a desperate class; violence is absolutely necessary to keep them from violence. The man had but strained a necessary severity; his fault, if any, was excess of zeal and too ardent love of discipline,' etc., etc.; and if the jury and the audience had had only heads to judge the case with, Mr. Sergeant Eitherside might have hoodvdnked them with these time-honoured falsehoods and confusions of ideas. But they had hearts, and their hearts enlightened their heads. They caught the true features of the massacre by instinct, and astounded by their emotion the cold hearts and muddy understandings that had up to this point dealt with the case but never grasped it.

Then came another phenomenon of this strange

business. The judge instead of completing the case and taking his share in the day's business (as the counsel and the jury had theirs) by passing sentence on the evidence and on the spot, deferred his judgment.

Now this was an act opposed to the custom of English courts in criminal cases. A judge is a slave of precedents.

Why then did the slave of precedent defy precedent ?

We shall see. -

Three mortal months after the trial the promised judgment was pronounced. Where? In London, a hundred miles from the jury and the public that had heard the evidence. The judgment was not only deferred, it was transferred. Thus two objects were gained: the honest heart of the public had time to cool, fresh events in an eventful age had displaced the memory of murdered Josephs and his fellow martyrs, and so the prisoner-slayer was to be shuffled away safe unnoticed, and the absence secured of the English public from a judgment which the judge knew would insult their hearts and consciences.

The judgment thus smuggled into law, delivered on the sly before a handful of people who could not judge the judgment because they were not the people that had heard the evidence.* This judgment what was it when it came ?

* This deferring and transferring of a judgment was unconstitutional. No English judge has a right to try a man in one locality and judge him in another. Such a mutilation of a judicial proceeding is opposed to all recent precedent, and to the spirit of English law: for its effect is clandestine judgment.

It was the sort of thing this trickery had led discerning men to expect.

It was three months' imprisonment !

Three months' imprisonment for prisoner-slaughter, for destroying souls as well as bodies, for destroying creatures from whom the law has taken self-defence presuming that of all men its own officers would be incapable of abusing that circumstance to their destruction.

Three months' imprisonment for man-slaughter in its

Since it matters little whether the doors are closed upon the people altogether, or the judge runs away from the people who have heard the evidence, and delivers it on the sly in a distant corner. Both these tricks are evasions of publicity. The law does not acknowledge the readers of " The Times " as the people before whom trials are conducted and verdicts thereon delivered. Not the reader of the evidence abridged for sale, but the hearer of the evidence in all its purity is the public recognized by the law ; and this public that judge evaded. It was an act of great weight and danger if not checked, for it was a retrograde step in law, in liberty, and in public policy and security for justice.

Open courts and public surveillance of all trials from the beginning to the end are essential to judicial purity. Not to know this is neither to have read history nor observed mankind.

Above all, open courts are the acknov.'ledged safeguard of English subjects and English justice. The act was unlawful on yet another score. There is a limit to the discretionary power of judges. No judge has a right to postpone his acts of justice unreasonably, or to expose justice unnecessarily to risks and accidents. Suppose this old man had died during the three months he so rashly interposed between the body and head of a judicial proceeding. Why not ? Death takes noodles as well as the wise. All that horse-hair cannot always keep out a little death, any more than it can a great deal of jocose levity and sheer stupidity.

VOL. III. Q •

worst and blackest and most heartless and cowardly form, except infanticide. For to compare beast with beast, the savage who tortures a woman to death attacks a creature who though weak has some defence, and encounters the opinion of all mankind; but the caitiff who destroys a prisoner attacks a creature who has no defence at all, a man prostrate already under a great and pitiful calamity, and has the prejudices of all the thoughtless to back him in his cowardly attack.

This judgment rested on two main blunders. The law withdraws its protection from a malefactor while actually engaged in illegal acts, but at any other moment it protects his person and property as impartially as it does yours and mine.

For instance if a burglar breaks into my house I may then and there cut him down like a dog. If a pickpocket puts his hand in my pocket I may knock him down like a bullock. But if I break into a notorious felon's house and rob him, I am just as great a felon in the law's eye as if I so robbed an honest citizen; and so I am if I attack a burglar's or a pickpocket's person and life at any moment when he is not feloniously engaged. I am none the less a villain in the law's clear eye because my villainy is aimed at an habitual villain. And here the law is not only just but expedient, for were such fatal partialities once admitted, we should soon advance from doing acts of villainy upon villains to calling any one a villain whom we wislicd to wrong, and then wronging him.

For want of comprehending the above plain distinc-
tion judge muddlehead condemned a murderer of non-offending malefactors to three months' imprisonment.

The second fallacy was a parallel one.

' Prisoners are under the lash of the law, therefore they cannot be so completely under its shield as other citizens are.'

Why not?

Tliis was an unfortunate assumption, for they happen to be one shade more sacred than the good citizen.

The good citizen is under the protection of the law, but the prisoner is under the especial protection of the law.

The good citizen has the law and his own hands to protect him.

The prisoner the law only, his hands are tied.

The good citizen is protected from violence only by general laws.

But the prisoner by general laws and by a specific act of the law, viz. by his sentence; that sentence by determining precisely what violence or suffering he is to suffer expressly excludes all lawless violence.

It is hard that I must come with such primitive remarks as these after the steps of a judge. I should not have needed to after a lawyer.

A penal sentence has two ends in view—public example, and the correction and if possible amendment of the culprit.

Now as far as public example was concerned this sentence might be compressed in two words.

Fiat c^des !!

But perhaps the other end might be gained by it. Three months in a separate cell would at least show this Hawes the horrors of that punishment, to whose horrors he had added unlawful cruelties; and by enlightening his understanding awaken his conscience, and improve his heart.

Honest man, honest woman, who have burned or wept with me over these poor victims, you are not yet at the bottom of the British hireling.

They sent the man-slayer not to a separate cell, not to a penal prison at all, they sent him to the most luxurious debtors' prison in Europe, and turned this tiger loose among the extravagant, the confiding, and the merely unfortunate. Among these not among

CRIMINALS WAS THE PLACE THEY ASSIGNED THE PRISONER-SLAYER.

The vermin thought they were in the dark and could do anything now with impunity. Nobody will track our steps any further than the want-of-judgment-seat, thought they, and I confess that I for one was weak enough to track them no further. Fools! They had heard of God's eye to which the darkness is no darkness, but did not believe it; but He saw and revealed it to me by one of those things that men call strange accidents.

He revealed to me too, that the debtors in that prison shrank with horror from this cruel insult, and from the horrible companion attempted to be forced upon them, and so they virtually altered his sentence to separate confinement by refusing all communication with
him. The men were composed of erring men, silly men, reckless men, improvident men, mifortmiate men, scampish men; but they were not utterly heartless, or lost to all feeling of self-

respect and public morality.

* Que voulez vous ?' This was a portion of the public : not a bright sample, but still a portion of the public, and therefore a god in intellect and in morals compared with our hirelings.

It now remains for me, who am a public functionary though not a hireling, to do the rest of my duty.

I revoke that sentence with all the blunders on which it was founded. Instead of becoming as other judicial decisions do a precedent for future judges, I condemn it to be a beacon they shall avoid. It shall lie among the decisions of lawyers, but it shall never mix with them. It shall stand alone in all its oblique pity, its straightforward cruelty and absurdity; and no judge shall dare copy it while I am alive; for if he does, I swear to him by the God that made me, that all I have yet said is to what I will print of Jdm as a lady's whip to a thresher's flail. I promise him on my honour as a writer and no hireling, that I will buy a sheet of paper as big as a barn-door, and nail him to it by his name as we nail a pole-cat by the throat. I will take him by one ear to Calcutta, and from Calcutta to Sydney ; and by the other from London via Liverpool to New York and Boston. The sun shall never set upon his gibbet, and when his bones are rotten his shame shall live—Ay! though he was thirty years upon the bench posterity shall know little about his name, and

feel nothing about it but this—that it is the name of a muddle-head, who gained and merited my loathing, my horror, and my scorn !

The civilized races, and I their temporary representative revoke that sentence from the rising to the setting sun in every land where the English tongue is spoken.

We pity not the murderer but the poor murdered child, driven to death by tortures without a parallel in modem England—driven to death in spite of all those strong instincts which while the body is yet growing fight in the heart against its unnatural destruction. And we lay down for the guidance of her Majesty's judges in all future cases this plain axiom of a law which has no muddle-headed partialities: That slaughter committed on a felon not actually engaged in felony is felony. That a prisoner under penal sentence is at least as much under the shield of the law as is an honest citizen. That the gaoler who destroys his helpless prisoner by starvation, violence, solitary confinement, slow tortures, etc., and the father who destroys his child by similar means are one felon of the Brownrigge school.

To this I add as a corollary, that the judges who hanged Brownrigge in England and the judges who hanged the gaoler in Paris for Hawes's offence on a smaller scale knew their business and did their duty, and acted upon a truer and wiser humanity than that which tells a class of men who hold so many little-valued lives in their hands in dark places not inspected

by the public, that they may kill without being killed for it. Our verdict is—" Non fiat csedes in tenebrosis locis." Let not slaughter be done in dark places. And that verdict we will find means to enforce if need be.

And now let us turn our backs on muddle-heads and hirelings and soothe our vexed souls and end in pure air among the daisies.

It is nine in the evening. A little party is collected of farmers and their wives and daughters. Mrs. Greorge Fielding rises and says, ' Now I must go home.' Remonstrance of hostess. ' George will be at home by now.'

' Well, wait till he comes for you.'

' Oh, he won't come, for fear of shortening my pleasure.'

Susan then explains that George is so fullish that he never will go into the house when she is not in it. ' And here is a drizzle come on, and there he will be sitting out in it I know if I don't go and drive him in.'

Events justify the prediction. The good wife finds her husband sitting on the gate kicking his heels quite contented and peaceable, only he would not pay the house the compliment of going into it when she was not there. He told her once he looked on it as no better than a coal-hole when she was not shining up and down it. They have been two years married.— NB. A calm but very tender conjugal love sits at this innocent hearth.

George has made a great concession for an English-]nan. He has solemnly deposited before witnesses his

sobriquet of " Unlucky George," not (he was careful to explain) because he found the great nugget, nor because the meadow he bought in Bathurst for two hundred pounds has just been sold by Robinson for twelve thousand pounds, but on account of his being Susan's husband.

And Susan is very happy. Besides the pleasure of loving and being loved, she is in her place in creation. The class of woman (a very large one) to which she belongs comes into the world to make others happy. Susan is skilful at this and very successful. She makes everybody happy round her, ' and that is so pleasant.' She makes the man she loves happy, and that is delightful.

My reader shall laugh at her: my unfriendly critic shall sneer at her. As a heroine of a novel she deserves it, but I hope for their own sakes neither will undervalue the original in their passage through life. These average women are not the spice of fiction, but they are the salt of real life.

William Fielding is god-father to Susan's little boy.

He can stand by his brother's side and look without compunction on Anne Fielding's grave, and think without an unmanly shudder of his own.

THE END.

Printed in Great Britain
by Amazon